PARADISE

FORBIDDEN

RC KNIPSTEIN

ISBN: 978-1-61296-378-5

PUBLISHED BY BLACK ROSE WRITING

www.blackrosewriting.com

Printed in the United States of America

Suggested retail price $17.95

Paradise Forbidden is printed in Calibri

To those who would heal

Primum no nocere

Paradise

Forbidden

1

Tommy Kirkland was a busy lad. He was in the earth moving business. One of his larger trucks was in the process of moving a load of sand away from the excavation site. He had ridden his Big Wheel down the driveway to the sandbox his dad had built for him to start his day's work. It was six feet square and bordered by 2"x 10" planks nailed at the corners. The enclosure was piled high with sand, of course, and there were several diminutive vehicles scattered inside with which to move it. Earlier, Tommy's mother had told him that a good breakfast was needed for such hard work, so he grudgingly ate his cereal before heading outdoors.

Tommy was now well into his workday with his trucks, loaders, shovels, and scoops in full utility as piles of sand were disappearing from one part of his sandbox only to reappear in another. At first he did not notice the distant whine and thunder-like rumbling sounds, but as they came closer and grew louder, he stopped his excavating and looked up to the sky.

Two huge black aircraft flying side by side were approaching Tommy's backyard and looked to his widening eyes as though they might land there. The planes were several hundred feet above the ground, but their immense size made them appear much closer. At first, Tommy just looked up in awe at the curious spectacle, but as the planes came closer, he sprang up from his sandbox and went racing into his house. His mother met him at the door as the now deafening roar of the planes' engines had alarmed her as well. The house shuddered as the two aircraft lumbered over it and then continued on past. Tommy held his mother's hand and clung to her skirt until the noise stopped and he was sure the big planes were gone.

* * *

Alex Madison was making love to his wife but thinking of another woman. He had loved his wife since the day they first met, so it was not as if he wanted to be with anyone else. He had read somewhere that some men and women too, fantasized about others as they were having intercourse with their wives, husbands, or significant others; and this practice heightened their enjoyment of sex as well as further bonding them with their sexual partner. All Alex knew was that this universal rhythmical dance that joined his body with Maria's in moments of shared excitement was something that they both participated in hungrily. All it took when he was tired, angry, distracted, or otherwise indisposed was a glance at her slender body with its graceful curves, or to touch her bronzed skin, to renew his intense desire for his next close encounter with her. They were one of those unique couples whose appetites for physical closeness were exquisitely compatible. Once the touching started and their hormones were awakened, they could not seem to get enough of each other.

Alex and Maria had been married almost twenty years and had two teenagers, aged thirteen and seventeen. John, the oldest, was a junior in high school, and Charlotte was in the throes of emerging pubescence. John was rather quiet and studious, but had a sharp wit and a bent toward the sarcastic, while Charlotte was more talky and beginning to be what her best friend Amy described as "boy crazy." This apparently meant that Charlotte was beginning to acknowledge that the masculine gender existed at all, something that up to that point Amy had taken no meaningful notice of.

As he kissed and caressed his wife while their bodies ebbed and flowed together, the woman in Alex's thoughts was in fact not an object of sexual interest to him, but a rather dowdy, overweight, but congenial patient he had seen in his office earlier in the day. He could say with truth and conviction that in his twelve years of clinical practice as a psychiatrist, there may have been two or three women patients that had stimulated him sexually. His training had prepared him for such eventualities which his mentors had assured him would appear from time to time. Acting on such feelings was in every way contrary to good clinical care and breeched every canon of ethics in medical practice. Alex had never actually seriously considered being physically inappropriate with a patient, but he knew some doctors who had; and, he also knew he was not immune to certain feelings that blessed and cursed the human psyche. Still, it unnerved him at times when he began to notice how attractive a woman patient was; or, as was sometimes the case, if her behavior was in any way seductive and he might be consciously or unconsciously responding to her.

Another benefit of Alex's lovemaking with Maria was that it seemed to liberate his mind as it relaxed him. Thoughts would come to him from many different directions and from many aspects of his life. He was somewhat introspective, although not overly so, and he tried not to let himself get too immersed in psychologically based ruminations. Sigmund Freud and others had made significant contributions to medical and mental health science and thought; but as time had proven, psychoanalysis and psychotherapy did not become the universal panacea for the world's ills as had been once trumpeted with great enthusiasm. People were suffering with neuroses, psychoses, anxiety, and depression as never before. While understanding some people's emotional or unconscious motivations was sometimes helpful, many patients were not relieved of their symptoms by such understanding, and the origin and stimulus for much of human behavior remained largely unexplained. What Alex had told himself again and again when he had chosen psychiatry as a profession was that he wanted to be seen as a physician first and a psychiatrist secondarily. He wished to be thought of by his colleagues and patients as a normal person and not as some kind of kind of eccentric screwball with endless, esoteric psychological explanations for emotional ills without having a clue as to how to resolve them.

As a wave of warm, satisfying, relaxing sensations bathed his body, he once again found himself exhausted in that soothing, tingling way that only sexual stimulation can bring about. He and

Maria consummated their lovemaking with a lingering kiss and a long, warm embrace before he fell back on his side of the bed and sighed deeply.

"That was pretty close, tonight, honey. We'll have to try to get it right one of these nights soon," he said as his hands roamed over Maria's soft skin. She laughed softly as she put her head on his chest.

"Well, I'm glad we're getting closer. We haven't had near enough practice... only twenty years now. I guess we have to keep on trying though," she replied.

Alex smiled and pulled her toward him. He thought of how his desire for her had waxed and waned at times, but never stayed gone long. He had endured many hours of whining complaint from his patients as to how they could no longer stand to look at or be with their spouse or partner. Making love to one another was the last thing they wanted to do. Still, there were those who had relationships that were satisfying and fulfilling. The differences and the reasons for them were often inexplicable and mystifying.

As Alex was looking at the ceiling in their bedroom, his mind was still on the woman he had seen in his office earlier in the day. He wasn't sure why she had stuck in his mind this way. Usually, he didn't bring his work home. And her history was remarkable for its absence of any compelling reasons for her to be suffering from depression. That one thing in itself was not unusual, in that Alex had often heard people say they had no reason to be depressed or unhappy. Their lives were going well; they had no family or work problems; there were no financial stresses. But, when he heard stories like that, he immediately began to think and ask about other things such as a family history of depression. It was often there in some form or fashion. People did not usually become clinically depressed without some reason. It was a matter of ferreting out those reasons that were most often the problem.

Understanding why people became depressed was, after all, less important than doing something to make depression go away. From Freud's time and after, it was widely believed that the causes for depression were usually emotional and psychological.

Treatment was based on that premise. Other treatments like electroshock therapy or insulin shock therapy were widely used from the 1940's and into the 1960's and beyond. Early in the 1960's, effective medications became available, but they were only effective less than half the time and they were deadly in overdose. Toward the end of the 1980's newer kinds of antidepressants were developed that were safer to use, but no more effective than the previous, older ones.

Alex's training had commenced in the late 1970's. He had been schooled with psychodynamic explanations for emotional disorders being the most likely and important harbinger of their appearance. As his experience widened in actual practice, it became clearer that while psychological factors were important, there were other equally important things to know in understanding all mental and emotional disease, and depression in particular. The practice of, and training for, the practice of psychiatry began to change dramatically. Some training programs completely abandoned teaching psychotherapy and its variants. Psychoanalysis and psychotherapy took a back seat as pharmacology began to do the driving. The quest for newer and more effective medications with fewer negative side effects would take hold not only of psychiatry, but all branches of medicine.

Psychiatrists in general and Alex in particular began to think that all of those developments should make for happier patients and more successful treatment outcomes. There were certainly treatment successes but it seemed, to Alex anyway, that far too many people did not respond to treatments that should by every measure and expectation be helping them. In addition, many people did not like the idea of having to take medication to feel normal; and many people suffered side effects from the medications that were supposed to help them.

As Alex lay in bed, the lady he had seen that day seemed to bring into relief for him some of the perplexities he was encountering as he attempted to treat depression. It also seemed to him that depression was almost all he was treating as the days went by. He was not surprised to find out from his colleagues that they were experiencing similar things. The lady he had seen in his office had no current stresses or issues, no significant life changes, and no past or family history of depression. *Then why was she depressed?* Alex wondered. He rolled over and kissed Maria on the cheek.

"Good night, baby," he said as he sank into welcome sleep.

2

Happiness, Alex thought as he stood fiddling with a ball point pen in his hand.

It was a word, a state of mind, an emotion, a wish, a fantasy, and for some, a reality. People did not usually come to a psychiatrist because they were happy, but nevertheless some who found their way into his office were in such a state. He had seen many patients who, despite the emotional turmoil that may have been the reason for their coming, were truly happy with their lives. It was something of an oxymoronic state of affairs associated with the human condition. People without fail said they wanted to be happy; or, it was the only thing that was missing in their existence; but they often had no clue of how to find it, or get it, as though it was some tangible object to possess.

Alex was standing in front of one of the expansive windows in his fourth floor office in the Plaza Tower Building that stood next to and overlooked the Interstate. It was mid-morning and the traffic flow had ebbed a bit. It was a prestigious location that he was able to afford only because he had gone to college with the owner of the complex who had given him a really sweetheart deal on the rent.

His momentary reverie was interrupted by a buzz from the telephone on his desk. When he picked it up, he was greeted by a familiar voice.

"Mrs. Whitmore is ill and has cancelled her appointment, Dr. Madison. So, you have forty five minutes before your next patient. Would you like to leave a wakeup call?"

A smile crept across Alex's face as he listened. Emily Northcutt was his office manager. Among other things, she was bright, efficient, likeable, and possessed a sense of humor that was engaging but also sharp and incisive.

"No, Mrs. Northcutt," he intoned with feigned seriousness, "I think I'll play a couple of games of handball off the walls in my office while I have some time. I hope the noise won't bother you."

"Very good, sir. Don't hurt yourself," she answered and hung up.

Alex walked back over to the window and resumed his ruminations. He was thinking about when he was a resident. He and the other residents would endlessly argue over and discuss issues that then seemed so essentially monumental to their training and understanding of the nature of man and his behavior. Could people really change? How do we help them change? Is it even worth trying?

One of his mentors, Dr. Flagg, had said, "We put on patches with adults. If you want to really have a chance of changing someone, you need to start with adolescents. It's only with them that you can do some good for the rest of their lives."

At the time, Alex remembered how skeptical he had been. He felt Dr. Flagg was being far too pessimistic about what psychiatry could do. Now, however, after some dozen years of practice, he was not so confident. Slowly, grudgingly, he had come to a place in his career where, while he was no less idealistic and hopeful about helping his patients, he realized there were limits to what he could do; and, sadly, he did not believe in miracles any more. He would do what he could: say what he thought would help people, and hope the seeds he planted would bring forth some fruit. That was the best he could come up with while still keeping some of his idealistic nature and not giving in to hopelessness and disillusionment.

Happiness and clinical depression had a relationship to each other, but they were not necessarily antonyms. Sometimes people did not feel unhappy until something changed in their life and they experienced real unhappiness. Sometimes a person fell into clinical depression and did not realize it. A husband, wife, friend, or a psychiatrist had to point it out to them. Most people were simply not able to be objective about themselves and their emotional lives no matter how introspective or bright they might be. Alex often pointed out to his patients that emotions had nothing to do with how smart or dimwitted someone was. Slow witted people were sometimes far smarter at managing their emotions than those with triple digit IQ's. That fact was one of the great levelers among the human race.

As he went about his clinical work, Alex had to keep reminding himself that clinical depression and what people often thought of as depression were two different things. Even for a clinician, it could be a troublesome distinction. Sadness, unhappiness, being grumpy or disgruntled in life were not necessarily depression. Falling into clinical depression was a life changing event that threw an unseen cloud of misery over its victims and changed their entire being, sometimes forever. Sometimes it even cost them their very life just as surely as if they had a deadly, incurable cancer.

As a huge red tractor-trailer passed below him on the freeway, Alex thought back to a day when he was in his third year of medical school—the first time that med students were actually on the wards at Parkland and under the tutelage of experienced, respected physicians who were oftentimes clinical researchers as well. Dr. Raymond Bondurant, an internist and world authority on diabetes mellitus, was listening to an intern relate the symptoms of a recently admitted patient. The young doctor pointed out that in addition to the patient's chest pain and shortness of breath, the patient's family had reported that the middle aged man had also been withdrawn and less active in recent weeks.

The older doctor listened for a moment and said, "Oh, that's just depression," as though he might have been saying, "Oh, that's just a head cold," thus relegating clinical depression to some throw away category of medical diagnoses.

It seemed a sadly pervasive truth that the only time anyone, including some doctors, paid attention to someone's depressive state of mind was if he threatened to jump off a building or blow his brains out. Another dreadfully tragic, inescapable truth was that some people did just that without any warning or indication of their deadly intentions whatsoever. For the psychiatrist, or any physician for that matter, whenever he or she was confronted with patients with depressive symptoms, there was the possibility of a fatal outcome just as surely as if they had a late stage malignancy. No one, doctors or patients, liked to dwell on such thoughts for long.

Man, I'm getting morose here, Alex thought as he walked over and sat down on his couch. He took several deep, long breaths as he stretched his arms and yawned. He could still catch a momentary whiff of the aroma of Maria's perfumed hair from last night and early this morning as they lay together before he slowly got up and headed for the shower. Alex had never been a morning person, and it took him awhile until he was up to speed in the AM.

It seemed worse lately, though. Alex had noticed his patient load was increasing to the point where he had told Emily to hold off scheduling new people which he seldom, if ever, did. Having more people to see was a good problem for any physician to be sure, but for a psychiatrist, it could become a burdensome stress that no amount of added income could ever fully compensate. Alex tried not to worry about money, but he did anyway, as he knew college was on the horizon for both his kids, and it was only getting more expensive like everything else he could think of. Maria did some substitute teaching occasionally but, thankfully, they did not have to rely on that income. She just enjoyed the change of routine and a few extra bucks to spend. But, with what appeared to be happening with the increased demands for mental health treatment, finances were not the immediate issue. There would be far more encompassing concerns looming ahead for the Madisons, and everyone else for that matter.

* * *

She had been sitting at a table in the noisy, crowded club where the youth of that era were wont to gather frequently, especially on the weekends. Alex had noticed her shortly after he had come in and headed to the bar with a couple of his friends. He was not a pick up artist by any stretch, but he held out for the possibility of lightning striking sometime. Conversation was not his thing, especially with strangers, and he always felt just plain stupid trying to make small talk. He thought that every woman in the place knew what he was really after, so why bother? It just never occurred to him that a woman might want the same thing. Somehow that possibility never entered his mind and thus never came about.

Alex casually surveyed the room as he tapped his foot to the intoxicating cadence of the never-ending rhythms coming from the blaring speakers that seemed to be located all around his head at the moment. The more he tried to avoid looking in her direction, the more she came into his view, although he did not think she had noticed him. She had on a dark colored sweater over a white blouse that was buttoned up to her neck. Both of her hands were under the table, and she looked anything but comfortable as she gazed around the room as though she might have been lost. Occasionally she would manage a forced smile when one of her companions said something to her. Otherwise, she seemed like she might have been on another planet. She definitely did not have that carefree, "I'm having fun" look of some of the other young women in the place.

Alex had always thought that a person's eyes were the thing. Hers were dark, and though they were for the most part unsmiling, they were also lively and alluring. Long, dark hair framed her face and settled gently over her shoulders and around the front of her blouse. Her skin was a captivating shade of olive brown. Alex could not look away from her face once he had fixed on it. He had been to this place several times but had never seen her before-he would have remembered.

Alex did not usually think of himself as a man of action, but tonight would be different. He had convinced himself in just a few short minutes at the bar at *Shady's Club* that if he did not meet this woman, the most beautiful woman he had ever encountered, he was no man at all. So, he put his drink down on the bar, walked over to her table, tripped on a chair leg, and fell sprawling on the floor at her feet.

* * *

Alex laughed out loud as he sat on his couch thinking of his first encounter with Maria. Instead of laughing and leering like everyone else who had seen his ungainly spectacle, the dark eyed woman stood and helped him up.

"Are you Ok?" she asked as he had managed to get back to his feet. His buddies at the bar were whistling and clapping as they blew him kisses amid their paroxysms of laughter.

"Those guys are just jealous because they can't think of such creative ways to make a first impression," he said as he looked into her dark eyes and then started laughing himself. "I'm fine, thank you." She just looked at him a moment and smiled and began laughing too.

"I must admit, that's the most original pick up technique I've seen yet," as she reached over and smoothed the collar of his shirt. The touch of her soft hands on Alex's neck sent waves of indescribable sensations through his body that he hoped would last forever and then some. He smiled wanly to conceal his embarrassment before he spoke.

"Well, I know you're just dying to have me sit down after such an unforgettable introduction," he said, feeling he didn't have much to lose at that point. "My name is Alex Madison."

* * *

Maybe Sartre had something after all with his existential thing, Alex thought. How many people could claim with any truthfulness to having such a chance meeting with their intended that turned into a twenty one year marriage and two kids? Life was indeed strange. Eight billion human beings on the planet, and he landed right at the feet of Maria Marisol Benivides in a night club she had never visited before or since. She had been there only at the behest of some of her friends who almost literally dragged her out of the dorm to go with them. Maria wasn't a prude, but she wasn't a party girl either. She had not come to college just to find a husband. She wanted to become a teacher. Her parents made sacrifices for her to go to school, so she wasn't about to disappoint them. But, when she met one Alexander Edward Madison, she wanted to be with him so much that she wasn't sure what, if anything, she would not do to make such an eventuality likely. Both of them never really had a chance after they first laid eyes on each other.

3

It seemed to be the kind of thing that most people could only look back on and wonder what had really happened and why anyone hadn't seen it coming. It did not take a giant leap of insight or imagination to recall other events in recent history that were similar. The AIDS epidemic, for example, seemed to come out of nowhere and snowballed into a worldwide panic while everyone was looking on, but not paying much attention; or, in psychiatric jargon, exhibiting a great deal of denial. Adolph Hitler had risen to power in the 1930's in Germany while the rest of the world observed with a casualness that ushered in World War Two and its attendant devastation.

Perhaps it was partly due to the fact that most people in the medical community did not look at psychiatric illnesses in epidemiological terms like plague, or polio, or, influenza, or encephalitis. Doctors and lay people alike did not usually conceive of things like epidemics of depression, or anxiety, or psychoses. Physicians, including psychiatrists, wanted to see people with illnesses they could treat. Many family practitioners, internists, and surgeons sent patients off to the psychiatrist only when they felt the basis of the complaints were not physical. The practice of medicine had changed to the extent that the "real" doctors—the family practitioners, internists, and surgeons—had in truth little time to be counselors to their patients any longer and get to know and understand their needs as people. Medical care had become a commodity bought and sold just like the items on the shelf at the grocery or hardware store. Doctors and hospitals now advertised on the radio and TV as well as in the newspapers. It seemed all too clear, now that there was very little of the "art" left in the art of practicing medicine. Whatever the patient's complaint might be, there had to be an intervention to cure it, whether it be a pill or a scalpel; and, furthermore, it needed to be done quickly and at the least possible cost. Medical science had come to a turning point in history, and everyone including the doctors, hospitals, and medical insurance companies was sure they were each headed in the right direction, but agreement among them was scarce.

* * *

Alex was bewildered as he once again stood looking out his office window at the passing traffic. He had added hours to his schedule, but still he could not keep up with the people that were lining up to see him. Every psychiatrist he knew was in the same boat. In the past two years, three new psychiatric hospitals had been built, in the city and there were plans for more. The admissions at the small hospital where he worked had tripled in the last six months, which made the owners ecstatic, but was killing the staff.

One of the major television networks had prepared and shown a two hour special on what could only be called an epidemic of depression in America. This was not just limited to one particular part of the country either. From east to west, from coast to coast, the United States was falling victim to an unprecedented onslaught of emotional misery. In addition to the increased hospital admissions and psychiatric patient visits, the suicide rate had started a steady upward climb in the preceding two years that had affected every socioeconomic group in the country. It seemed that clinical depression was not just for the rich or poor; it treated everybody the same regardless of race, creed, age, or anything else. It appeared no one was immune.

The buzz of his desk telephone startled Alex as he was contemplating his increasing work load and the fact he was seeing less of his family as the months crept by. He slowly picked up the phone, "Yes, Emily," he answered and yawned.

"It's Dr. Nelson, sir," the office manager said.

"Ok, put him through, Emily," Alex replied and rubbed his eyes. "Hey, John, what's the word, man?"

"Oh, man, Alex. I'm on call today and we're overwhelmed here. Could you take a few more patients?" he asked plaintively. Competition among the psychiatrists at the hospital, though generally friendly, had always been acute; but to ask a colleague to take patients was unheard of only a few months ago. Now, everybody had all they could handle most all the time. It was a good problem to have, but was beginning to tell on the small group of doctors on the hospital staff.

"Sure, John, if you need the help. It must be really gangbusters over there," Alex ventured.

"I can't begin to tell you, man. I've never seen it like this. Maybe it's the moon or something, but I hope it slows down soon. I can't imagine this going on much longer. It's going to kill us all," he said with a tone of exasperation. John Nelson was one of the doctors on staff with whom Alex had only a passing acquaintance. They were not friends; they only spoke if they saw one another in the hall. Alex did not particularly like him. Dr. Nelson took little interest in his patients except for the revenue they ultimately provided him.

"Just tell Gloria in intake that I will take the patients you can't manage," Alex replied.

"Thanks, Alex. I won't forget it, man," Dr. Nelson said and hung up.

* * *

The next patient had been seated on the couch as Alex sat down in his chair. Mrs. Alice Dayton was an anxious, middle aged woman with a worried expression she wore like a mask that had not changed in the two years she had been coming to see Alex. She had a never ending litany of complaints about her husband, children, neighbors, the mailman, and everyone else with whom she had any contact whatsoever. Her medications were always ineffective and in need of changing in her view. Alex frankly did not know why she kept coming to see him, as she was forever casting not so veiled complaints toward him as well. Alex leaned back in his chair and waited for the latest cascade of indignities the world had been pouring down on her.

Mrs. Dayton just looked at the handbag in her lap for a minute or more without saying anything. She wrapped the handkerchief in her hands around her palm in a circular motion. Then she began to dab it at the corners of her eyes as tears began to flow in small rivulets down her cheeks.

"What is it, Mrs. Dayton?" Alex finally ventured to ask. He was genuinely puzzled at this kind of thing coming from her. Although she complained a lot and tended to dramatize things, she seldom, if ever, cried openly. Anger was her emotion of choice, not sadness.

"I don't know, Dr. Madison. I've just been feeling so down. I talked a long time to my husband last night about it. He told me to be sure I told you today." Now the wheels were turning in earnest in Alex's mind. She usually did not exchange ten words a day with her spouse, or so she had been saying for the last two years. Like many unhappy couples, they lived in a state of self-imposed imprisonment with one another, but dared not take any meaningful steps to change things.

Alex was so stunned, he just looked at her for a long moment mostly because he could not think of anything to say to her. He shuffled his feet and cleared his throat several times.

"Have you been taking your medication, Mrs. Dayton?" was all that he could manage.

"Yes, sir, just like it says on the bottle and the way you told me to," she was now looking at him and wiping her face at the same time. "I don't think they're working though. I just keep feeling the same...unhappy." She looked down at her handbag again and the tears kept coming. Her body was shaking with the rhythm of her sobbing.

Alex was searching his mind, and he recalled that he had given her every antidepressant at his disposal without any real success.

In truth, he felt that most of her symptoms were from the nature of her personality, and she was not, and likely never had been, clinically depressed. In the past, he had felt he had little to lose in trying the medications. This, however, was another story. For the first time since he had known Mrs. Dayton, he felt like he might be able to develop some actual rapport with her. With some patients developing an alliance was easy, but with others it was hard to come by. Mrs. Dayton was in the latter category.

By the time she left his office a little while later, Mrs. Dayton's tears had dried up some. Alex had adjusted her medication as well as recommending she bring her husband on her next visit as well. He wasn't so sure about the patient, but he felt much better about her treatment and his role as her doctor. It was at times such as this that he remembered why he wanted to be a psychiatrist.

* * *

For Alex, the episode with Mrs. Dayton was like a small, green, verdant island in the middle of an endless ocean in which the horizon only revealed bleak images of dark, forbidding waters. The burgeoning numbers seeking help for crippling symptoms of depression became like a great tide assaulting the shoreline of America in unceasing, relentless waves.

Hospitals were now overflowing with patients they could not safely contain. New hospital construction had no way of keeping up with the need for more treatment facilities. Psychiatric patients were being housed in general medical hospitals when there was no room for them on the psychiatric wards. Word was coming from Europe and Asia as well that similar things were happening there. It would seem that this epidemic had now become a pandemic. Governments and medical organizations worldwide began to meet, but there was little they could do but talk, since there was no real explanation for what might be causing this catastrophe, or what could effectively be done about it.

In the United States, the federal government began to issue charges to the pharmaceutical industry to come up with more effective treatments for depression. Academic researchers and pharmaceutical manufacturers were given incentives for finding some answers to this nightmare that now had the entire world in its grip. All the world was looking for answers but had no clue from where they would come.

4

The Federal Pharmaceutical Administration, or FPA as it was usually called, was the national agency in the United States that oversaw the development and marketing of prescription drugs that could legally be given to patients by licensed physicians. This particular agency had a long and storied past which varied a great deal depending on who was telling the history. The agency saw itself, and oftentimes justifiably so, as protecting the nation from medicinal substances that could potentially do harm to the public rather than provide whatever remedies for whatever ailments the drugs were designed to placate or cure.

The pharmaceutical manufacturers often saw the agency as an overly zealous, unrealistic watchdog with vast powers that prevented this industry from providing the American public with medications that they desperately needed to combat a myriad of maladies, and therefore depriving these same companies of vast profits in the marketplace.

Physicians were somewhere in the middle of this struggle between free market enterprise and the protection of the masses from possible unscrupulous manufacturers and marketers of pharmaceuticals of dubious or no value in medicine. If anything could be said regarding the nature of the world and its inhabitants concerning people's health and wellbeing, it must surely be that there was always someone promising everlasting happiness through some drug or miracle cure for every ailment that had been evidenced in the history of mankind. Alex was reminded of a lecture he had attended in medical school given by a psychiatrist who had glibly said that if someone claimed that stump water had cured him of cancer, there would be a hundred people lined up waiting to testify that such a thing was true and the government was trying to keep it quiet, thus preventing Nirvana for all.

It would seem that America's good health and how to bring it about and sustain it was the subject of a vast array of disparate opinions. The contention only worsened as the population grew; and with it, more sufferers of ill health, both physical and emotional. But, as far as the FPA was concerned, the agency was viewed by many as a ponderously bloated government entity that was heavy handed and inefficient at the task for which it had been created. As would soon be evident to everyone in America and abroad, such a characterization of that particular government agency would become only a sidebar to history and a moot point, indeed.

* * *

There were reasons the FPA had come to be viewed with such ambivalence by the drug manufacturers and the medical community at large.

On the one hand, it was a large government agency charged with overseeing a vast number of therapeutic drugs that were prescribed by physicians for the benefit and betterment of people's health. To perform that formidable task, it employed thousands of bureaucrats who in turn needed to justify their continued presence on the payroll by doing what bureaucrats usually did for the federal government; namely, make any and everyone who came under their purview dance to their tune with veiled and not so veiled threats of disapproval of products which could make a pharmaceutical company millions or billions of dollars, or ruin their business altogether.

On the other hand, however, the FPA had a past to live down.

In the decade of the 1960's, there was a drug which had been approved by the FPA for infertility called pedazerine. As was almost always true with any new medication released to the market place, certain side effects that did not show up in the clinical trials appeared when the drug began to be prescribed to many patients in the general population. Often times these unexpected effects were mild and not serious. However, sometimes the results were life-threatening and even tragic.

In the case of pedazerine, infants born to mothers who had taken the drug often appeared at delivery without a major portion of their brain. The medical term was *Anencephaly*. It happened sometimes spontaneously in some infants' gestation, but it was a complication in virtually every child born to mothers who had taken pedazerine. But whatever the condition was called, it resulted in financial ruin for the manufacturer of the compound in an avalanche of lawsuits that came about when expectant parents saw that their newborn joys were born with a condition that in most cases was incompatible with life.

As could be expected in cases of such ghastly consequence, the FPA came under such excruciatingly intense criticism and scrutiny, that it retreated into a defensive stance so as to be virtually impregnable to the possibility of future problems with medications they approved. The FPA was determined to never have another pedazerine allowed onto the market again. It was at least understandable how the agency morphed into an entity that was seen as dictatorial, autocratic, and arrogant owing to the weight of responsibility it shouldered.

For this and other reasons, the pharmaceutical manufacturers and the FPA from that day to the present lapsed into a relationship in which each viewed the other warily. Their uneasy coexistence had been marked by years of mutual mistrust. They were like two veteran, grizzled, professional football teams with a long standing rivalry. Sometimes they gave each other grudging respect, but they did not like each other.

* * *

"Dr. Madison, there is a man on the phone from Washington. He says he would like to speak to you about an important matter. He sounds serious," Emily said over the intercom on the phone in Alex's office. "Do you want me to put him through, or are you indisposed again?"

"Very amusing, Emily. What's his name?" Alex responded with a sigh and a yawn of fatigue, not disinterest.

"It's a Mr. Branch, sir. He says he is with the Department of the Interior," Emily answered flatly.

"Ok, put him on, Emily. Thank you," Alex replied and listened as he cleared his throat.

A deep, baritone voice came on the line. "Dr. Madison?"

"Yes, this is Alex Madison, sir. To whom am I speaking, please?"

"Dr. Madison, this is Congressman Sherman Branch. I am the chairman of the president's newly formed Committee on Healthcare Emergency. I wanted to speak to you regarding the outbreak of depressive disorders in the country. It appears to be something like the plague of the Middle Ages, don't you think?" Mr. Branch said with a nervous laugh under his breath. "Our committee is attempting to put together a plan to deal with it."

"There is a serious problem to be sure, Mr. Branch, but I'm not sure how I can be of help to you, sir. I'm not a researcher, or a pharmacologist. I'm a practitioner of general psychiatry," Alex intoned in response. The last thing he needed or wanted right now was some sort of a political discussion with a congressman he did not know from Adam, and without any notion of why this man would be calling him.

"Yes, yes, I know you are likely surprised I would call, but I need some help from people like you who are on the front lines, so to speak, in dealing with this thing that is eating us alive right now. I need someone who can tell me what we can do to help the country rid itself of this menace."

Oh, brother, Alex thought, *now he is sounding like the politician he must be.*

"Well, I don't know quite what to say, sir. We obviously need better treatments than we have at our disposal now. Where they are likely to come from, though, I'm not at all sure," Alex said trying to sound scholarly and learned. "It would also help if we had some kind of an idea what has been causing this onslaught of depressive suffering. I don't think anybody has come up with so much as a good guess as to the cause of the outbreak."

"I'm sure that's true, Doctor, but we have to start somewhere if we're going to get anywhere; wouldn't you agree, sir?" the congressman asked and was clearly waiting for a thoughtful reply. Alex squirmed in his chair as he tried to think of something to say that wasn't totally clichéd.

"Of course, you're correct, Mr. Branch. I think that all of us in the trenches, as you say, are frustrated and bewildered at the scope of the problem we're facing. No one of us has, frankly, seen anything remotely like this before, so we're ill-equipped to deal with it, sir," Alex responded. He was somewhat proud of himself for thinking of anything at all that might have sounded intelligent. At the same time, he wondered why the congressman would be calling him. He was not famous or published, had written no books or clinical papers, but was a day in, day out, garden variety practitioner of psychiatry. Why wasn't Mr. Branch asking these things of the leaders in the field?

"That's why I am calling you, Doctor, in case you're wondering. We're all in the same boat here. I have talked to some of the notable doctors in your area, and several of them suggested you might be a good person to speak with as you have a busy practice and are well respected by your colleagues," Mr. Branch paused for a moment and continued. "Would you consider being a consultant for my committee?" Alex was stunned and gratified at the same instant in time. He thought for a moment before he spoke.

"You do me a great honor, Congressman Branch. I'm not sure I could be of much help, however. Let me talk it over with my wife before I make such an important commitment," Alex answered.

"Of course, Dr. Madison. I know I'm asking a lot on such

short notice, but we're in a serious dilemma here as I'm sure you are aware. I want to proceed with some meetings quickly so, hopefully, we can find some direction here soon."

"Yes, sir, I understand perfectly. I would certainly be of help if I could be. If you will give me, say, three days, I will call you back with my answer," Alex replied and let out a long sigh he hoped the congressman could not hear.

"That would be fine, sir. I will look forward to talking with you again," Mr. Branch replied. He then gave Alex a contact number and hung up the phone.

Wow! Alex thought as he slumped back in his chair and rotated it around so he could look out his window. He began to wonder who the colleagues might be who recommended him to the congressman. Alex's best friend was a plumber, not a doctor, and Alex was not particularly tight with any of the better known psychiatrists in the area. He had made it a point to attend meetings of the psychiatric society on a somewhat regular basis, but he was not what one might call active. He enjoyed too many other things in life to devote much time to the politics of the local medical society. But, he tried to practice good medicine, and it was important to him that he had the respect of his contemporaries in the field. Despite all of this, Alex felt in his gut that he was seen as something of a maverick.

He smiled to himself and thought of that Bible verse that read, "Woe, be unto you if all men speak well of you." Alex did not think he had anything to worry about on that score. He laughed to himself as he arose from his chair and went to greet his next patient.

* * *

Charlotte Madison wasn't sure what was going on with her best friend Amy. All Charlotte had said was that Roger Bentley was cute. You would think she had renounced God or committed the unpardonable sin or something of similar magnitude. Amy huffed and stuck her nose in the air and walked away from her like she didn't even know her. They were both thirteen now and had been inseparable since they were in the second grade. Although the two girls had in fact sworn a blood oath to never have a boyfriend several years before, Charlotte was now thinking that she might have been premature in that decision. She at least wanted to reconsider the life long, completely binding agreement she had entered into with Amy.

Charlotte was lost in thinking about these matters as she walked slowly down the hall toward the cafeteria. She seemed oblivious to the hordes of teenagers all around her. A strident voice pierced the air among the noisy, moving mass of young bodies bustling down the hallway.

"Charlotte!...Charlotte!" the scream resounded in the hall as Amy came rushing alongside her. Amy thrust her round face into Charlotte's with a glare that Charlotte had come to recognize only too clearly when Amy was beside herself with some earth trembling issue on her mind. "Don't walk so fast!" she barked. Charlotte stopped for a brief moment before she continued on down the hall. Amy tended to dominate in their relationship, but Charlotte held her own when she was pushed. In her adolescent mind, this was one of those instances.

"Don't yell at me!" Charlotte riposted with an authority in her voice that did not often show itself as she turned her face away from her friend and continued walking. Amy hesitated for an instant and then took a few hurried steps to catch her.

"Ok, Ok, slow down and talk to me...PLEASE!" Amy conceded.

"Why should I talk to you, huh?" Charlotte said angrily. "You'd just go stomping off like some two year old." Amy's eyes flashed and a cold glare froze on her face as the two girls stopped dead in their tracks in the hall almost nose to nose. They were both dressed in jeans and had on matching jerseys with school colors along with their ever present sneakers.

"You're so beautiful when you're angry," Amy said as a grin started to spread from her mouth to her cheeks despite her best efforts to prevent it. Charlotte's dark eyes remained riveted into

Amy's for a pregnant moment before she broke into a giggle.

"You screwball! Why can't I ever stay mad at you for more than a millisecond? Huh?" she said as the two friends were now laughing as they bumped shoulders like they always did when they were in tune with each other.

"I think they call that friendship in case you didn't know, you nut case," Amy retorted.

"Oh, friendship, huh? Is that when you stomp off from your supposed best friend when you're mad? Huh? Huh?" Charlotte shot back with an edge in her voice.

"Ok, Ok, I get it. But, you ventured into that land where we said we would never go, Charlotte. It just surprised me, that's all," Amy said somewhat plaintively.

"Good grief, girl. We're both thirteen now...practically grown. Is it your intention that we head for the convent right now without ever even getting a first kiss?" Charlotte said and looked at her friend as the smile was fading from her face. Amy had no answer. She just looked down at her sneakers for a long moment.

"I don't know, Charlotte. All I know is that when you talked about Roger Bentley, I got this terrible feeling inside...a feeling like you were leaving me or something," Amy replied as she looked back down at her feet which were shuffling back and forth across the tile floor. Charlotte looked back at her with a smirk.

"Just where would I go? We're stuck with each other 'til we graduate high school," she said and grinned. Amy just looked into Charlotte's face. There was not a hint of mirth in her expression.

Finally, she spoke.

"I'm the one who's supposed to make the jokes, sister. Let's go to lunch."

The two teenagers then turned and started walking with purpose down the crowded hallway.

5

It was a fall day in Washington DC. The sky was a clear, crisp kodachrome blue that provided a striking contrast to the multicolored leaves on the trees outside the austere edifice that housed the FPA. Lauren Marsh, however, didn't have the privilege of being outdoors this colorful autumn day in DC. As was usual for her, she was cloistered in her cubicle in an immense room of similar cubicles with her gaze affixed to her computer screen looking at endless rows and columns of figures and other types of data that flickered before her eyes. She would occasionally strike a key on her keyboard, look at the screen for a moment, and then do the same thing again.

Lauren was not unhappy or bored. The truth was quite the contrary; she enjoyed her work and went at it with an enthusiasm that did not escape the notice of her superiors. Whenever her direct supervisor needed something done with thoroughness and accuracy—something he needed to be sure was done in exhaustive detail—he went to Lauren. The other truth of the situation was that, as was so often the case with dependable, capable employees like Lauren, the reward for their skills and dedication to their tasks seldom showed up in their paychecks. Occasionally Lauren's name and photograph would appear on the wall of the break room as an "employee of the month." It was an Agency recognition which allowed her to park her compact car in a specially marked spot nearer to the entrance of the building for a month.

Such career slights did not keep Lauren up nights; she hardly took any notice. Whatever feelings she may have harbored about such things were well hidden. Nor did she think much about whether such things *should* matter to her. Lauren soldiered on in her world of esoteric data on blinking computer screens that occupied her days and sometimes her nights as well. She took great interest in her work and made a decent living from her employment at the FPA.

Lauren had a brief marriage in her early twenties to a man who was bright, handsome, and forever unfaithful during their three year liaison. She loved him despite his meandering, but one day decided to pull the plug before both of them became totally encased in a fossilized relationship from which neither one would be able to break free—and before there were children that would bring other kinds of complications. The dissolution of her marriage was easily enough accomplished but left a deep, dulling, palpable pain that despite what her friends told her, she feared would never subside. It finally did, however, and there were no scars remaining that anyone could see; but that did not mean none were there. Despite her independence of mind and a rather iconoclastic spirit, there was a streak of domesticity in Lauren that she found bothersome and comforting at the same time.

Lauren was now forty. She had not totally ruled out ever being in love again, but she knew her chances would diminish as she aged. She was not unattractive, but she did little to gild her own lily. Her chestnut brown hair was usually pulled back from her face and pinned, or sometimes if she was feeling more reckless, in a ponytail. Though her face was rarely animated, her light blue eyes could be expressive. Her skin was light toned giving her a rather fresh faced, girlish look.

Lauren had always been slender at five feet four, but now she was beginning to notice some fullness in her hips that had not been there before. Her waist, however, remained tiny which accentuated her prominent, fulsome breasts which were the reason most men bothered to look in her direction nowadays. She was only too aware of that fact, which resulted in her ever increasing determination to avoid menfolk altogether.

Lauren wondered if there was a man left in the world who

would look directly into her eyes when they met, and forgo introducing himself to the melon-like mountains pushing out the front of her blouse. If there was one incontrovertible truism among the women she had known present and past, it was that those who possessed small breasts wanted bigger ones, and those who had large breasts wished them to be smaller. People always wanted what they did not or could not have. It was one of life's ironies for which there seemed to be no exception.

Whenever the subject arose between them, her best friend Ann Brady would say, "Count your blessings, honey, those things will take you a long way," to which Lauren would only sigh.

"Well, they've already taken me through one unfaithful husband," she would say, "I wonder where they will take me next?"

She paid only passing attention to her clothing and other accoutrements that most women found sacred. She presented herself to her rather cloistered world as neatly appropriate, but unadorned. Most men would call her plain; most women who liked her at least would have said she could have been more attractive if she bothered to make the effort.

Sometimes when she looked into her mirror in the morning, Lauren considered putting on more makeup or trying a different hairstyle; but those intentions usually melted from her mind before she left for work. Ann would tease her encouragingly to look to her appearance more, but Lauren would just smile, take a drag from her cigarette, and smile again without saying anything. Still she appreciated Ann for trying.

"I guess you know Art has been eyeing you pretty good for quite a while now," Ann said as she and Lauren walked across the busy street in front of their office building heading to a café for lunch. Lauren appeared to have not heard her friend's comment, but suddenly spoke.

"Art who?" she asked, looking genuinely puzzled.

"My God, Lauren, for such an intelligent woman, you're impossibly out of it sometimes," Ann replied as they walked.

"He's the guy that keeps stopping by your desk all the time to ask you things that he already knows. You haven't figured that out yet? Good grief, Lauren, you're worse off than I thought," Ann said as she shook her head from side to side.

"I just didn't think he was very bright, Ann," Lauren said with a straight face.

Ann just kept walking.

"Well, he's not half bad. I mean he's nice looking and he seems Ok to me. Maybe you should give him a chance," Ann added knowing what Lauren's response would likely be.

"You know how it is when you date someone at work, Ann. If it doesn't work out, it becomes uncomfortable, and then you have two unhappy campers at the office, not just one," Lauren said and let out an exasperated sigh.

"But what if it does work out? You ever think of that?" Lauren turned to look at Ann and pursed her lips. "Lord, why do I even try with you, honey? You're determined to die an old maid. Don't say I didn't warn you, though," Ann cautioned as they walked inside the small café and sat down.

"I'll keep it in mind," Lauren replied and half smiled.

* * *

"They want me to consult on some committee in Washington," Alex said as he stared at the ceiling in the bedroom as he and Maria were lying together quietly in their big four poster bed. "A Congressman Branch called my office and spoke to me about it," he continued.

"Well, I knew you would get into politics one day, honey," Maria said and laughed as she rolled over and put her head on Alex's shoulder.

"I'm afraid the man doesn't know what he's in for," Alex said and let out a kind of sarcastic giggle. "I'd love to speak my mind to some of those windbags up there. Could you imagine me sitting in some committee meeting in Washington? Maybe I'll be on the late news." With that, Alex laughed and rolled his eyes.

"I think it's an honor, baby. You should be proud that the congressman would ask you," Maria offered and kissed him on the cheek. "They'll get a good man."

"I don't know what they want me for, though, baby, or what I can do. This thing about an epidemic of depression is real enough, but I don't know that anybody has the faintest idea of what to do about it," Alex sighed. "It will be like the blind leading the blind."

"That's the point of the committee though isn't it...to find some answers?"

"Sure, but I don't know where they will come from, short of someone coming up with some miracle drug that will stop half the world from getting depressed," Alex answered. "It's just getting worse and worse."

"I know, honey, I know," Maria said and let out a long breath. "Maybe something good will come of it. I'm tired. Let's get some sleep."

"But I don't feel like sleeping, baby."

"Oh, I see. Feel like something else, do you?" Maria replied.

"You're getting the idea now," Alex said as he put his arm around her and nuzzled her cheek with his. Maria said nothing. She looked into Alex's eyes which in the dark were just black recesses in his shadowy face. She then put her arm around his neck and held him close to her silently.

* * *

Maria's optimism was not to be rewarded, however. Things did not get better as Alex and every other psychiatrist became inundated with new patients daily seeking relief from this scourge that quite literally had taken the country by the throat and was showing no sign of letting go. Some cities had initiated outreach programs which offered group meetings that were more or less like twelve step type gatherings that had been proven effective in the treatment of addictions.

Such measures helped, but nothing seemed to dent the rising

tide of forces that few if any understood or knew how to avert. It seemed the world was getting sicker and sadder with each passing day. And beyond that, it also appeared that no one was immune.

* * *

Alex had decided that he would accept the appointment to the committee that the congressman had offered if for no other reason than it would get him out of town from time to time and away from his practice which for him had fallen into the same category as a daily root canal. He had always loved his work; it challenged him and sometimes even inspired him as well. It now upset him that he felt as though he needed to get away from it. For Alex, being in a helping profession had always seemed something like a high calling. He felt as though he might be able to make a difference at least some of the time.

To be sure, there were days when he did not feel so filled with idealism and altruism and had nagging thoughts that he had not helped anyone, ever. He thought of a movie he had seen while he was in med school in which a prominent doctor who practiced in a large hospital had fallen into disillusionment with medicine and in a drunken stupor started yelling from a window of the hospital that medicine and doctors never healed anyone or cured anything. Certainly the events of the last two years could easily lead someone to make such pronouncements. The battle lines had been drawn and medicine and psychiatry were being defeated decisively.

With such weighty matters clattering in his head, Alex picked up the phone to call Congressman Branch to say he would sign on to continue the battle even though he had precious little hope of a victorious outcome. He laughed to himself as he was thinking that the Christians in the Coliseum of Rome in the first century AD likely had a better chance against the lions. As he punched in the congressman's number, he sighed and his smile faded.

* * *

Lauren tried to duck out of sight, but she was too late. Art Loman was just a few steps away walking toward her cubicle and had already seen her. She hoped in vain that he would keep going, but of course that was not likely to happen either. She buttoned the top button of her blouse and straightened her skirt as she reached down under her desk and feigned getting something out of her purse. She then heard his voice.

"You're not trying to hide under there, are you?" he asked. Lauren slowly raised her head and was greeted by two rows of white teeth as Art's face broadened into a wide smile. She managed a wan half smile and hit a key on her computer keypad.

"Just trying to look busy for the boss," she answered flatly. "But, I would hide if I thought I could get away with it." The grin that appeared to be pasted on Art's face only widened.

"You shouldn't work so hard, Lauren," he added. "Take a break sometime. Have dinner with me," he continued and then broke into a rather forced laugh that sounded like he had recorded it on tape for the occasion. Lauren did not answer, but only looked up at him standing above her computer screen as she was hoping her feelings of indifference toward him and her facial expression were in perfect agreement. Ann was right; he wasn't bad looking, but no bells were ringing for Lauren. It was like the slate was blank and nothing was likely to appear on it.

Just as Lauren was about to speak, she suddenly did not need to. The looming figure of her supervisor, Harold Janes, appeared without notice next to Art and said, "Lauren, I need to talk to you in my office right away, please." He turned just as abruptly and strode back in the direction of his glassed-in cubicle that was about ten times the size of Lauren's.

"Excuse me, Art, I had better go see what he wants," she offered and started away from her desk.

"Well, don't forget what I said, Lauren. Please think about it," he said as she walked past him. She just looked toward him as she passed, nodding her head once but saying nothing. Art took the few steps back to his own desk and stood with his eyes fixed on Lauren's hips as they swayed away from him down the corridor.

Harold Jane's office was about twenty or so paces from her desk, and when Lauren reached it, she tapped on the glass door. He nodded his head, and she entered and closed the door behind her. Her boss sat down and motioned for her to do the same. Trim and with carefully combed graying dark hair, he looked all of his fifty five years.. He was dressed in his standard uniform, a dark double breasted suit, white shirt, and dark tie. Lauren instantly recognized the very familiar focused gaze he had fixed on her. It usually meant even more unwelcome work.

"I've been assigned to a new committee, the Healthcare Emergency Committee to be precise, by Congressman Branch. The first meeting is next Thursday. Lauren, I want you to go with me as an assistant if that is acceptable to you," he said in his usual terse, direct manner that left little room for misunderstanding or rebuttal for that matter. Lauren knew that although he posed it as a request, it was in fact a directive she couldn't refuse. Harold Janes was retired military, and all his "requests" sounded like orders which, in fact, they were. It did not usually bother Lauren, as she liked Harold, but sometimes she wished he would loosen up a bit. As she was thinking this, she was also thinking she could not believe those thoughts were coming from her. He probably thought the same thing about her.

"Of course, Harold. I will be glad to accompany you to the meeting," she said. Lauren and her boss had been on a first name basis for some time. It was a privilege he did not grant often or lightly. It was reserved for those under him who had earned his trust and respect in the heat of battle, so to speak.

"Good, Lauren, I knew I could count on you. These meetings will have to do mostly with this fearful epidemic of depressive disorders the country has been experiencing. As you know, the pharmaceutical companies have been given some incentives to find better antidepressant agents. I think the Secretary had little choice but to take that road due to the growing number of

41

cases and the seriousness of the situation. The suicide rate is now twice what it was eighteen months ago. The president himself has made it a priority for us. The heat is on, and I'm afraid we're going to be the ones in the oven."

Harold leaned back in his chair, let out an uncharacteristic sigh, and steepled his fingers as he looked past Lauren and out into the huge room surrounding his office. "Lauren, I hope you will accept this in the spirit in which it's intended; but I wanted to say that I have appreciated your dedication and good work the years we've been here together, and I've not ever put it in just those words. But, before we launch into this task together, I wanted you to know how much you mean to the Agency and to me as your supervisor. Your work is superlative in every way, and there is no other person here I would rather have assisting me."

Lauren sat listening to him without so much as blinking her eyes. It was as though this man sitting across the desk was an alien just alighting from a distant planet. She thought she knew him at least to some degree, but she was now convinced there must be layers to this man she could never have imagined. It was either that, or someone or something had struck unimagined fear in his heart that brought about this incredulous metamorphosis.

Lauren continued to stare at him until it became obvious to even her that she was in this trance-like state. She cleared her throat and looked down at her hands that had been folded in her lap. "My goodness, Harold, I don't know what to say except thank you for your confidence in me. I have always tried to be a credit to the Agency and to you as well." She paused a moment before continuing, "You do me great honor, sir." They both just looked at each other for a pregnant moment.

"I'm just telling it like it is, Lauren. I wanted to thank you for what you do. I'm afraid, though, that this thing before us now is going to be bad news and you may not thank me for taking you along. I've been in combat, and even then I wasn't as anxious as I am now. I'm afraid we're in for even more troubling times, Lauren. It's just a feeling I have," he said as his eyes turned directly into hers. Lauren's heart was now pounding against her chest as Harold's piercing gaze was fixated on her.

"You'd better get back to your desk, Lauren, before everybody in here thinks we're having an affair," he added as one of his infrequent smiles was forming on his face. Lauren let out a little laugh as the tension inside her began to ebb away.

"Harold, the way you talk!" Lauren replied as she felt her face flush. "I should call your wife," she said and smiled somewhat self-consciously. She then gathered herself and added, "I hope you know you can count on me."

Harold just grinned and said, "I never doubted that, Lauren."

Lauren then arose from her chair, left her boss's office, and walked back to her desk with something like a smile on her face. Lauren did not know then that it would be some time before she felt like smiling again.

6

"Why did you want to become a doctor, Dad?"

Alex was reading the paper in the den while Maria was only a few steps away standing at the sink in the kitchen as the words came tumbling out of John's mouth. The two parents turned their heads in unison to look at their firstborn who was sitting on the couch in the den watching television. Alex was not even sure John had said anything as his son's attention appeared to be riveted to the flickering TV screen.

"What's that, son?" Alex asked rather rhetorically. John turned to look at his dad.

"Why did you want to be a doctor?" John repeated. "My science teacher asked us all to ask that of our fathers when we got home from school today," he added. "So, I'm doing my homework. Aren't you proud, Dad?" Alex let out some of the air that had stalled in his lungs for a few seconds. His anxiety level fell back down close to normal again and his pulse eased a bit. He wasn't sure why the question punched him in the gut like it did.

"And what about your mother? Don't I count in this homework assignment?" Maria asked.

"He didn't say anything about mothers, Mom," John answered, dragging out the "mom."

"Oh, I see," Maria said and went back to her dinner preparations.

"Well, son, I guess I thought it would be the best and fastest way I could make a million dollars," Alex replied and looked back to his newspaper. John shuffled his feet and smiled.

"Well, do you have it yet? I would like to be the son of a very rich doctor and never have to work a day in my life. I think I'll just be a playboy and have an Italian sports car, Dad," John said while trying to keep a straight face. "I don't like the idea of going to college anyway."

"Well, son, you'd better get used to the idea, if you want to go on eating. I'm not going to support you forever, you know."

"Aw, come on, Dad. You can do it. I know you can. Don't you love me?" John laughed and giggled as he rolled around on the couch.

"I would love you more if you went to college and got out and earned a living," Alex said with his face still behind the newspaper.

"You're no fun, Dad. Just a stick in the mud. Don't you know supporting your children is a parent's responsibility?"

"Only 'til they're grown. Then they're on their own. I'm going to keep my million dollars for myself. Your mom and I want to go on some cruises when I retire."

"I'm glad to hear that," Maria said as she was listening in the kitchen. "Where will we go first?... How about Rome?"

"Yeah, you can buy me a Lamborghini while you're over there, Dad. That would be cool," John interjected. "Good idea, Mom."

"Glad you liked it, John. When do we leave, honey? I can be ready in about an hour," Maria added as she was setting the table for dinner.

"You two are a laugh a minute," Alex said and paused. "I said after I retire. That will be in about a hundred years. You all don't hear very well," Alex retorted.

"See, I told you, Dad. You're just a party pooper. A real wet blanket," John said as he went back to his TV watching.

"By the way, Dad, why did you become a doctor?"

* * *

"Have you been tracking any of those new antidepressants, Lauren? It looks like one or two might be promising," Ann Brady asked as she and Lauren were having their lunch outdoors on an unusually warm fall day in Washington. "Some of the preliminary clinical trials look very good so far."

"Yes, I've been following some of them. The drug companies have been cranking them out since things have gotten so crazy," Lauren replied. "The early clinicals can be misleading and even inaccurate sometimes, though. I worry about that. You just can't rush those things, Ann. I hope we aren't going to get too lax on the scrutiny. That would be worse than the problem we're trying to correct."

"I know, Lauren, but when someone's really depressed, they want to feel better. Who cares if the medicine also gives them a dry mouth or some other side effect?" Ann came back. "I've been taking Pantozine for the past two years. It's changed my life. You wouldn't believe the difference."

Lauren looked like she had been slapped in the face.

"My goodness, Ann. I never knew that. I never even knew you were depressed," Lauren replied with her eyes wide and riveted on her friend.

"I know, honey. Depression is something that can sneak up on you, and it's got you before you know it. I felt terrible for about six months before I went to the doctor. I think my father was also depressed, but he never got any kind of treatment. I don't think he would have gone even if he knew he needed to. There's still such a stigma with emotional problems. Nobody wants anybody else to know. We all want people to think we're normal." Ann stopped for a moment to take a bite of her sandwich. "My doctor said that depression can run in families just like heart disease or diabetes. A lot of people don't know that. They think that if they get depressed they're just crazy or something." Lauren just listened and said nothing. She was thinking that even best friends kept secrets from each other. As Lauren looked at Ann, warm sensations flowed through her body like waves. She was thinking that there were no feelings like the feelings you share with a friend. The whole world might be falling into depression, but right now, Lauren was happy to be alive and here with Ann.

* * *

Alex did not much like flying. He knew it was probably the safest form of mass transit statistically, but the thought of being thousands of feet in the air in a rather fragile tube with wings full of flammable fuel did not give him much comfort. The thought of falling those thousands of feet to the unyielding earth below was no less than terrifying to him. But, thousands of poor souls trusted their lives and fate to the airlines every day, and the great majority of them came through the ordeal unharmed. He had seen a number of patients in his practice that needed to take muscle relaxers or antianxiety medications every time they boarded an aircraft. For some, it was just an occasional vacation trip, but for others who traveled as a part of their livelihood, the medications had become a routine necessity.

Anxiety was likely the most common of the emotional complaints of patients and ironically the least understood. People could tolerate being miserable for years on end but could not stand to be anxious for more than a few minutes at a time. The vulnerability and helplessness most people felt when they were anxious tended to make them say and do things they would never dream of otherwise. Alex conjectured it was likely that fact alone that made people so afraid of it. Having been anxious himself on more than a few occasions, he felt for them.

Of course, there was no denying the fact that he was indeed vulnerable while thirty thousand feet in the air in what amounted to a glorified kite.

Sometimes there were damn good reasons to be anxious, he thought.

If a rattlesnake was at his feet, he would be anxious. If someone was pointing a gun at his nose, he would be anxious, so why not when he was in the sky at some ungodly altitude in a contraption that someone else was controlling? He could find nothing wrong with that logic.

Alex had hoped Maria would come with him on this trip, but

she begged off at the last moment. That was a bit surprising to him as Maria was usually like a racehorse at the starting gate when it came to going anywhere. And especially if it involved a ride on an airplane. She had told him many times that one of her fantasies was to be a flight attendant so she could travel more. He was stunned when she said she would stay home and look after the kids. She did add, however, that if he went back for some follow up meetings, they could take some extra days and see the sights around Washington, DC.

The other thing that was on his mind was what, if anything, he was going to be able to contribute to this committee when he arrived in Washington. Alex had been mulling that over for some time. He had settled on a preliminary plan to just listen and speak when he was spoken to; but he knew that he was going to be expected to know something of value; produce it for the committee; and be able to offer helpful suggestions. He would be entering the corridors of power-enormous power. Whether these congressmen were windbags or not, they were going to be looking to him as an expert in the field of mental health. This was not just some political exercise over funding or power. The country and the world were falling into a serious crisis that needed to be defused, and quickly. Alex did not want to think about the possibility of not getting control of this ogre that looked like it was going to engulf the entire planet. It was like the most abhorrent, frightening monster movie one could imagine; only, this was the real thing, even though the beast had no scales or foot long teeth, fangs, or talons.

"Please fasten your seatbelt, doctor, we're about to land," the flight attendant interrupted Alex's self-imposed trance.

He then started to think, *Takeoffs and landings: the most dangerous part of flying,* as the huge aircraft began to lumber down toward the waiting runway outlined by glistening white lights.

* * *

"Mom, is Dad going to be on the news?" Charlotte asked as she, John, and Maria settled down at the supper table.

"Sure, Sis, they're going to swear him in as the new president," John answered before Maria could. Charlotte took a deep breath of obvious disgust and glared at her brother.

"You are so retarded, John. I don't know how you could have possibly made it to the eleventh grade. I guess they just moved you along anyway because you are so hopeless," Charlotte replied and looked to her mother for her reply. But, John kept talking.

"No, they recognized that they had genius material here. They've actually been holding me back. I should already be in college," John said and took a big bite of his mashed potatoes.

"Why don't you two practice your sibling rivalry somewhere else besides the supper table," Maria said rather sternly. "I'm not in the mood for your sarcasm tonight, John, or yours either, Charlotte. Can't we just have dinner without the usual fireworks display?" Maria added and took a great interest in her soup.

The two siblings both paused and looked at their mother as though there might have been a stranger at the table. Maria was not given to such displays of irritability. A few minutes of uneasiness passed at the silent table until Charlotte ventured to speak.

"I'm sorry, Mom. It's just that some kids at school asked me today whether Dad would be on TV because I told them he was going to Washington DC to be on a committee. I didn't know it would upset you."

Maria looked up from her meal and gave her daughter a meek smile. "It doesn't upset me, honey. I guess I'm not in a great mood tonight. I've had a headache all day and one of the commodes is stopped up. You know, some of a housewife's little unexpected pleasures. And to cap it off, your dad's gone. I didn't mean to be

49

gruff."

"I can fix the commode, Mom," John said. "I watched Dad the last time it happened. I know what to do."

"I appreciate that, John, but let's wait for the plumber. He comes tomorrow," Maria said and smiled. "It can wait, honey. It's been happening for a while now, and I think it may be a bigger problem with the drain or something. We better find out for sure."

"I've heard plumbers make more money than doctors do, Mom," John added. Maria just smiled and stirred her soup.

"I wouldn't be a bit surprised, sweetheart."

* * *

The committee room was quite large with a long, imposing table of dark wood that ran almost the entire length of the enclosure. There were large windows along the exterior wall that let in welcome sunlight. The weather had been blustery, and the days had been gray and gloomy in Washington for the last week or so until the morning of the committee meeting, which had dawned with bursting sunlight.

Lauren was hopeful that the turn in the weather might be an omen of sorts; but she had always been a dedicated romantic. She had spared no effort to disprove that particular trait to those who worked around and with her, however. Somehow, she was more comforted by the notion that she should be seen as an unemotional, no nonsense, realist by others. She wasn't sure what that would prove, but she was convinced it must be something of great importance about the strength and genuineness of her character.

Alex had been met by Congressman Branch outside the committee room as planned. They talked for a few minutes before entering the large room. The congressman asked Alex to sit in one of the chairs around the outside walls of the room until he was introduced as a consultant, at which time he would be asked to come sit at the large table. He thought that odd, but he was not one to question Washington protocol, so he did as he was directed.

Alex had on his most expensive dark gray suit with a pale blue shirt and a red patterned tie and his best pair of wing tipped shoes. Even if he had nothing of value to report to the committee, at least he would be well dressed for the occasion.

There was a lot of talking and handshaking among the throng of people surrounding the table. Some had taken their seats at the table and were reading what Alex guessed was the proposed agenda. He was sure of only one thing about committees—he hated to be a part of them. Invariably there was a lot of talk and posturing and sometimes an argument or two if the pot got stirred a bit. The other thing he knew about committees was that there was always someone, or some group of someones, who would try to take control of the proceedings; and it was not always the person officially in charge. Alex was wondering if a meeting in the Nation's Capital would be any different. He would soon know more than he had any desire to know about Washington committees.

* * *

The promising sunlight that started the day had proven short lived. By noon the clouds had returned and a gloomy gray sky had covered the city. By evening, a chilling rain had begun to fall. Alex sat in his hotel room and looked out the window as the rainwater was streaking across the glass. Even though the lights of the city had come on, it was dark and cold looking outside. He felt lonely , out of place, and he missed Maria. He was still baffled as to why she did not want to come along. His puzzlement was festering inside him and feeling more like anger.

As much as Alex loved his wife, he was disquieted by the fact that he was also quite dependent on Maria. She had always been his confidante, his lover, his friend, his companion, and his steadfast due north no matter which direction life had taken him. Alex had always thought he was his own man, but when Maria was not there with him, he felt an uneasiness that felt like he was about to be cast adrift. It would be all too easy to blame his present apprehension on her.

Alex reminded himself he was a grown man, not to mention a doctor, as he picked up his cell phone to call his wife.

"Ola, Chiquita. Como esta?" Alex asked after he heard Maria's voice. He loved the sound of Spanish, though he only knew the few words and phrases Maria had taught him over the years.

"Ola, Señor Doctor. You're not going to like this report, I'm afraid," she said with a sigh.

"What is it, baby? One of the kids? What's going on?" his voice was getting louder as he spoke.

"Relax, sweetheart, the kids are Ok, it's the plumbing in this house we bought that's about to drive me crazy. It looks like we're going to have to replace the sewer drain out to the street. It's clogged with tree roots and some of the pipes are broken. It'll only be a few thousand dollars he says," Maria finished her report and exhaled loudly.

"Well, it's always something," Alex responded somewhat relieved. "Man, I can't believe this. Here I am wanting to shake your tree, and all you can talk about is waste disposal. You're so romantic."

"Well, my darling, it deals with one of our body's other basic functions. Imagine where we would be without it." Maria dragged out the "other" as she spoke.

"Why do you have to always be so practical? And always right? You're making me feel inferior."

"Remember, dear, I can't make you feel anything. At least that's what you've always told me."

"I must have been nuts. You can make me feel a lot of things, like you're doing right now," Alex said and sighed.

"Oh, baby, I love it when you talk to me like that, but phone sex is just not the same thing, my love."

"I should hope not. Virtual technology has not progressed that far yet. I hope it never does," Alex retorted and grinned. "So, what did you tell the plumber?"

"I just told him I would talk to you first. I don't know that we have much choice, honey."

"I guess we'll have to bite the bullet, baby. How are you doing? I miss you. Still wish you were in my warm bed tonight." There was something of a pause before Maria answered.

"I know. Me, too, sugar. I wanted to come. I still don't know why I stayed home. I guess the thought of going to Washington put me off. I was a bit addled when I thought about it. Now I'm sorry you're up there by yourself. Please come home soon." Maria was now sounding further and further away as Alex listened.

"Well, we're supposed to have a short follow up meeting tomorrow, and then I'll be on the plane again," Alex answered. "Tell the plumber to go ahead and don't worry about it. I think we have enough in savings to cover it if the insurance doesn't pay. I love you, baby. Tell the kids hello. Tell them I haven't made it on the evening news yet, but don't stop watching. Their old man may be a TV star yet," he said and laughed. His smile faded as he looked out the window of his room while the rain streaked the glass.

"See you tomorrow night, honey. I love you," Maria said and hung up.

Alex touched the "End" button on his phone and put it down on the table by the couch where he was sitting. The cold looking rain made the lights out on the street sparkle.

* * *

The meeting the next day, a Friday, was indeed a short one. Alex was grateful he was not called on to give any comments. Mr. Branch told him later his time would come, however, and that the first few meetings were largely organizational to give members of the committee assignments and such. Alex was given a large packet of bound documents listing committee members and an ongoing agenda. The committee would be reconvening in only two weeks in order to start formulating a plan to actually do something. The only thing that Alex could imagine that would be, was to start prodding the pharmaceutical companies to come up with more and more effective antidepressants. He couldn't see what else they could really do.

As the meeting closed, Alex bid farewell to Congressman Branch before leaving for the airport. He had shaken the congressman's hand and as he turned to leave the committee room, he walked right into a woman who was standing behind him, knocking her back on her heels. Alex instinctively grabbed her shoulders to keep her from falling.

"My goodness, I am sorry. I hope you aren't hurt, ma'am," he said. The woman just looked at him blankly at first through her pale blue eyes before she spoke.

"I guess I'm Ok," she said as she looked right into Alex's eyes. He relaxed his grip on her shoulders as she straightened her skirt.

"I was afraid I might have caused you to fall, miss," Alex continued. He was embarrassed and went on, "I usually don't grab strange women when I'm in Washington for the first time. I usually wait for the second or third visit to start doing that," he said and smiled. Again, she just looked at him for a moment before a faint smile began to lighten her face. She then started to laugh.

"You're the doctor from Texas, aren't you?" Lauren asked.

"Yes, ma'am, but we're not all so clumsy in that part of the country," Alex answered. "I'll try to look where I'm going next time... I'm Alex Madison."

"Lauren Marsh, Dr. Madison. I'm an assistant to Mr. Janes of the FPA."

"I'm happy to know you, Ms. Marsh. I hope when we see one another again, it won't be on a collision course," Alex replied.

"No harm done, doctor," Lauren replied.

"Well, I'd better get to the airport. I'll be back for the next meeting. Perhaps we can run into one another again at that time," Alex said and laughed.

"Perhaps so. Have a good trip, doctor."

7

Fall turned into winter and the days seemed colder and grayer even for Texas as the weeks elapsed with little respite for Alex in his office or at the hospital. He had attended several meetings in Washington of the Healthcare Emergency Committee in which nothing much had happened with the exception of a lot of rhetoric and handwringing.

The situation for the nation had worsened to the point in which employee absences in industry both large and small had become staggering. Some now feared that the country would have to face a slowdown (or even the shutdown) of the production of some goods and the provision of some services in both the public and private sector. There were shortages at grocery stores, dry goods stores, department stores, hardware stores, and just about every other kind of businesses that depended on deliveries to replenish their inventory. Employees who were still unaffected by the epidemic, were required to work longer hours to service a more demanding public. A tragedy no one could have possibly imagined only five years before had settled on beleaguered America and the world beyond America's shores.

Although none had yet erupted, there was nationwide fear there would be riots and other forms of anarchy erupting on the streets of the US. The military was on full alert along with all state and local law enforcement agencies. It was almost as if the nature of the epidemic was preventing any civil unrest. People had been felled by an emotional condition, depression, and did not seem to care what was to happen to them or the country for that matter.

Although the suicide rate had escalated to levels never seen before, the crime rate overall had come down and the murder rate had precipitously fallen. It was an irony that defied any known explanation or understanding. Sigmund Freud was no doubt spinning in his grave.

The president had pulled out all stops and demanded something be done and quickly. The FPA was on notice that whatever measures needed to be taken to end this self-destruction of the nation should be implemented immediately.

It was only too clear that the Agency did not know what more to do. Research could not go any faster than it could go. Incentives given to the drug companies could only accomplish so much. Who cared how many billions they would make if there was no society left in which to live? A civilization in which money would have no value had never been really contemplated before except by poor deluded souls who harbored dreams of some sort of an altruistic utopia. It looked like the earth would soon be populated by a dull, listless, uncaring humanity that seemed to be retreating back to a society that would soon become uncivilized and regressive. If there was a more unlikely, crazier scenario to be contemplated, no one had come up with it in the thousands of years since the first species that could be called human emerged from the savannahs of Africa. A world that had produced a Michelangelo, a Da Vinci, a Shakespeare, and an Einstein was most assuredly not supposed to turn out like this.

* * *

Alex pulled into his driveway fighting drooping eyelids after being up for almost eighteen hours or so. He had his office patients, but also was doing extra duty at the hospital where the patients were now being housed in the hallways on cots. The government agency that accredited hospitals would have been appalled, but there was nothing they were likely to do about it. In fact, there was nothing they really could do about it. If there had been any one positive effect of this catastrophe, it had nullified or otherwise silenced the functioning of many governmental bureaucrats. Alex smiled when he thought of that.

Alex was an optimistic person by nature, but he felt himself slipping away. There was not anything anybody could do as far as he could see. The world was in disarray now in a way he could never have imagined. He thought of what things must have been like during the Second World War in Europe when so many people lost everything with the collapse of their society and the destruction of the world they had known just a short time before. It was incredible that such a thing could befall the world again, yet here it was. Humanity now needed a miracle.

Alex parked his car and went inside to find Charlotte sitting in the den on the couch. She turned to look toward him as he walked in.

"Hello, sweetheart, doin' your homework?" he asked.

"Dad, Mom must be tired, I think she's in the bedroom asleep. I knocked on the door, but she didn't answer," she replied and frowned.

"I don't doubt it, Charlotte. We've all been pretty beat these last few months. Have you had your dinner, yet?"

"I fixed a sandwich, Dad," the teenager answered flatly.

"We all have to do more and pitch in and help with things the way they are now, honey," Alex added. "God knows when things are likely to change."

Charlotte just looked up at him with a somber frown on her face.

Alex put his coat on the back of the couch and slowly walked to the hallway that led to the bedrooms. It was quiet and dark without the light on.

Maria must be really tired, he thought as he opened the door to the master bedroom.

As he tiptoed in on the soft carpet, he looked to his left toward the bed. Maria was dressed in jeans and a sweater and no shoes as she lay with her back toward him facing the far wall. Alex thought it odd she was lying on his side of the bed and that she would even be in bed at this hour. It was just a few minutes past eight. Maria was more of a night person and always had been. They shared that trait which had led to many late night discussions before they ended up entwined in each other's arms.

"You tired tonight, baby?" he asked as he walked toward his wardrobe to empty his pockets on one of the shelves. He finished the ritual he performed every evening of taking his billfold out of his pants pocket and storing it and then putting his pocket change in a plastic jar on the shelf. Alex thought of the latter practice as sort of a forced savings account that he took to the bank every year or so to retrieve the cash he had accumulated. He then started the process all over again.

Maria had made no reply, so Alex went to his lavatory and washed his face and hands and dried them thoroughly. He stood for a moment until he realized that Maria had not moved and he could not hear her breathing. He took the few steps over to the bed and put his hand on her shoulder.

"Come on, baby, you won't sleep a wink tonight. Let's get some supper. Rise and shine," he continued and gently shook her shoulder. It was then Alex noticed how cool she was to his touch; her skin did not have its usual soft, silky feel. His throat tightened and suddenly became raspy dry. Something like fear, anxiety, and panic flowed from his stomach up to his mouth as he shook Maria harder. Her body just bounced on the bed, but she did not move. Alex seized her by the shoulder and pulled her toward him. Her face was sallow and waxy and her mouth was partly open. Her eyes were closed. Instinctively, he felt her neck for a pulse.

"No! No!" he screamed, and turned his wife on her back. He forced her mouth open and tried to breathe into it, hoping to resuscitate her. He pressed on her chest forcefully several times and tried to breathe for her again. Charlotte suddenly appeared at the bedroom door.

"Daddy, what is it? What's the matter?" she asked frantically.

"Call an ambulance, honey! Call 911! Call 911!" Alex

screamed at her. The teenager stood as though petrified for a moment and then turned and ran down the hallway. Alex wrapped Maria in his arms and sobbed as he held her. Outside, it was getting much colder as a frigid wind was assaulting Texas from the north.

* * *

Maria Marisol Benivides Madison was forty one years of age when her heart stopped beating as a result of an overdose of antidepressant medication she had taken. She had left no letter or note to anyone, but the medicine bottle found on her bedside table left no real doubt as to what had happened. The almost empty bottle was the only evidence that remained as to the condition that had led her spirit to depart the confines of her mortal body.

This vibrant, smart, engaging, and likeable woman was the last person anyone including her family would have believed could take her own life, and yet, she was gone with only a cold, gray, stone marker left as an earthly reminder of the reality of her absence to a host of devastated and inconsolable family, friends, and loved ones.

No one knew Maria had been depressed except Maria herself.

There was no one to blame, no one to scream at, no one to get mad at, except perhaps Maria herself, if, of course, one did not count the condition of depression itself. When that ghoulish, destructive cloud fell over a human being, there was no reasoning, logic, explanation, or clever escape from its devastating consequences in some people; or so it would seem. Medical science had thus far not devised a treatment that was always effective even if it could be applied.

* * *

Those kinds of concerns were far from Alex's mind as he stood by his wife's wooden casket on a cold, blustery, rainy day at Oakwood

59

Gardens Memorial Park. He was huddled with John and Charlotte, along with Maria's family as they watched helplessly as her earthly remains were lowered into the frigid ground. Alex thought of a line from a song that was one of Maria's favorites.

Life's full of loss; who counts the cost?

Alex knew only too well who would be counting the cost of Maria's death. He had never contemplated the possibility that she would not be with him. As many patients as he had seen over the years that had lost spouses and loved ones, Alex had never once considered he might be among them. He need not be concerned any more about the possibility of the world coming to a bad end; his world had already done so.

8

John was looking at the trees outside his classroom window that were now beginning to show the small, pale yellow-green leaves that were uncurling on the ends of the branches. The bare, barren look of winter was beginning to take on the first color of the coming spring. But it didn't feel much like spring to him. The past weeks had become months now since his mother's death. It seemed like it had been forever, and he was having a hard time remembering what she looked like. He and his friend James had gone to a movie the day she died and by the time he got home, the ambulance had already taken her away. Charlotte had been able to watch her go and say goodbye, or at least see her before she was transported from the house for the last time- a privilege he was denied.

When he saw her in her coffin later, she no longer seemed like his mother. Her eyes were closed; even though she had makeup on her face, she still looked waxy and pale. Despite the efforts the funeral home had expended to make her look otherwise, his mother still looked dead. He wanted to be able to say something to her and to have her talk to him again. He wanted to say he was sorry for every sarcastic, angry word he had ever said to her, or for every time he disappointed her. He wanted to scream at her for doing what she did; for not letting him know how bad she was feeling; for leaving all of them. He wanted to ask her why she couldn't tell him. Now, he and dad and Charlotte would never know, and what was worse, they could never, ever do anything about it but hurt. It was unimaginable; it was unspeakable; it was done.

She was gone, but he still couldn't believe it.

* * *

Lauren knocked softly on Harold Jane's glass door just as he looked up and motioned for her to come in. Before she could say anything, Harold stood up.

"I think we may have a winner, here, Lauren. This new drug from Gardner looks to be a good one. The clinicals are all in the green. In the trials, there was an almost ninety percent improvement across the board. I've never seen anything to compare with it, ever," he said as he turned his gaze toward her.

"I know, Harold, I've been following it closely, too. It's hard to imagine those clinical trial totals could be so positive. It's a completely novel compound. It's not a tricyclic or a SSRI. It apparently has a totally different mode of action than any antidepressant we have seen before. I hesitate to say so, but it almost sounds too good to be true," Lauren said with more enthusiasm than was usual for her.

"Oh, Lauren, don't even think that. We need something that works, and we need it yesterday. But, I know I'm preaching to the choir here."

"I'm on your side, Harold. I hope it works, too. I don't know how the country has been able to hold it together so far. How do you think we need to proceed?" Lauren asked.

"I talked to Sherman Branch and we have an emergency called meeting of the committee on Thursday. That's only two days away and we need to be ready with a workable plan," Harold said as he looked at some papers on his desk. "The biggest drawback with this agent is the time it takes to work. In the clinicals, it was at least two months and closer to three before most people showed a response with the oral dosing. The company thinks they may be able to come up with an aerosol form of the compound which may be faster acting. It apparently can enter the blood stream through special receptors in the nasal passages. It's the best option by any stretch that we have seen yet. If it works as we all hope, it will be a Godsend," he finished and let out a long sigh. "God help us if it doesn't."

"Amen, to that," Lauren said. "I'll get started on the data for the committee." Lauren turned, headed out the door, and started walking toward her desk. As she reached Art Loman's cubicle, he stood up suddenly.

"Hey, Lauren, is something going on?" he asked. Lauren just looked at him blankly for a moment.

"Well, it looks like we may have something like a breakthrough, Art. We'll soon know for sure," she said as she stopped in front of his desk.

"That's great, Lauren. Would you like to have some lunch today?" he asked.

"Thanks, Art, but I have to prepare some data for a committee meeting Thursday. I appreciate your asking, though," she added and smiled at him. As she turned and made her way toward her desk, she was unsure of why she had said what she did. Maybe Ann's incessant, good natured nagging was beginning to take effect at last. Or maybe she was just lonely. Whatever the case, she felt Art Loman's eyes on her back as she meandered on toward her cubicle. At least he was interested, and a woman could do worse.

I'm sounding like Ann, she thought.

Lauren sat down at her computer and started striking some keys. Something like a smile began to spread across her face.

* * *

Alex was once again on an airplane, but this time he was not bothered by any concerns about safety or the fragility of the huge aircraft, or even if it would descend back to earth in one piece or ten thousand. He knew that people navigated grief and loss in many different ways; in fact, he had piously told many of his patients that very thing. What's more, he meant every word of it at the time, and he would have done anything he could to ease their suffering. Now, he hadn't the least idea what he could do to mitigate his own. It was an irony not lost on him.

Physician, heal thyself, he thought as the big airplane shuddered against the wind as it lost altitude and began falling toward the airport runway. As the flight attendant had said when she made her announcement in preparation for landing, they would be on the ground in just a few short minutes. Of course, she didn't say if it would be in one piece or ten thousand, but either way, Alex didn't much care.

* * *

The recent meetings of the committee had been sparsely attended as morale had ebbed as the hope for any kind of quick resolution to the epidemic had evaporated like the memory of a smiling politician's campaign speech made the day before. This day, however, the room was bustling with activity and humanity as well. It was a called meeting, which alerted everyone that something was in the wind. Congressman Branch was busily talking to some people at the head of the table. Suddenly, he sent everyone to their respective places around the table and called the meeting open.

"Members, I am pleased to report that Gardner Pharmaceuticals has an announcement to make at this time. So as to not waste any more time, I am going to ask the company's chief of product development, Dr. Gene Harris, to speak at this time. Mr. Harris, go ahead, please," Congressman Branch finished and sat down.

A stocky man in a brown suit, white shirt, dark green tie, and wearing small, wire framed glasses stood up and cleared his throat. He seemed ill at ease as he looked down at a sheaf of papers in front of him on the table.

"I'm afraid I'm not a public speaker, so bear with me folks. I'm a researcher primarily," he stammered. "I am glad to be able to tell you all, though, that we have a very promising drug in development. It is a type of antidepressant no one has seen before. Or, at least we think no one has seen before. If it was known to anyone heretofore, they have kept very quiet about it," he cleared his throat again and drank from a glass in front of him on the table. He carefully wiped his mouth with a handkerchief, and cleared his throat again.

"The chemical name of the compound is desoxybutasane and the trade name is Dynasane. As I said, it is a different type of antidepressant medication. All the other types of antidepressant medications have acted on chemicals in the body at the nerve synapses, or the tiny space between nerve endings, or on the enzyme system in the human body in the case of the monoamine oxidase inhibitors." Dr. Harris paused again before he continued.

"To be perfectly frank, ladies and gentlemen, we don't really know what the mode of action of this compound is. We initially thought it was going to act like an SSRI, that is to say, on the reuptake of serotonin at the synapse, but as it turns out, it has no effect on serotonin at all. All we know is that it is quite effective against depression. The clinical trials have been so incredibly positive that it has astounded us all. No treatment for depression heretofore has been so positive. The clinical trials have shown that up to ninety per cent of recipients of this drug have shown clinical improvement and resolution of symptoms. Nothing we have in our pipeline has shown anything like the effectiveness of this drug. We have communicated with other drug companies and nothing any of them have can compare to Dynasane for clinical efficacy. I think it may be the answer the country and the world has been anxiously awaiting. Thank you for your attention," Looking a good deal relieved, Dr. Harris then sat down.

There were a few seconds of hushed silence, and then a burgeoning of many voices that began to crescendo around the room as committee members began to talk among themselves. The voices became louder until Congressman Branch waved his hand.

Alex had been looking out the window during most of the doctor's presentation. He had heard many just like it at many meetings, many times. When releasing a new drug on the market, the pharmaceutical companies were always anxious to tell everyone how marvelous it was and that there had never been anything like it before. And no matter what kind of drug it was, or what it was supposed to do, it would likely cure everything including athlete's foot. Furthermore, it had practically no side effects to speak of. Alex just shook his head and chided himself for becoming so jaded. He had to remind himself that this was not just business as usual any more. The future of the planet was at risk. But somehow on this day in late March, even that meant little to Alex as he continued to look out the window as Congressman Branch stood up now and asked for quiet.

"Thank you, Dr. Harris. We will forgo any questions right now, ladies and gentlemen. I want a chance to meet with the subcommittee on clinical implementation before we have any further discussion and make any final decisions. The subcommittee will meet this afternoon at two o'clock. We will adjourn for now. I want to thank everyone for coming."

The crowd slowly began to leave the room with most if not all involved in animated discussion. Alex was the one exception. As everyone made their way out of the room, he remained seated at the huge table. He continued to look absently at the trees outside with their branches bending and swaying to a brisk March wind.

"Hello, Dr. Madison," a voice came over Alex's left shoulder that momentarily, at least, shook him into some semblance of being in the here and now again. He turned to see a woman whose pale blue eyes were rather pleasantly fixed upon his as she spoke. "It's good to see you again, sir. How are things down in Texas?" she asked as she straightened the collar of her white silk blouse. Her long brown hair framed her face and cascaded down over her narrow shoulders. Alex was obviously taken aback as he turned further around to face her.

"Oh, hello, Ms... ah...."

"Marsh, sir, Lauren Marsh. We met at the first meeting of the committee some several months ago last fall," she reminded him.

"Oh, of course, Ms. Marsh. I'm afraid my memory isn't what it used to be. I hope you are well. You're with the FPA aren't you?" he asked.

"Yes, sir. I'm Harold Jane's assistant." Lauren could see that Alex was uncomfortable, so she did not linger. In fact she was not sure why she had spoken to him anymore than she knew why she had been so friendly recently to Art. All she knew right now was that she was feeling uncomfortable and a bit foolish. "You looked kind of lonely sitting there by yourself, sir. I just thought I would say hello," she added and started to turn to leave.

"Oh, please, Ms. Marsh, I'm sorry. I don't mean to be inhospitable. My mind was far away for a moment, I'm afraid. I guess I'm a bit tired from the trip, and work has been a bear the last number of months. I guess you've been experiencing the same thing, though," Alex said as he came to his feet.

"Well, I'll forgive you this time if you will stop calling me Ms. Marsh. My name is Lauren," she said and looked into his eyes.

"That's small penance to pay, Lauren. My name is Alex. Please call me that, if you will." Lauren looked at him with some discomfort arising in her stomach. Calling a professional man she knew only casually at best by his first name was not in her book of standard operating procedures. It was also somewhat puzzling to Alex. He was not sure why he had granted her the privilege. It just seemed to come pouring out of his mouth.

Oh, well, he thought, *it's done.*

"Well, I suppose I will see you at the subcommittee meeting this afternoon," Lauren finally said after a brief period of some uncomfortable foot shuffling.

"Yes, I suppose so, Lauren," Alex answered. "It looks as though this new drug may have some promise."

"Yes, it sounds like it, Alex. I'll see you then," she said as she turned and left.

When this woman called his name, a flowing, tingling sensation began to cover Alex as if his body was being slowly submerged in a warm, comforting hot tub. It wasn't until later that he realized that while Lauren was there, Maria had slipped away from his thoughts. Those same sensations that had been warming him on the inside just a moment before suddenly turned to a chill.

* * *

"Your dad gone to Washington again?" Amy asked.

The warm spring day found Amy and Charlotte at one of the tables outside the cafeteria at Jamison Junior High during their lunch hour.

"Yes, he took off yesterday. It was a special meeting of some kind. My aunt Grace is staying with me and John at the house," Charlotte answered as she was toying with a potato chip held in her fingers. "He should be back tomorrow sometime, he said," she added. Amy frowned as she looked at her friend.

"What's that committee supposed to do anyway? Things just keep getting worse. My parents are both taking medication for depression now," the teenager barked as the two girls were squinting their eyes in the noonday sun.

"Dad says they are looking for some new treatments for depression. So far, they have come up with zip," Charlotte explained. "I don't know what's going to happen, Amy. Everything has gone to crap. I hope there is still a world going on when we graduate high school." The two girls then just looked at each other.

Amy knew that Charlotte was hurting, but Amy was also well aware that she was just not the consoling type. Sad, serious things just left her confused. Still, it bothered her that she could not help her friend. She knew that Charlotte and her mother had been close. Amy envied that. Amy and her mother on the other hand, had, at best, an angry, adversarial struggle over everything from clothing to chores to how she fixed her hair. If it had to do with anything

Amy did or did not do, or anything she was even planning to do, an inevitable struggle ensued. To make things worse, when Amy appealed to her father, he invariably sent her back to her mother. She was trapped. Why couldn't her mother have committed suicide instead of Charlotte's so she could be free of these hindrances to her happiness? All she could do right now was pray for the day when she graduated high school and left home. She would find her own way in the world. No one was going to stop her, either.

The clanging of the school bell signaling the end of lunch interrupted Amy's thoughts of her friend and family as she and Charlotte got up from the table and deposited their trash into the plastic bin by the sidewalk.

"Where you going now, Charlotte?" Amy asked.

"English," she answered.

"Oh, yeah, you've got that old bitch Anderson, don't you?" Amy sneered. "I had her last term and, God, I hated her. She's such a prude and I wonder who she thinks she's fooling with that dyed hair," Amy went on with a gleeful cackle.

A scowl formed on Charlotte's face as she stopped on the walkway with her books in her arms. She now stood facing her best friend.

"Amy, do you ever stop to listen to the horrible sounding things you say about people? All Mrs. Anderson ever did was try to teach you English. You talk like she was trying to murder you or something."

Charlotte then turned and strutted away. Amy stood and watched Charlotte until she disappeared into the building.

"Bitch!"

Amy then turned and walked the other way.

* * *

By two o'clock the sun was still shining through the glass windows of the committee room as the participants began taking their seats around the large table for the called meeting scheduled by Congressman Branch. There were about a dozen people in all. As he sat down, Alex noticed that Lauren Marsh took a seat in one of the chairs around the periphery of the room. He nodded in her direction with a faint smile and quickly turned his attention back to the head of the table. If she returned his greeting, he did not see it.

Lauren had noticed the gold band on Alex's finger the first time they met, and after the initial disappointment she felt, did her utmost to delete it from her mind. Just another of life's curveballs she had to face. She just assumed he was married and let it go. The trouble was, it would not let her go. During the ensuing meetings of the committee, she found herself looking in his direction as though her eyes couldn't find anything or anyone else to look at. It did not appear that he noticed her at all, and that notion was corroborated when she had spoken to him earlier in the day. He did not even remember her name. Lauren sighed deeply and turned her attention to the notes in her lap.

There were three other psychiatrists on the committee from other parts of the country, none of whom Alex knew personally, but he had become acquainted with all three since he had been attending the meetings. He learned they all had private practices and one was an active researcher as well. Two of them were, in Alex's opinion, bright, thoughtful, realistic, and concerned about the problem at hand, while the other, the researcher, was a bag of wind with no real grasp of the depth and far reaching consequences of the problem they were trying to end. All the man could seem to do was make inappropriate jokes and self-aggrandizing statements suggesting his central role in ending the crisis that left Alex and the other two psychiatrists either looking at the ceiling or shuffling their feet.

Alex suspected someone so glaringly misguided about the purposes of their task must have had a friend or cohort in politics who wanted to be in the headlines if anything came of these proceedings. It was just the kind of thing that made Alex never want to be a part of the political system or anywhere near it. Where there was credit to be claimed for worthwhile achievement, there were always plenty of those who were willing to step forward and receive it. But, when there was blame to be laid for failure, no one ever had a clue, except of course that someone else was responsible. It was the way of the world and nothing that Alex was likely to do was going to change it any time soon. As much as he tried and wanted to be an objective, balanced realist, he was first and forever an idealist, and what was more telling, he knew it.

What would transpire in the next hour or so would be little more than logistics to implement the distribution of this new drug that was supposed to start the nation and the world on a path to healing; but what was to happen after that would throw into question every notion of what Alex ever considered sane and sacred.

9

Alex was sitting in the airport waiting area near his departure gate. It would be another twenty minutes or so before his flight would be boarding. The darkening sky would soon be totally black as only vestiges of gray hovered near the horizon as the day was slowly dying. Despite the coming of spring, it was getting colder outside. The artificial light coming up along the roadways and around the airport was beginning to illuminate the evening darkness.

Alex placed his carry-on luggage on a small table beside the chair he selected and sat down. His feet felt heavy and his stomach was tight and knotted as he stared out the expanse of tall windows in front of him. The plane was already parked at the gate with the accordion-like extension of the jet way resting against its side covering the entry door to the aircraft. Although he had been flying a good bit more than usual the last six months or so, he still didn't like it much. He would be glad to get home, even as lonely and deserted as the house was since Maria was not there anymore. Her absence was like a clamorous, deafening silence that he felt when he was at home. Although they never spoke of it, he knew Charlotte and John felt it, too.

Alex squirmed in his chair; no matter how he positioned his body he enjoyed no comfort. He was not sure how he was going to tolerate the several hours he would have to spend on the plane to get back home. It was not unlike the increasing number of nights which found him aimlessly writhing on wrinkled, twisted sheets with his arms groping and searching but finding nothing to grasp and hold. Maria's absence was a cruelty that conjured troubling, frightening emotions in Alex that he could never have imagined while she lived. His anger toward her overpowered and devastated him, and was then followed by waves of relentless, merciless guilt.

Now, there was no appeal, no absolution, no resolution, and no solace for him. Whoever came up with the term "survivor guilt" must have had firsthand experience with the condition, because those who were left behind surely suffered from it unless they were totally inhuman or complete sociopaths. If Maria wanted to hurt him, she had chosen the cruelest way possible. He had been victimized by his guileless love and devotion to her. His dependence on her constant self-effacing goodness through all their marriage had left him a pitiful victim of her final treachery. She had done this thing to him. He had been faithful. He had loved her and cared for her. He had never wavered. Maria had been weak. The most capable, resourceful woman Alex had ever known had proven to be weak when she needed to be her strongest. Alex hated her for that most of all. He had been convinced there was not another man in the entire universe that could have stolen Maria from him. But he had been wrong. She had been seduced by a far more cunning, enticing, and finally destructive suitor.

His name was Depression.

* * *

Lauren stood in the hallway, helplessly watching as he slowly walked away. If she were to obey her heart, she would go racing after him like some smitten schoolgirl. But, some forty plus years of carefully constructed inhibitions would not permit it. He had not stopped to speak to her as she had secretly hoped. Thoughts of this man from Texas had been invading her days and nights these past few months, and she had been unable to lift a finger to stop it. Never mind the fact that he was married to another woman. Lauren did not allow such a mundane consideration to spoil her excited but unwholesome fantasies.

Although it had been six months or so since it happened, she could still feel his hands gripping her shoulders to stop her from falling when he bumped into her that day they had met. From that first clumsy, serendipitous encounter, she became lost in the gaze of his emerald green eyes and his casually disarming smile. She was hardly the kind of woman who swooned over any man who walked by, yet Dr. Alex Madison was hardly just any man who walked by. Although she didn't understand it, his mere presence had reignited feelings she considered long buried, or at least never again accessible. Lauren even considered that her change of attitude toward Art had been because she was hoping he would distract her obsessing over the good doctor. If it were true, that plan had obviously not worked very well. If this madness was to continue, she guessed the next step would be to consult a psychoanalyst.

As these thoughts pressed on her mind, Lauren gripped the sheaf of documents she had in her arms tighter and pressed them against her breast until her fingernails were slicing into the defenseless pages. She stood motionless with her gaze fixed on the retreating doctor until he reached the end of the hall and rounded the corner disappearing from view.

"Lauren...Lauren," a voice of which she was only dimly aware made Lauren blink her eyes and turn her head suddenly. Harold Janes was looking intently at her. "Lauren, are you coming with me back to the office?" he asked. Lauren coughed and cleared her throat before she could answer.

"Yes, Harold, I'm ready when you are," she finally said, making an effort to disguise her embarrassment.

"You seemed distracted there for a moment, Lauren," he said as they started down the long hallway.

"Oh, I was just thinking of all the things I have to do when I get home, Harold. My house is a total wreck. I haven't straightened it in weeks." She was not actually lying, only avoiding telling the whole truth; but then again, she did not have to tell Harold everything even though they were somewhat closer than the everyday boss and employee.

"I guess we've all been pretty distracted these last months. I'm glad I have Annabelle to keep me grounded. Marrying her was the best decision I ever made in my life, Lauren," he added looking straight ahead as they walked together down the hall.

"She's such a lovely woman, Harold. You're a lucky man for sure," Lauren replied as her stomach tightened and sensations of discontent flowed through her body.

* * *

"Dr. Madison, there's a man on the phone...says he's from Washington. Should I put him through?" Emily Northcutt's voice came cutting over the intercom on Alex's office phone. It was Friday morning after Alex's arrival back from the meetings in DC. Alex had been lying back in his chair between patients. He opened his eyes and began rubbing them with his fingers.

"Did he say who he is, Emily?" Alex asked.

"No, sir. He just asked to talk to you...said it is quite important."

"Ok, Emily, put him through." Alex cleared his throat and sat up in his chair. He picked up his handset as an unfamiliar voice came into his ear.

"Dr. Madison?" the voice intoned.

"Yes, this is Alex Madison, to whom am I speaking?"

"This is Charles Danton, Dr. Madison. I am with the Department of Defense. I'm a member of the Special Operations Branch of the Defense Department. We're part of the CIA, but don't worry, we don't want you to do any spy work or anything like that," he said and laughed. "We do, however, want you to participate in a special project that is related to the Healthcare Emergency Committee for which you are a consultant. I don't wish to alarm you, but this assignment requires a high level security clearance. Congressman Branch has requested that you be a part of this operation. You are the only physician on the committee he has selected for participation. The president has approved your being included as well," Mr. Danton said as Alex's

75

ear had become glued to the phone. He had not moved or blinked his eyes since he heard Mr. Danton make mention of the CIA. Waves of both excitement and fear were washing over him.

Good grief, Alex thought, *what the hell is this?*

"If you do not want to sign on, Dr. Madison, you need to let me know now. I'm sorry to be so cryptic, sir, but confidentiality and security is a paramount consideration. I'm speaking to you on a secured line right now," the man said and stopped for a moment. Alex was not sure how he wanted to respond, but he thought he needed to say something. After a somewhat pregnant pause, Alex finally spoke.

"Mr. Danton, I hope you will understand my reticence, sir. It's not every day I get a call from someone saying they're with the CIA. I guess my first impression is that I certainly do not want to disprove Congressman Branch's confidence in me. Still, I'm concerned about the secrecy and what I might be asked to do. Can you give me an idea of what this is about?" Alex replied and let out the breath he had been holding even though he had been speaking.

"All I can really say, doctor, is that you will be involved in making decisions that bear on your country's wellbeing and future and perhaps even its survival; hence, the security issues. I'm afraid that is all I can say. What's more, I need your decision now. I cannot wait for you to consider it. I must know right now, at this moment, if you are in or out, sir," he said and the phone line fell into an eerie silence. Alex stood up from his chair, turned, and looked out onto the freeway. It was something he often did when he had to make decisions of some importance.

This one certainly qualifies for that distinction, he thought.

He continued to gaze out the window for a brief second or two, and just as a motorcycle cop sped by with his lights throbbing blue and red, Alex took a breath.

"I'm in," he said.

"As you wish, sir. Now, you must listen to me carefully. It is now 10:35 AM. At precisely 1:30 PM, a car will arrive at your home to pick you up. You may pack a small bag with whatever personal items you need. You will be given further instructions and information at that time," Mr. Danton said.

"How long will I be gone?" Alex asked.

"You likely will be back home tomorrow evening, but that is subject to change."

"What about my family? I have children that must be cared for."

"That has already been arranged. You will have an opportunity to speak with your son before you leave. Your children will be looked after by your wife's sister. We have already contacted her." Alex felt a curious mixture of amazement and anger as he listened.

"You must have been pretty sure of my decision, Mr. Danton," Alex said with and edge in his voice.

"Let's just say we were confident you would do the right thing, Dr. Madison," the man said curtly. "This is a matter of some considerable importance, sir."

"It must surely be," Alex answered. "I just don't like other people, even the CIA, making my decisions for me."

"I understand completely, sir. I hope you will appreciate the necessity for all the cloak and dagger aspects of this as time elapses. If you are not at your home at 1:30 PM, there will be no further contact with you from anyone from the government, and you will no longer be a consultant on the Healthcare Emergency Committee. We are hopeful you will give your country your complete loyalty and cooperation. The car will be at your home as I have instructed you. Best wishes, sir." With that, Alex's line went dead, and he sat motionless at his desk, clutching his phone in his hand with his knuckles blanched white.

As if suddenly animated from a forced inactivity, Alex arose from his desk, took his coat from the rack where he had hung it, and walked out of his office. He stopped at Emily's desk only long enough to tell her to cancel out the rest of the day and he needed to leave. She looked at him curiously for a moment, said, "Yes, sir," and returned to what she had been doing as Alex headed for the elevators.

10

"That's right, son, I should be back tomorrow night, but I'm not sure. I want you to look after your sister and do what your aunt Grace asks you to do. I know I can count on you, John. I wouldn't be going unless I had to. It's an emergency kind of thing again," Alex explained to his son by phone. John had received a notice in his last class before lunch that his dad would be calling him at school with an important message. John's pulse had quickened when he received that news, and he was relieved when his father came on the line to talk to him. Even though the school had banned cell phones on campus, he had one. He thought about making a joke when his dad came on the phone, but he thought better of it under the circumstances.

"Ok, Dad. What's going on anyway? This sounds kind of sudden. Are you alright?" John asked.

"I know, son. It surprised me, too. I'm fine. I don't want you to be worried. Just take care of Charlotte and I'll be back as soon as I can. Your aunt Grace will be there when you get home from school."

"Well, I don't know how Charlotte will feel about me taking care of her, but I won't tell her you said that. I'll just tell her you told us both to behave. Ok, Dad?" Alex laughed despite his anxiety. John could always seem to come up with something he didn't expect. John had his mother's wit and Alex's sarcastic bent of mind.

"That's probably a good way to put it, John. I'll see you tomorrow night." Alex put his phone down and continued to pack a small bag with a change of shirt, socks, and underwear. If he had to stay longer, he would just buy what he needed. He checked to see how much he had in his money clip and was satisfied that he had several hundred dollars in his pocket. Alex had assumed he would be going to Washington DC, but it had occurred to him that assumption might be wrong. Mr. Danton had only said he would get further instructions after he was in the car. If the situation were not so serious, this would be sounding more and more like a suspense novel—and not a real good one at that. Alex was excited, but also had an underlying feeling of dread he could have done without.

Alex glanced at the clock on Maria's bedside table and saw it was five minutes after one.

Baby, I wish you were here for this one, he thought. He closed his bag, walked to the dining room, and looked out one of the front windows.

No car as of yet.

He sat down on the couch in the den, took a deep breath, and slowly let it out. As he closed his eyes, he wished like hell that when he opened them, Maria would be sitting there with him once again.

* * *

"Did you get it all out of your system the other day? Huh? Huh? I guess you thought you were hot stuff prancing off like you did," Amy growled at Charlotte when she caught up with her in the hall between classes. "You can apologize anytime you're ready, Miss Priss."

Charlotte turned to look at her friend, but kept on walking.

"Please, Amy, could we have a little less drama? Not a whole lot less, maybe, but a little less?" Charlotte replied. "I think you've been watching too many soap operas, my dear. Can't we just make up like best friends are supposed to?"

Charlotte's comments took Amy by surprise. She was not used to Charlotte's being so cool under fire, especially when she was trying to be so intimidating.

Not to be bested, Amy regrouped and shot back, "Oh, listen to that! You must've eaten an extra bowl of Wheaties this morning, or is it that time of the month, little girl?"

Charlotte stopped abruptly and glared into Amy's dark eyes.

"My, my, Amy. Do you really want to know?"

Charlotte paused and a grin came over her face.

"I didn't know you knew about those things, Amy. Health class must be doing you some good after all," she added before her friend could mount a comeback.

Amy's face flushed as her eyes widened in anger.

"And I guess you're so smart, aren't you, Miss Priss? You make me sick! You're just a mousy little bitch with a rich daddy! No wonder your mother killed herself! She was probably sick of you!"

Without warning or hesitation, Charlotte leaped forward and pushed Amy back against the lockers that lined the hallway. There was a loud, metallic clang as the teen's body slammed against the metal doors. Before Amy could respond in any manner, Charlotte pushed her up against the lockers and began to use her notebook like a bludgeon, hitting Amy repeatedly on her face and chest until she fell to the floor on her back. Charlotte then threw her notebook down on Amy's prostrate body and stood over her like a victorious gladiator. Amy tried to get up, but when she did, Charlotte pushed her back down again with her foot.

"Go ahead, you selfish bitch! Get up and see what I do to you next! Go ahead!" Charlotte screamed as she stood over her best friend lying motionless on the floor.

Amy was stunned and shocked. She began to whimper and cry. Charlotte's face was a livid red color and her eyes were flashing like they were on fire. The students in the hallway stopped as if suddenly petrified. A teacher who had been only a few steps away when the incident started raced over and grabbed Charlotte by the arms to pull her back. She pulled herself loose from his grip and started back toward Amy who was still on the floor sobbing. By then, several students and another teacher came forward to get in between Charlotte and her fallen friend preventing any more mayhem between the two girls.

Several students and the teacher helped Amy to her feet as the teacher led her down the hall and away from Charlotte who was still angrily glaring at Amy's back. The other teacher had once again grabbed Charlotte's arms trying to restrain her from following Amy. Charlotte struggled against him for a moment, but his grip was firmer this time as she continued to scream at her best friend who was now surrounded by a small, excited coterie of students.

The whirling sensation in her head began to slow a bit as Charlotte stopped pulling against the teacher's restraining hold on her. Her breaths were quick and shallow as she watched the small crowd around Amy lead the tearful teenager away down the hall.

"Let go of me!" she shouted as the teacher tightened his hold on her arms.

"Settle yourself down, young lady!" the man barked at her.

Just at that moment, the vice principal hurried up alongside Charlotte and slid her arm around the teen. She then looked toward the other teacher and pursed her lips.

"I've got her now, Mr. Johnstone. Thank you for your help," she said as she ushered Charlotte to the side of the hallway in front of the lockers.

A group of classmates had gathered around them both watching intently.

"You all go on to class, now. Go on!" the vice principal commanded as the group only slowly showed any inclination to comply.

She then turned toward Charlotte.

"What on earth, honey? Are you alright? What happened?"

The bewildered woman was asking questions she really didn't expect to be answered as she tried to calm the girl. She knew Charlotte only as a name and a face, but she also knew she had never been a behavioral problem in the past.

Charlotte was still looking down the hall as Amy was being escorted away. She could no longer see her friend because of the crowd that had surrounded her like she was some kind of celebrity. Charlotte's head was clearing more now as the whirling slowed. She realized it was Vice Principal Barnette who was standing next to her. The teenager looked blankly into the woman's eyes and then back at the receding crowd around Amy.

Well, I guess I've done it now, she thought.

She expected her father would be surprised and angry. She also expected her mother would be shocked, disappointed, and ashamed if she were still alive. Charlotte also expected she was now going to be in world of trouble. What she had not expected as she stood in the hallway with the vice principal was how good she would feel.

* * *

The large, black vehicle pulled away from the curb as Alex was trying to get comfortable in the back seat.

The CIA really does use these black SUVs, he was thinking as the two young men in the front seat looked straight ahead and said nothing.

The driver had opened the door and greeted him flatly and then closed it securely after Alex was inside. He could think of at least a half a dozen movies in which he had seen similar-looking black vehicles used by various government agencies for nefarious purposes. The darkly tinted windows added to their rather sinister appearance.

The young man who was driving made his way over a number of surface streets until he turned onto I 30, one of the interstate highways that passed through town. At that point, Alex concluded they must be headed for the DFW International Airport. It was at that moment that the young man on the passenger side of the front seat turned and handed a red, letter-sized envelope to Alex.

"You need to read this now, Dr. Madison," the young man said.

His sunglasses were so dark that Alex could not tell if he was looking at him or not. Alex took the envelope, but said nothing. The dark red missive was secured by a closure that consisted of two dime-sized round plastic disks with a string attached to one that wound around and under both of them. Alex unraveled the string and opened the cardboard envelope.

There was a single sheet of white paper with the following message:

Dr. Madison:

You are not to speak to anyone other than the two men in the vehicle with you until you are inside the aircraft.

Charles Danton

Special Operations Division, CIA

Alex read the brief message, held it in his hand for a brief moment, and then returned it to the envelope.

"Do you understand the instructions, sir?" the man who handed him the envelope asked.

Alex was thinking, *What kind of a stupid question is that? I would have to be a moron not to understand it.*

Resisting the urge to make some sarcastic rejoinder, he simply replied, "Yes, sir, I do," and left it at that.

No smile appeared on his face, but he was smiling inwardly as he was thinking that maybe he was a moron to have agreed to this now questionable escapade. He then contented himself by looking out the window at the passing traffic.

The dark SUV made its way along I 30 until the driver turned on the exit to US 360 North. From there it headed toward the airport, but by a route that was unfamiliar to Alex. After passing through a guarded gate nestled in a grove of trees that was invisible from the freeway, the driver took several narrow roads until he suddenly pulled up to a small hangar on the periphery of the huge airfield. Alex conjectured that it probably could be seen from the air if one knew where to look.

There was a small passenger jet parked next to the hangar and two men dressed in dark suits standing beside it. The entry door to the plane was open and steps were in place beneath it. The sleek aircraft's engines were whining in the afternoon sun as the dark vehicle pulled up close to the plane's door.

"This is where you get off, Dr. Madison. Just go ahead and

board the plane, if you will, sir. Have a good flight, sir," the man in the passenger seat said as he continued to look straight ahead out the front windshield. The driver then got out and opened the door for Alex and motioned for him to get on the plane.

Alex stepped out of the door and after a brief hesitation, walked to the plane, climbed the steps, and went inside. Immediately, one of the pilots closed the cabin door and returned to the cockpit without speaking.

There were eight large, comfortable-looking seats inside, four on each side of a center aisle. Alex just stood for a moment as though disoriented, when a man in a dark suit suddenly appeared from behind a partition in the back of the aircraft.

"Good afternoon, Dr. Madison. Please take a seat wherever you like. We will be taking off momentarily, sir," he said in a somewhat cordial tone. "Please buckle your seat belt."

Alex did as he was asked and almost the moment he snapped his seat belt in place, the engines on the small jet began to whine at a higher pitch and the plane began to move.

The bizarre nature of this whole overdrawn scene left Alex with a discomfiting feeling of unreality; the same kind of disconnected, disjointed unreality he only felt when he was dreaming. The plane was beginning to gather some speed as it taxied toward one of the auxiliary runways on the edge of the airport. Alex felt as though his stomach was turning inside out as his fingers dug into the soft armrests of his seat. He pushed himself back against the soft cushions and thought of Maria.

11

It had caused something of a stir, but Harold Janes had insisted that Lauren was to be allowed to accompany him to the top-level conclave that had been called by Congressman Branch, approved by the president, and organized by the CIA. The issue was concerning her security clearance.

Lauren's maiden name was Calzone. Her father's brother Marcello Calzone had been a known associate of the Marco crime family that operated primarily in the Boston area where Lauren had grown up. As a child she had been only dimly aware of the significance of that family association. She had known her uncle Marcello as a friendly, gregarious man who visited her family in their home from time to time. He was known to the local, state, and national law enforcement community, however, as a particularly ruthless and merciless assassin for the Marco family.

To his credit, Marcello did his best to keep the Marco's unholy business away from his own family, but it was a case of guilt by association for Lauren, her mother, and father. Apparently her Uncle Marcello's occupation and ties to the Marcos were well known to the FBI, and there were files in abundance to document it. There had never been any problem for Lauren from this tainted family association until a red flag was raised as her background was screened for the special committee assignment as Harold Janes' assistant. Some very serious looking men in dark suits questioned her extensively about her family ties until they were satisfied that her inclusion and participation in the activities of the special committee would not be a threat to the security of the

United States of America. Lauren thought it all much ado about nothing, but she was unaware at the time of the actual nature of the special committee's responsibilities. All she knew for sure was that it was very hush-hush and she was instructed not to talk about it to anyone.

"I hope they didn't give you too hard a time, Lauren," Harold said as she was taking a seat in his office across the desk from him. Lauren just smiled faintly as she sat down.

"Oh, it wasn't anything, Harold, just a bunch of questions about my family," she answered with something like a smirk on her face. "I suppose you know my uncle was a crime figure in Boston when I was growing up. You do know, of course, that all Italian families are members of the Mafia, don't you, Harold?" She turned to look at her boss as her smirk turned into a broad smile.

"Well, I'm glad you're taking it with good humor, Lauren. I'm not sure what this upcoming meeting is all about, but it sounds like it will be quite important. I'm sure it has to do with the new drug. I'm having a hard time understanding why such secrecy and security is necessary, though," he replied and shook his head side to side. I guess the CIA knows best. I'm not going to second guess them. We'll just have to see what develops tomorrow at the meeting."

"Do I need to bring anything? Anything that they haven't seen before?"

"No, Lauren. They told me we are only to be in attendance. No more data is needed. I suspect some kind of announcement will be made and an agenda for the drug's distribution will be decided," he continued as he sat behind his desk with his hands steepled in front of his face. "I understand from the Interior Department that absenteeism in the work force is at an all-time high this last month. There were five congressmen who attempted suicide in the last two weeks. Fortunately, three of them survived." He stopped for a moment as his gaze turned away from Lauren.

"I tell you, Lauren, no one has ever seen anything like this in this country, or any other for that matter. The medical community is making heroic efforts, but there has been no progress. I don't know if you knew or not, but one of the doctors on the committee had his wife commit suicide several months ago. I think I saw you talking to him at the last meeting —Dr. Madison, I think is his name. The doctor from Texas." A sudden chill swept over Lauren. It suddenly became clear why Dr Madison had seemed so distant and indifferent in the meetings. Lauren was saddened but also felt relief to hear this. She dare not think what these unhappy tidings for Alex Madison might portend for her. It was not long before she would feel the inevitable pangs of guilt as this door she thought forever closed to her might now be unlocked. She squirmed in her chair and began to twist a lock of her long brown hair like she did as a child when she was thinking about something that made her happy.

"No, I didn't know about that. I don't really know him. We've just spoken briefly at some of the meetings," Lauren replied. "That poor man," she added as her voice trailed away.

"Yes," Harold said softly. "A tragedy indeed."

* * *

Thunderous sounds assaulted Alex's ears. He also felt something like a jolt against his shoulder.

"Dr. Madison...Dr. Madison," a bodiless voice echoed as Alex's eyes began to slowly open. He instinctively turned his head toward the source of the sound to see the dark suited man who had welcomed him on the plane earlier peering down at him. "We're here, Dr. Madison," the man added and turned to walk toward the front of the plane.

Alex was emerging from unconsciousness as he reached down to unbuckle his seat belt. He was surprised he slept so soundly. He could never sleep on planes or any other vehicle for that matter. The golden glare of the fading sunlight caused him to squint his eyes as he looked out the window of the plane.

One of the pilots came out of the cockpit and opened the door to the aircraft. He pushed the door to one side and returned to the cockpit without looking at or speaking to Alex.

"The car is ready for you now, Dr. Madison," a voice from behind Alex announced. He turned and saw it was the man who had awakened him. The unsmiling man gestured toward the door of the plane. Alex then picked up his bag and walked toward the open door.

An apparent clone of the SUV in Dallas that had taken him to the airport was waiting with one of the side doors open. A tall, lean man in a dark suit wearing sunglasses was standing stiffly by the vehicle as Alex walked toward it. "Good evening, Dr. Madison," the man said and placed his hand on the door of the SUV anticipating Alex's entry into the vehicle. With Alex inside, the man closed the door firmly and climbed onto the passenger seat of the SUV as it began to ease away from the plane. It proceeded past a large hangar and out the gate of a chain link fence where a uniformed guard was standing to the side. The guard raised his hand while the driver of the vehicle returned the gesture as he drove on through the gate and out onto a side street next to the airport. The sun was just disappearing as the black SUV gathered speed on the nearly deserted roadway.

* * *

"Where's Charlotte, aunt Grace?" John asked when he arrived home from school. "I heard she got into a fight at school today." He was looking anxiously at his aunt as she was setting the table for supper. She continued putting the dishes on the table and said nothing as the boy stood with his eyes glued on her.

"She's in her room, John, but I don't think you should bother her just now," she answered. Grace Gutiérrez was Maria's older sister by some ten years and had been helping Alex with the children since her sister's death. Her husband Armando had died two years earlier of a heart attack, and her three children had all left home either to marry or go to work, or both. She was alone and welcomed the opportunity to look after John and Charlotte whenever she could. Maria had often said that if ever there was a woman born to be a wife and mother, Grace was God's anointed one.

Grace continued fussing around her sister's kitchen while John continued to stand motionless by the counter. He watched his aunt walk back and forth to the table several times as he stood frowning.

"Is she Ok, Aunt Grace? I was worried. Some of the kids I talked to at school said she lost control and looked like she could have killed Amy. They've always been best friends. Did you talk to her?" he asked still watching as Grace stayed in constant motion preparing their evening meal. His aunt finally stopped, walked over to him, and put her arms around his shoulders.

"Your sister is Ok, John. She's just upset right now. She didn't say much and I thought it best not to question her. She was crying when she got home and went straight to her room. I talked to her a bit, and she said she was tired and wanted to sleep for a while. That's all I know. Now, go get ready for supper, honey. It'll be ready in a few minutes," Grace replied and started back in motion again.

John continued to stand frowning for a moment and then walked through the kitchen and den back to the hallway that led to the bedrooms. He stopped momentarily at Charlotte's closed door and just looked down at his sneakers before he tapped lightly on it. There was no response at first, but then a voice from inside the room said, "What?" rather gruffly. John slowly eased the door open and took a few reluctant steps inside. Charlotte was lying quietly on her bed with her back to the door. She still had on her school clothes—jeans, school jersey, the windbreaker she liked to wear, and her favorite pair of running shoes.

"Sis," he said and waited for her to respond. She said nothing, so he continued, "Are you alright?" and waited again. What she did next was the last thing he would have expected from Charlotte. She sprang up from her bed and quickly walked over to her brother thrusting her arms around his neck as she started to cry.

"Oh, John, I miss mom. I miss her so bad," she said as her wracking sobs were coming in short, staccato bursts. "I wish Dad was here," she continued as she held her brother closer. As stunned as he was, John stood and extended his arms around his sister as she wept. He could not remember a single time in the past that they had ever hugged each other. It felt strange to him being so physically close to her. He was shy with girls, but somehow holding Charlotte felt natural to him now. For a moment at least, he felt none of that brother/sister angst that was so often apparent between them; and he didn't feel like saying anything sarcastic either.

"I know, Charlotte, I miss her, too. Dad will be back tomorrow, I think. I talked to him before he left today." She relaxed her hold on his neck, walked to her bed, and sat down. John waited a few seconds and then followed her and sat down beside her. Charlotte put her face in her hands and started wiping away the tears on her cheeks. John just looked straight ahead not having any notion of what he could or might say. Their mother's absence was an invisible elephant in the house that everyone had been tiptoeing around for the last several months. John began to feel the tension draining from his body after Charlotte had spilled her grief all over him.

The two teenagers just sat on Charlotte's bed in silence.

"John, Charlotte, come on now for supper before it gets cold," Grace's voice came rolling down the hallway to shatter the calm in Charlotte's room. It was daylight savings time now and outside the sun was still high in the afternoon sky. John was thinking that it was too early for supper as he got up and walked toward the door.

"Come on, sis, eat a little something. I bet it will make you feel better. Tomorrow's Saturday. No school! You can relax all day and Dad will be home tomorrow night," John said after he reached the door to Charlotte's room where he had stopped for a moment. Charlotte just looked at him without much

90

expression.

"I'm afraid he's going to be mad at me, John. I really went off on Amy. She just kept railing on me and I just went off. I felt good after it happened, but I feel terrible now. I was just so mad, I couldn't stop," Charlotte replied as though she was talking to the wall in front of her. "I might have hurt her... I was just so mad!" Charlotte paused for a moment. "It was horrible. She'll never forgive me now. We'll never be friends again, I just know it." The tears that had disappeared from her face now made a reappearance in her reddened eyes.

John did not know Amy well, but he knew her well enough to know Charlotte could be right. Amy was not a forgiving person. She was bright and oftentimes likeable and witty; but she could also be rude, hateful, and cynical at times, even to Charlotte who was her best friend. It had always been puzzling to John why Charlotte put up with her. He thought that maybe it would be best if he said nothing at all about Amy.

"Come on, sis, Aunt Grace is waiting for us. Let's go and eat something." John then turned and started down the hall as Charlotte slowly stood up from the bed and trudged out of her room behind him. She walked like her feet weighed a hundred pounds apiece. Mirth would be a scarce commodity in the Madison household that evening.

12

"Dr. Strangelove," Alex was thinking as he walked into the smallish room with dark, wood paneled walls and a circular table in the center surrounded by ten high backed chairs. This room was smaller than the one he remembered from the movie, but it had the same dimly lit, somewhat bare and cold atmosphere. But he was seeing it in color instead of the austere black and white of the film. Still, the room was colorless in character and Alex guessed in purpose as well.

One of the chairs placed around the table stood with its back to a large rectangular screen which occupied one entire wall of the small room. The chair was larger and wider than the others and had a higher back as well. Alex correctly concluded that whoever was to lead these solemn proceedings would likely be seated there. The room had the unmistakable, intoxicating aroma of aged wood and leather.

* * *

The evening before, Alex had been delivered to a bungalow located in a spacious compound containing several similar cottages along with some larger, austere looking structures surrounded by a looming stone wall covered with ivy and other greenery. The huge gate constructed of dressed oak timbers was guarded by armed, helmeted, uniformed men in pressed battle fatigues with their trousers bloused over shiny black combat boots with crisp white laces. The driver of the SUV in which Alex was a passenger stopped in front of the gate and showed a packet of papers to one of the guards who looked through them thoroughly until he was apparently satisfied. He signaled one of the other soldiers to open the gate and let them pass. After the black vehicle passed into the compound, the soldier who had examined the papers looked at one of his comrades in arms and said, "We can all turn in our weapons and rest easy tonight, boys; the CIA is on the case." The two soldiers grinned as they walked back to their posts by the gate.

Alex was given a zippered case by a young man as he got out of the SUV. He then said, "Your instructions are inside the case, Dr. Madison. I hope you enjoy your stay in Washington, sir." With that he closed the door behind the psychiatrist and climbed back into the passenger side of the black SUV. It departed without fanfare, leaving Alex standing alone in front of one of the small stone cottages.

Once inside the bungalow, Alex found a tray of food on a table in a small nook off to one side of the spacious room. It consisted of a turkey sandwich, a bag of potato chips, and two large chocolate chip cookies. He found some cold drinks and milk in a small refrigerator near the table. While Uncle Sam apparently did not want Alex to starve, he also apparently did not want him to eat too high on the hog, either. At any rate, he was not all that hungry.

An inspection of the documents in the case given him by the young man in the SUV revealed a rather straightforward rendition of the events to take place the next day. Breakfast would be available at eight am in the large building in the center of the compound, and afterwards the meeting he was to attend would begin in the conference room promptly at nine. Unless something unforeseen should occur, the meeting should be over by noon at the latest, and he would be flown back to DFW at that time. It seemed to Alex that this could have just as easily been a meeting of the local bird watching society as a top level, CIA sponsored, secret conclave in which the security of the country was at issue. But no one had asked him for his views on the matter. Not yet, anyway. Mr.

Danton had told Alex that the necessity for all the cloak and dagger stuff would become evident, but thus far Alex was still in the dark as to why all these elaborate measures were being taken in preparation for the upcoming meeting.

* * *

Although he had been to Washington, DC, several times in the last six months or so, Alex had no idea where he was presently. He wasn't even sure he was in Washington. He had just assumed so after the plane had landed and he had been brought to this place. The driver of the SUV that delivered him there had welcomed him to Washington, but that might have been some kind of misdirection. He had been asleep when the plane landed, so he concluded that he might be in Georgia for all he knew for sure.

As Alex was thinking all these things, he also concluded that it really didn't matter too much, either. He was here and there was not much he could do about it even if he wanted to. After all, he had agreed to all this intrigue. Something told him that if he were to try to leave the compound without consent, those guards would shoot him without a moment's hesitation. Alex always tried to see humor in things, but he was coming up empty in his current situation.

Alex had slept so soundly on the plane that sleep evaded him now as he lay in the comfortable bed in the cottage. With the rustic wooden furniture and the dark timbered beams crossing the room from one wall to the other and supporting the knotty pine ceiling, the place looked like a hunting lodge. If it were, he would have been a lot happier. But all he was hunting now was some welcome slumber, and he feared it would not come.

* * *

There was a gathering of solemn faced people standing around the entrance to the meeting room a few minutes before nine the next morning. The building itself was constructed of dark stone with a lot of exposed wooden beams and other rustic touches similar to those of the bungalow where Alex had spent his sleepless night. He recognized all but two of the somber faced participants at this gathering. Harold Janes and his assistant Lauren were there along with the doctor from the pharmaceutical company. Alex was unsuccessfully trying to remember his name. There were three other members of Congressman Branch's committee present whom Alex recognized but only knew well enough to greet politely. Mr. Danton was correct in that Alex was the only physician on the committee present at this assembly. Congressman Branch was the only other notable who had not arrived as of yet.

The two people who Alex did not know were military men attired in the full regalia of their respective branches of service. One had on a blue uniform and the other sported a uniform of dark green. They both had a chest full of small, rectangular, multicolored ribbons aligned in rows and columns on the left front breast of their coats. Alex did not know much about the military and its insignia, but he had heard of these collections of decoration called "fruit salad" in the past. They apparently represented types of service and campaigns the wearers had been a part of in their careers. Both men wore the traditional dress caps of the military with round, flat crowns and shiny black bills. They were standing quietly side by side and spoke to no one.

Alex was beginning to feel uncomfortable, shifting his weight from one foot to the other, when the front door to the building opened and Congressman Branch swept in along with another man walking a pace or two behind him. The congressman did not speak to anyone at first but walked directly to the conference room, opened the door, and went inside. After a brief moment in which all the participants left outside had turned to look at the closed door, it opened and Congressman Branch appeared and motioned for everyone to come in.

As Alex surmised, the congressman took the larger chair at the table and invited everyone else to sit down in the chairs that remained. The two military men sat to the right of Congressman

Branch and next to one another. Everyone else just scattered around the table and sat down wherever they could find an empty seat. Alex ended up sitting between two of the members of the committee he did not know. He noticed that Harold Janes and Lauren were sitting across the table from him. He nodded briefly to her when their eyes met. Lauren smiled faintly and nodded back.

"Gentlemen and ladies," Congressman Branch said as he turned and smiled at Lauren. "I want to introduce General Andrew Markward of The United States Air Force, and General Sheridan Brightman of The United States Army. Both are on special assignment to the president for the purposes of the charged responsibility of our committee and this particular meeting today." Both men nodded their heads only slightly at the congressman's introduction. He then continued.

"Our nation has been attacked by a sinister force which has enslaved a multitude of our populace. Our efforts to combat this force have met with dismal and in many cases heartbreaking failure." He turned his gaze momentarily toward Alex whose eyes were cast downward as he remained motionless in his chair. "I know I am only telling you what you already know only too well. It is a crisis the magnitude of which we as a nation have never had to face before. I remember when I was a boy as the great polio epidemic swept our country and people were lined up in the halls of hospitals in iron lungs. It was then that our medical community stepped up and thankfully found a desperately sought-after cure. The situation we find ourselves in today makes that long ago memory pale by comparison. I never imagined in my lifetime I could make a statement like that, and it would not be the least bit exaggerated. Yet, here we are today with just such a calamitous state of affairs on our hands." Congressman Branch stopped for a moment as he averted his gaze down to the table in front of him. The others around the table were sitting as though they might be fearful of moving.

"There is not a single phase of American life that has not

been affected by the events of the last two years or more. Our government and industry have both suffered grievous slowdowns and our economy is weakened to the point of impending collapse. Our very way of life has been challenged and our families have suffered. If we cannot stem this dysfunction that has imperiled the country, our very survival is at dire risk. I wish I was eloquent enough to convince you of the necessity of the next steps we must take." The congressman paused and cleared his throat.

"Ladies and gentlemen, we are going to inoculate our entire population against the ravages of clinical depression with this new drug Dynasane."

Everyone sitting around the table began to come to life as though they were suddenly activated by some sort of unseen current. There was a flurry of spontaneous conversation among the shocked participants. Only the congressman and the two generals were not reacting with animated surprise. Congressman Branch sat quietly for more than a few moments as he allowed his announcement to permeate the minds of the stunned committee members.

Alex did not believe or even comprehend what he had just heard. How do you inoculate anyone against depression? People were inoculated against things like viral, bacterial, or other kinds of infections, not emotional conditions. You might as well try to inoculate people from getting tired or hungry. What the congressman had just said had no scientific basis whatever, and Alex had never heard of such a concept in the history of medicine or psychiatry. He was a medical consultant to the committee and no one had even asked him anything as to the feasibility of such a scheme.

The buzzing din of conversation among those present began to subside a bit as Congressman Branch drew his chair closer to the table. "I know you are all surprised at this announcement and I can well imagine why. I know you have questions as well. I'm going to ask that you hold your questions for a moment until Dr. Harris of Gardner Pharmaceuticals has a chance to elaborate on this plan.

Doctor, will you go ahead please," the congressman said and pushed his chair back from the table a bit.

The stocky man who had made the presentation at the regular meeting two weeks previously massaged his chin with his hand before he spoke. "One of the drawbacks of Dynasane is that when it is given orally, it takes two to three months to bring about clinical improvement in patients. We are not sure why that is any more than we know why the conventional antidepressants take four to six weeks to begin to take effect in most people. We needed to find a way for the drug to enter the body to deliver its therapeutic effects faster and more efficiently. Our labs have come up with an aerosol preparation that we think will accomplish that. The urgency of this situation has not permitted the usual clinical trials, but we do have the aerosol preparation developed, and we feel that there is no reason to believe that it will not be just as effective as the oral compound and much faster acting." The uncomfortable doctor began to cough and squirm in his chair as he tried to clear his throat to continue.

"I must say in all candor that this whole situation sounds like something you would see in a science fiction movie, but the gravity of our nation's condition warrants drastic measures. As I said at the meeting a few weeks ago, none of the other drugs developed have shown the effectiveness and promise of Dynasane. Unless some other solution shows itself quickly, this is the best we have been able to conjure up that has any chance of saving our nation and, indeed, our world." The doctor looked down as he concluded his remarks. All those listening to him just offered unblinking stares. He then pushed his chair back from the table and folded his hands in his lap.

Congressman Branch looked around the table in obvious expectation of some reaction. The two generals sat listening quietly, their faces betraying no trace of emotion or expression.

"Well, folks, if you have questions or comments, now is the time," the congressman offered.

The small congregation of solemn faces around the table remained motionless until Alex suddenly straightened himself in his chair. He looked down into his lap and drew a breath, "How do you propose to deliver this medication to the whole of the population?" His eyes were now leveled at the congressman.

"I'm going to ask General Markward to answer that," the congressman said and leaned back in his chair. Both of the military men had placed their hats on the table in front of them. Before he began to speak, General Markward reached forward and touched the bill of his cap as though he might pick it up. He rubbed his thumb over the shiny insignia attached to the front of the hat.

"We are going to use some especially equipped aircraft to dispense the drug by air," he said in a rather monotonous baritone. "We should be able to cover the entire country with this type of saturation spraying in about one week's time," he intoned and leaned back in his chair.

Good grief, they're serious, Alex thought, but he hardly felt the government would go through all this rigmarole and include two high ranking generals to make jokes at this point. Alex paused a moment, then spoke again:

"The first thing any doctor learns in his training is to do no harm. Is this stuff going to hurt anybody? What about those who might be allergic to the drug, Dr. Harris?" he asked. It was then that Alex felt Lauren's eyes riveted on him as he listened for an answer.

"We have not had a single allergic reaction to the drug so far except for a few minor rashes that responded to topical treatment. We feel the overall possible benefit to our society is worth the small risk involved in this case," Dr. Harris answered. The obviously nervous doctor then cleared his throat again. Alex just stared at him. He wanted to believe what this man was saying, but legions of doubt began to emerge in his mind and then settled as an uneasiness in his gut. Before Alex could say anything else, another voice was heard:

"When is all this going to take place?" Harold Janes asked. Congressman Branch turned to General Markward.

"When does the Air Force start the runs, general?" he asked.

"The planes are being prepared now, sir, and we will begin the operation day after tomorrow, Monday morning," he answered without moving in his chair. One of the committee members sitting next to Alex then spoke:

"Will the public be informed, Mr. Branch?" he asked.

"We discussed that very thing at great length, sir," he replied. "We concluded that any explanation we could make would just be confusing and could possibly alarm the populace to panic or worse. It was a very difficult call, but we think we've made the right one. No one is trying to play God here; our country is distressed and dying, and we need to take action. I know it's drastic and some of you may not agree, but this is the best option we could devise. I hope you will join with me in praying that it will be a success and our nation will recover. The president has granted final approval for us to begin." The congressman once again scanned all those sitting around the table with his unblinking gaze. "Is there any further discussion?" he asked. No one spoke.

The congressman put both of his hands on the table and exhaled visibly as though he was somehow relieved. "Well, then, I wish you all Godspeed and I do not need to remind anyone, I trust, of the absolute need for discretion with this information you have been entrusted with." He then pushed himself away from the round table, stood up, and walked out of the room.

The military men sat for a brief moment and spoke to each other quietly before they, too, arose and left. Everyone else around the table remained seated as though they might be waiting for a bell signaling that the class was dismissed.

"Well, that's it then," Harold Janes said as he stood up. Everyone else slowly followed suit and seven souls slowly departed the dimly lit room.

* * *

The instructions in the small case Alex had received when he arrived had included a short paragraph that said he would be met outside of his bungalow after the conclusion of the meeting for transport to the airfield. Alex started out the front door of the building and took the walkway that led toward his cabin. He glanced to his left and saw Lauren walking out toward one of the black SUVs parked in front. "Hello, again, Lauren," Alex said as she was only a step or two away, off to his left. She stopped and turned to look his direction.

"Oh, hello, Dr. Madison," she replied. She then turned to Harold Janes and said, "Go ahead, Harold, I'll be there in just a minute." She then looked back at Alex and smiled. "I hope you are well, doctor."

"I asked you to call me Alex. This is no time for formalities. The world's a serious enough place right now," he said. Lauren looked at him with eyes that suddenly turned dark as the smile faded from her face.

"Yes, Alex, you're right about that. There's not much to celebrate these days," she said. Lauren hesitated a moment, but then added, "I was so dreadfully sorry to hear of your wife's death. I'm so sorry. I hope you will accept my condolences." She then looked down at the stone walkway.

"Thank you, Lauren. It's kind of you to say so. Maria was a lovely woman. We were married twenty one years. I miss her every day."

"I know you must. I hope your grief will not linger."

"Lauren, the car is waiting. We need to go now," Harold Janes' voice came from a few steps away as he was standing by the door of the dark vehicle. Lauren turned and nodded.

"You'd better go now, Lauren. It was good to see you again. I hope the next time the circumstances will be happier," Alex said.

"Have a good trip, Alex," she replied as a warm smile reappeared to brighten her face once again. Lauren hesitated a lingering moment, looking directly into Alex's receptive eyes. She then turned and took the few steps to the SUV. A young man in a dark suit closed the door behind her and got in on the passenger side of the front seat. Alex just stood and watched as the vehicle rolled away down the drive.

13

Alex didn't know if it was the guilt or the excitement he was feeling that kept him from being able to sleep on the plane ride back to DFW. He had assumed he would lapse into a coma once the small jet was airborne. Sleep had evaded him all the night before, and he was exhausted from the intensity and insanity of the meeting. When he had agreed to serve on this committee several months ago, he could not have imagined a more unlikely or preposterous course of action to deal with a national emergency. It was, as Dr. Harris had put it, something that rightfully belonged in a preposterous science fiction movie.

The small aircraft began to shudder like a motorboat on choppy waters, which made Alex grab the armrests of his seat with both hands. His disdain for air travel had been revived when the jet entered some turbulent air, disrupting a smooth flight up until that point. A moment or two later, the dour faced, dark suited man who had welcomed Alex back on the plane for the return fight to DFW appeared in the aisle.

"Be sure your seat belt is fastened, Dr. Madison. We may have some tough going for a while. We're just entering a cell of bad weather on our route," he said as though it might have been a recorded announcement. The man then disappeared again behind the partition at the back of the plane. Alex pulled the free end of his seat belt to snug it across his lap and leaned back in his seat. He thought if the plane crashed, it might be his just punishment for what he had been thinking and feeling about Lauren. Maria was dead now about four months and he was already looking to replace her. He then looked out his window at the dark sky with its roiling, black clouds and smiled to himself.

What a numbskull, he thought. Maria would laugh at his thinking such a thing and likely make a joke about it.

She was the least likely woman he had ever known to exhibit any jealousy whatsoever. He knew that all that stuff was coming from him. Still, the thought of another woman in his arms or in his bed excited him, but gave him pause as if it was something unseemly. It happened every day; spouses died; people fell in love again and remarried. It just didn't happen every day to Alex Madison.

* * *

"When is Dad getting home?" Charlotte asked her Aunt Grace as the older woman continued in her usual state of constant motion about the house, cleaning, dusting, straightening pillows, and anything else she could see that was in dire need of domestic realignment.

The woman stopped and looked at her niece as though her power supply might have been interrupted.

"I don't know, sweetheart. I think sometime this afternoon. He said he wasn't sure." The teenager put her thumb up to her mouth and started biting on her thumbnail.

"I wish he would get home, Aunt Grace. Do you think he's going to be mad at me?" she asked.

"For what, baby?" Grace asked.

"You know, for the thing at school. I've never been in trouble at school before. I've never even had to go to the principal's office or been in detention. He's going to be mad, I know it," she said as she threw herself down on the couch.

"He might be, honey. I don't know, but your dad will want to know what happened and why you got mad at your friend. That's not like you."

Charlotte grabbed one of the pillows from the couch and clutched it tightly against her chest.

"I can get mad, too, Aunt Grace, just like anybody else," she blurted out angrily. "I'm no goody-goody like everybody thinks."

"Well, you're a good girl, though, Charlotte, and you usually don't go around hitting your friends when you get mad. Your dad's going to want to know why you did that. What are you going to tell him?" Grace asked and looked intently at the girl who was now glowering at the magazines on the coffee table in front of her. A long moment went by in silence. Charlotte then abruptly stood up.

"I'm not a good girl, Aunt Grace! I'm not! I can be bad, too, like other girls I know. I hate having to be good all the time!" she shouted and ran down the hall toward her room. Grace stood for a moment and then heard the inevitable crash of Charlotte's slamming door.

"Oh, Lord. I wish Alex was home, too," Grace said. She then looked up at the large family portrait of Alex, Maria, and the children on the wall of the den.

"Porque, Maria? Porque?" she whispered in Spanish as she crossed herself.

Thoughts of her own two girls came surging into her mind from a place she thought was long buried. She did not want to go there again.

* * *

Although he could not sleep on the plane, Alex began to yawn and doze almost from the moment he climbed into the black SUV for the trip home from the airport. He tried to put Washington, the committee, and even Lauren, too, out of his mind.

He was thinking of Charlotte and John and what might be going on at home. Then he thought maybe he didn't really want to know. His children had not been any trouble at all so far; but he had been holding his breath and waiting for the bubble to burst, especially since Maria's death. It didn't seem to matter as much if a surgeon's kids turned out bad, but if you were a psychiatrist and your kids started screwing up, everybody knew it and wondered why. It was kind of like being a minister in a way; people expected your offspring to be perfect. It was damned unfair to be sure, but there was little in life that was fair, no matter how much people wanted it or deserved it.

As the sinister looking vehicle turned the corner onto Alex's street, he saw John in the front yard throwing a baseball to one of his friends. John was the shortstop on his high school team and the coach had told Alex that he had a good chance of a scholarship to a major university. He was that good. Alex was glad of that, but now he was only hoping there would be a college for John to go to when the time came.

"Those your kids, Dr. Madison?" the young man driving the SUV asked flatly.

"One of them is; that's my son, John in the red cap," Alex answered.

"Your boy a baseball player?" the young man asked. Alex was so surprised at the sudden interest shown by the young man, he was having a hard time getting in tune with the conversation. Both of the agents in the front seat had said nothing since they had departed DFW.

"Uh, yeah, he plays shortstop for his high school team." Alex hesitated. "He's pretty good."

"Baseball was my game, too, Dr. Madison," the young man said with some liveliness in his voice. "I was an outfielder. I played two years in the Dodgers' farm system. Finally decided I'd try and find some honest work. Look where I ended up," he added and laughed as he looked over at the other man in the passenger seat.

"That's not what you told me, Ed," the other young man said. "You said you couldn't hit a curve ball," he added and laughed.

"You don't have to tell everything you know, Bill," the driver replied as they both started to laugh. Alex laughed too, as the three men enjoyed a light moment in the heretofore solemn journey. "Well, here we are, Dr. Madison. Home again, sir," he said as he pulled up in front of Alex's house.

"Thanks for the ride, you guys," Alex said as he was climbing out of the SUV. "Best wishes to you both."

"Thank you, sir. To you as well," the driver said and managed a faint smile as his partner was getting back into the vehicle after opening Alex's door. Once the door was closed, the dark SUV eased away down the street.

"Hi, Dad. Did you get to meet the Prez, or anything exciting?" John asked as he walked toward his father.

"Yeah, we played a round of golf and some gin rummy, too," Alex answered and posted a broad grin across his face. He then put his arm around his son's shoulder and the two laughed as they bumped shoulders together. "Did you win your game last night?"

"Naw, one of their guys who usually hits about .150 got lucky and parked one in the top of the ninth with two on. We just gave it away," John answered as he screwed his face into a scowl.

"Well, a blind hog gets an acorn sometime," Alex replied as he started walking to the front door.

"Dad, come here a minute," John said and motioned toward Alex. Father and son stood face to face as John spoke in a low voice:

"Charlotte wants to talk to you, but she's probably too scared. She had an incident at school Friday. Don't tell her I told you. She's worried, Dad." Alex just looked into his son's eyes.

"Is she Ok, John?"

"I don't know, Dad. She's just worried and scared. She and Amy had a humongous fight." John hesitated. "I'd better shut up. She needs to tell you about it."

"Ok, son. Thanks for giving me a head's up. You did the right thing." Alex then turned and slowly walked to the front door of the house. He hesitated a moment before he turned the knob and went in.

Grace had been in the kitchen when she heard the front door close. She came half running through the den to intercept Alex. "How was your trip?" she asked as she reached for his bag and took it from him.

"Oh, it was alright, Grace. Everything Ok here?" he asked. Grace turned and put his bag down on the floor in the entryway and slowly looked up at Alex.

"Oh, I don't know, Alex. Charlotte is upset. She had a problem at school with her friend Amy. I think she's afraid you will be angry with her," Grace said in hushed tones.

"That kind of news travels fast. John already mentioned it to me," Alex replied. "Where is she?"

"I think she is still in her room sleeping. Are you hungry? Want something to eat, Alex?" she asked and looked at him.

"I could use a cold drink or something, Grace, but I'll get it. Don't bother yourself. I'm going to put my stuff in the bedroom and look in on Charlotte," he answered and headed down the hallway.

Alex deposited his things in the bedroom and changed into some sweats and his running shoes. He hadn't been doing much running in them lately for which he chided himself under his breath. Since he reached forty, he had told himself he wouldn't fall into physical decline like so many other men he had seen approaching middle age. He had begun to understand though how easily the passage of time overtook a man.

Alex washed his face, scooping the cool water from the running tap with his cupped hands. He turned off the water, dried his face, and sat down in the inviting chair not far from the foot of his bed. Although he had hoped to deceive himself, he knew it would not work. He was only prolonging the dreaded necessity of talking to Charlotte. Sometimes he hated his penchant for self-evaluation that had become so ingrained during his training.

Alex had been hoping for a serene evening of reading the paper or maybe watching an old movie, rather than having to deal with some family issue. But he didn't have Maria anymore to help him arbitrate things like this. He was it now, the only voice of parental authority his children now had; and that sobering reality made him miss Maria even more-and hate her even more for leaving him. Although he talked to his patients about it all the time, he was surprised at how easily his anger toward someone he had loved so completely and unselfishly could surface. But, he was the grownup in the family; he was supposed to teach his children how to manage life's dark days.

"Damn!" he whispered under his breath as he got up and headed for the door to the hallway.

* * *

Lauren unbuttoned her skirt and let it fall to the carpet of her bedroom floor. She then began to unfasten the small buttons of her dark, silk blouse one by one until she reached the top one which she had some difficulty sliding through the buttonhole which was just small enough to make it irritating. She managed it though, and pulled her arms out of the sleeves and dropped the garment on her bed. Lauren was left standing in her pantyhose and the black, lace-trimmed brassiere she had purchased at a specialty lingerie shop only recently. She then stepped out of her skirt lying on the floor and walked over to the full length mirror mounted on the inside of her closet door.

Scanning her body in the mirror, Lauren wondered how long it had been since a man had seen her in such a state of undress. Despite her marriage ending in failure, she vividly remembered the last time she and her then-husband, James, made love; how his powerful hands roamed over her body; how hungrily his lips pressed against hers; how their bodies joined in that ultimate pleasure shared by a man and a woman. Most disturbingly, she was thinking how readily she would welcome him right then to do it all once again. He couldn't be faithful, but he could take her to paradise every time he touched her. But what her heart so desperately wanted, her head told her would not sustain their relationship for the duration; so, she chose painful heartbreak over a marriage that was destined to leave her empty and disillusioned. That was seventeen years ago, and Lauren wasn't sure even now she had chosen correctly or wisely.

As she critically examined herself, Lauren noted her hips were too wide for the legs that supported them, but her waist was still tiny for a woman of her build which made her voluptuous breasts look even larger. As a girl, she was teased by the boys who wanted to see and touch them; and teased even worse by envious girls who longed to have them. Instead of being the desirable asset everyone else thought they would be, Lauren only found her breasts to be a ponderous nuisance.

She wasn't even sure why she bought the bra. Alluring undergarments had never held much appeal for her even when she was younger. Lauren's cynical side made her wonder why she even bothered. She knew she wasn't pretty, so if a man looked at her, she presumed he wasn't looking at her face.

Lauren's thoughts then turned to that man again. That man from Texas who had been hounding her consciousness every waking minute for the last few weeks. He had not entered her dreams yet, but she expected him to appear there at any time. And when Harold told her of Alex's wife's death, it was like her heart and mind went into another gear entirely. Lauren took some solace in the fact she was hardly old at forty one. Maybe she could have something like a life again after all.

A nauseous ache began crawling through Lauren's gut. Could she dare to allow herself to be hopeful? When she thought such things, a rare optimism began to rise in her as though it was trying to come up out of her chest. But life had cruelly taught her that when there was hope there always seemed to be disappointment and disillusionment waiting to pounce.

There had been other men. Lauren had never suffered from a lack of male attention despite her efforts at times to make herself unattractive by neglecting her appearance. She dated occasionally and even allowed one gentleman into her bed, but it had been hollow, cold, and unfulfilling. It only made her think of James and how she missed his intoxicating, stimulating caresses. He could bring her passionately to life like no man she had ever known. His memory just reinforced the notion for Lauren that no other man would ever be his equal in her heart or her bed.

Lauren continued to look at the woman in the mirror, staring into her light blue eyes with glowering intensity.

"What do you want, Lauren?" she asked the solemn faced, familiar looking stranger in the looking glass. "What is it that you're waiting for?"

She just stood motionless for a long moment and then sighed heavily. Finally, she turned away making the questioning woman disappear from the glass as well.

Right then, and despite what Lauren truly believed in the most remote recess of her mind, the answer to her query was deceptively simple. It did not depend on some dark, esoteric, Freudian interpretation of her unconscious. She wanted what everybody breathing air wanted: Someone to love her and someone she could love back without fear or doubt. Earlier in the day when she had looked into Alex Madison's hazel eyes, she knew she need look no further. Her search was at an end.

She had found him.

Lauren slipped out of her pantyhose and took off her pretty new bra. She then put on a cotton jersey pullover and a pair of panties before she pulled on her favorite velour jogging pants that became softer and more comforting every time she washed them. She was now in her favored costume for a Saturday evening at home. The soft carpet felt good under her bare feet as she made her way out of the bedroom and headed toward her small kitchen where she made some coffee.

A few minutes later, Lauren had gathered her coffee and a novel she was trying to finish before settling into her favorite spot on her soft, overstuffed couch. But by the time she opened her book and lit a cigarette, her interest in reading had waned. She was now only thinking of a certain man.

14

It was maybe four or five steps down the hallway to Charlotte's door, but it seemed to Alex that he would never get there. He was going in blind to whatever was going on with his thirteen year old, but he was not without some educated guesses. John and Grace had both given him some facts, but Alex figured there was going to be much more to it. He had always known Charlotte to be a friendly, talkative, but somewhat passive child who was good natured and always eager to please. It bothered him, then, that she had been so quiet about Maria's death. She had been unusually taciturn in her acceptance of her mother's sudden disappearance. Charlotte was not given to fits of emotion or hysterics like some teens; at least not in the thirteen years Alex had known her, but nonetheless, he suspicioned that her silence and emotional distance spoke volumes.

In the past, Alex had satisfied himself with the notion that he could not be a psychiatrist to his own family. Maria's death had laid the truth of it on his doorstep in spades. He feared, though, that as a parent, he was not helping his children when they needed him most. As a doctor, he knew what to do and say; but, as a father, he was at a loss and he felt clueless most of the time. He had the uneasy feeling this was certain to be another of those times.

Alex softly tapped on Charlotte's door and waited. There was no response. He then rapped on the door with more vigor.

"Charlotte, honey. Are you awake? It's Dad, baby," he spoke louder now as he waited at her door.

After what he thought was a reasonable time to wait, Alex opened the door and slowly walked in. He looked around and noticed that Charlotte's bedcovers were a bit rumpled, but she was not there. He turned and walked out of her room and down the hall toward the den. As he was midway through the den, Grace appeared in the entrance to the kitchen area.

"She's outside on the swing in the back yard," Grace said. "I'm going home now, Alex, if you don't need me anymore."

"We always need you, Grace, but I know you're anxious to get home. Go ahead and thank you, again," Alex replied and kissed her cheek. Grace blushed and kissed him back.

"You can call me anytime, Alex. You know that," Grace said. "I love you and the kids, and it gives me something to do. I never seem to see my children much anymore. They're always so busy." Alex opened his arms and hugged her.

"You're always welcome here, Grace. We love you, too." Their eyes met for an uncomfortable moment before Grace scurried off to the kitchen to get her purse.

Alex looked out one of the windows in the den with a view of the back yard. There, he saw Charlotte sitting in the swing suspended from a large oak near the edge of the small lake behind the house. The sun was hovering over the rooftops of the row of homes across the water. Alex loved this time of the day which made him more reluctant than ever to go and see Charlotte. What was to come could not possibly be pleasant. He said goodbye again to Grace before he went out the back door and trudged across the lawn toward where Charlotte was sitting in the swing.

"Hi, sweetheart. You're all alone out here," he said rather cheerfully. Charlotte turned suddenly and looked up at him frowning.

"Hi, Dad. I didn't know you were home. It was a pretty quick trip this time, huh?" she asked and looked out at some ducks swimming over to the water's edge.

"Only one day, honey. What did you do today?" he asked. Charlotte didn't answer for a moment, but only continued looking at the ducks that had now left the water and were walking across the grass.

"I just stayed home all day. I was kind of tired," she said

quietly. Alex then walked around and sat down next to his daughter on the big swing.

"Are you feeling alright?" he asked.

"I've just been tired, Dad. I had a bad day at school yesterday," she replied and let out a long, labored breath. "I got in a fight with Amy. I hit her and pushed her down in the hall. I was just so mad. I don't know what happened to me, Dad. I'm sorry now, but I was just so mad," she said as she clinched her hands together in her lap. "Please don't be mad at me, Dad. I won't do it again. I promise!" she added quickly as she stared out at the water.

Alex was now feeling disconnected from his emotions. Charlotte was laying things out for him so plainly, he found himself off stride. He had not expected that. He wasn't angry; he was more worried than anything else. He just looked at his daughter and put his arm around her shoulder and pulled her closer to him. "What were you so mad about?" he ventured.

"Oh, Amy was just being the way she always is," she replied, "bossy and pushy and sarcastic. And she said some horrible things about mom. I just got tired of it and decided to push back, but I lost control, Dad. I started hitting her, and I didn't want to stop I was so mad," she offered and looked up again at her dad. "Getting mad is scary, Dad. It makes you do things you really shouldn't do." She stopped for a moment and looked out at the lake. "I want to tell Amy I'm sorry, but I don't know if I'd really mean it. Sometimes I hate her when she acts so sarcastic and hateful."

Alex just listened. He knew Charlotte needed to resolve this for herself. He wasn't sure he could help her do that by saying anything. Alex also knew that Charlotte could take a big step toward maturity as a result of this incident, or a giant step backward if he gave her some ill-advised scolding. He looked out across the lake at the setting sun and wished that Maria could whisper in his ear. She could tell him what to do and what to say. But Alex also knew that his wife's absence was at least partly the reason for Charlotte's lapse into anger and rage toward her friend. The rest was probably being thirteen and the telltale effects of a fresh supply of new and unfamiliar hormones in her maturing body.

"What are you going to do, sweetheart" he asked and leaned back in the swing.

"I guess I need to talk to Amy, Dad, but I'm scared. What if she won't listen to me? What if she stays mad at me?" she asked plaintively. "We've been best friends since kindergarten, Dad!" Alex felt a gnawing in his gut. He remembered thirteen, too.

"Well, honey. It's a terrible thing to lose a friend, but there are some things that we don't have control over. If Amy is truly your friend, don't you think you can work it out?" Alex answered and asked as truthfully and optimistically as he could.

Charlotte looked away again as the sun was now barely visible over the distant houses. "I hope so, Dad. I'll need to talk to her. But she can be hard headed when she wants to. Maybe that's why I like her. She's stronger than I am."

"Oh, I don't know about that," Alex offered. "You're both strong in different ways. You have a quiet strength. Amy is just louder than you are." Charlotte looked up at her father like he had uttered some great truth. She just stared into his face. Finally, she looked back out at the lake as a smile grew across her face.

"She's loud, alright. That's for sure, dad," she said and began to laugh. Alex smiled and began laughing too. Alex felt a sense of relief, although he suspected Charlotte's issue with Amy would not be so easily settled. He decided not to push his luck.

"Are you hungry?" he asked.

Charlotte nodded.

"A little bit."

"Come on, sweetheart. Let's go in. Aunt Grace made us some sandwiches for supper." The two got up off the swing and walked across the lawn toward the house. The sun was now completely gone leaving the gray cast of twilight covering the evening sky. It was that time of year when a refreshing coolness lingered in the air before the steamy summer nights came and drove people back indoors to the welcome relief of conditioned air.

Alex stopped and breathed in the unmistakable aroma of steaks sizzling on his neighbor's grill. "Looks like Fred is cooking tonight," he said as he looked toward the back yard of the house next door.

"Every Saturday night, Dad," Charlotte said. "Mr. Martin cooks out every Saturday night. You know," she reminded him.

"I know, baby. I guess I just forgot for a minute." That gnawing ache started to settle in his gut again as he and his daughter went into the house and closed the door.

* * *

"Do you know what this stuff is, sarge?" the airman asked as he and some of his comrades were hoisting a large canister-looking apparatus up under the airplane's wing.

"Don't know, don't care, and neither should you," the sergeant barked in reply to the young soldier's question. "We need to have this baby ready to go at 0600 tomorrow. That's all I know for sure, so get your ass in gear," he sneered and walked on toward the other wing of the huge aircraft.

"Is Schmidt always such a dick?" the airman asked one of his fellows.

"Only when he's awake," the other young man replied.

"Do you know what this stuff is, Hardy?" the airman asked his companion.

"Don't really know, but I've heard these bombers are going to be huge crop dusters tomorrow. They're going to spray some kind of crap everywhere."

"No shit? That sounds like something in a spy movie, man," the other airman said and laughed.

"Yeah? Maybe Schmidt is really James Bond in disguise."

"Yeah, right. Could you imagine some dynamite blond cozying up to that prick?"

"Only in his wet dreams," the other airman replied.

"You asswipes get to work or you'll be on report in about

five minutes!" the sergeant yelled as he walked back in their direction.

"Yes, sir, Sergeant Schmidt, sir," the young airman replied grinning.

* * *

"Yes, sir. Yes, Mr. President, everything is ready. The project starts in the morning at six," Congressman Branch spoke into his phone. His brow was furrowed and his craggy face revealed the unrevealing stoicism of years of political responses to political questions. In this case, the voice on the other end of the line belonged to the Commander in Chief of the United States Armed Forces. Things didn't get much more political than that. "I appreciate that very much, sir," he said and put the phone down in its cradle.

The congressman then looked across his desk at the two uniformed men sitting quietly in his office. They, too, had the inscrutable demeanor of those who were accustomed to the unblinking demands of leadership.

"Well, gentlemen," Congressman Branch offered in his soothing baritone, "everything is ready and it's all a go from the White House. All I know to say is I hope this thing works. It's the damndest idea I've ever heard proposed in my life. I know it may sound like a campaign speech, men, but this may be a turning point in our nation's history, " he concluded and sighed.

The two officers across the desk squirmed in their chairs before one spoke:

"Well, congressman, I'm not sure we have much choice. We're up against it, I'd say," General Markward replied. "Like that doctor said in the meeting, I hope this stuff we're spraying over the country doesn't hurt anybody. Maybe it will do some good. The planes will be ready at 0600." The congressman just listened and swiveled his chair side to side.

"The ground forces are on alert, Mr. Branch, should we have any problems anywhere. I can't imagine why we would, but, you never can tell. Those big planes flying so low will have some people wondering," General Brightman added and looked over at his comrade in uniform. "Is that drug going to be visible when it's sprayed? Will people be able to see it?" he asked.

"It's colorless and won't be visible," the congressman answered. "They tell me it has a sweet odor and will linger in the air for about eight hours or so after it's sprayed. We'll know if it has done any good in about two weeks."

"Has the medical community been apprised of what we're doing?" General Brightman asked. Congressman Branch took a deep breath.

"Only the doctor from Texas, Dr. Madison, knows about the spraying project. He was present at the meeting Saturday morning. The two other doctors on the committee know about the drug, but not about this project. I felt that the fewer people who knew about this thing, the better. If anything goes haywire, gentlemen, we will be in for a lot of heat. I don't think I need to explain that to both of you," the congressman answered. Congressman Branch's words then died in the air and a deathly silence descended over the three men.

"It's out of our hands now, congressman," General Markward said somberly. "I think some prayer would not be out of order."

"Amen to that," the congressman said as the three men stood and shook hands. "Godspeed, gentlemen," he added as the two military men turned and left his office.

After the generals had left, the congressman just stood for a time at his large window that overlooked the city. It was a few minutes after midnight. Washington was a maze of lights like white dots on a huge black grid stretching into the distance.

The weary lawmaker rubbed his eyes and then turned and walked to a cabinet a short distance from his desk, opened the door, and took out a tall bottle and a glass. He poured a generous amount of the dark amber potion into the glass and sat down in a large, leather covered chair in the corner of his office. He slowly lifted the glass to his lips and drank. The scotch both soothed and stimulated as it flowed into his throat. He sank back into his big, soft chair and closed his eyes.

15

Sundays had always been special for as many reasons as there were souls living in America For many, the events of the past two or so years had not changed that, but there were nevertheless signs that things were not the same. Churches of all denominations and faiths lamented the dwindling numbers attending services. Places that offered pleasure and diversion like parks, movie theaters, sports stadiums, and similar venues all reported decreased attendance. People were staying at home in vast hordes. It would seem that pleasure itself had taken a long holiday. This creeping disease of inactivity had spared no part of the country.

Those whose voices were fond of sounding social and spiritual alarm did not shrink from pronouncing that God's wrath had at last been visited on America with this plague and that repentance was the only path to healing for the nation. Others whose perceptions favored paranoia proclaimed that a conspiracy existed both known and perpetrated by the highest ranking officials of the government to enslave the populace and insure the allegiance of the ignorant masses. Still others proposed that unseen aliens from space had poisoned the world leaving the human race their helpless victims. It seemed there was no shortage of explanations for the nation's woes except one that might actually bear critical scrutiny and, thus, possibly provide some hope for a solution.

The truth of the matter was, however, that all the camps offering their views and opinions were, in fact, in the same boat as far as what could be done. The government, the scientific community, the religious community, the medical community, as well as the lunatic fringe were all impotent to help a great nation and the rest of the world that was dying a little more with each day that passed. Those with a degree of wisdom became more fearful that without some effective intervention, the country would succumb to social and political instability and collapse into chaos.

If such an unspeakable likelihood should develop, there would then exist the apocalyptic America that had often been depicted in science fiction movies and novels. And it all could come about without the necessity of a nuclear holocaust. Sociologists and philosophers could then have free rein prognosticating what kind of society would then develop; and, indeed, if mankind would have any chance of survival. As it was now, this "sky is falling" and "back to the stone age" kind of rhetoric could be heard in many pulpits, in the media, and on any number of street corners already. But whatever viewpoint or theory one held, and unbeknownst but to a precious few, there would be changes to come.

They would be borne on the wind.

* * *

Alex put down the Sunday paper after he finished it, thinking how much it had dwindled in size over the last year or so. He knew the print media was holding off a severe challenge from the ever growing electronic media in all its forms, but he didn't think that was the entire explanation for the paper's shrinkage. He was also thinking it really didn't matter; it was only another indicator that the world he knew was slipping away.

Sunday mornings were different now that Maria was gone. She had been Catholic and he Baptist when they married. They both agreed that religious faith was important, but he was uncomfortable with the Catholic way, and Maria was uncomfortable with the Baptist way, so they settled on the Presbyterian way in the end. It was a happy compromise for them both, and they agreed they had learned something as a result of the change. Although the faith was important, Alex knew that the church was really the people who were there; and he liked the congregation at Grace Presbyterian. Well, most of them anyway.

Even though Jesus said to love one another, Alex knew there were limits. He also suspicioned that even though He didn't say so in the scriptures, Jesus knew that as well. He was trying to get everyone to respect everyone else and live together peaceably. There were many who repeated what Jesus said as the holy truth, but, unfortunately, very few who actually did what he recommended.

Since Maria died, Alex had not been consistent in attending church. For one thing, it was painful. Everyone and everything he saw at the church reminded him that his wife was dead. He knew that the Catholics believed that suicide was a mortal sin. It made Maria's death more intolerably sad and harder to understand. It also made him intolerably angry with her and being angry in church was not a comfortable thing for Alex. He could practice self-analysis until he was dizzy, but it changed nothing. The anger was still there. Freud and the Bible both could not purge it from him. He knew he would have to work out his own salvation on that score; and he knew the only way to do that was to find some way to forgive Maria for being so selfish as to leave him and the children.

If he was still in psychotherapy, Alex knew his therapist would point out, or lead him to conclude, that Maria's death was a narcissistic insult that he could not tolerate emotionally, and that it was preventing him from resolving his grief over her death. Just knowing that, however, did not stop the pain that arose in the pit of his stomach every time he sat in a church pew.

"Dad, I'm going over to Ray's," John said as he was opening the front door of the house. There was no response from Alex. "Dad! Hey, Dad!" John repeated, only louder. Alex was only aware of the dark paneling on the den wall coming into focus. He turned his head toward what he thought was a noise coming from the foyer to see John looking at him quizzically.

"Dad, are you there?" John asked.

"Oh, hi, son, I was in La La Land there for a minute. What did you say?" Alex replied.

"I'm going over to Ray's. We're going to the mall and we'll probably see a movie, Ok?" John repeated and waited for a response from his father.

"Ok. You guys be careful and have a good time," Alex answered. John then skipped out the front door and closed it behind him.

Alex looked at his watch. It was already a few minutes past noon. He was thinking that it was a few minutes past one in Washington. He wondered what Lauren might be doing. The memory of her light blue eyes the day before sent warm sensations through his body. He could feel his hands wanting to roam over her and longing to brush his lips against her soft skin. He remembered the scent of her perfume lingering in the morning air after she had walked away from him. Alex sat motionless and mesmerized as though he was rendered helpless by his recollections. He consciously tried to stop thinking of Lauren, but that was a hopeless impossibility. So he pushed himself back against the soft cushions of the couch and wondered how long it would take for the guilt to come and shatter his intoxicating fantasies of Lauren.

He wished he had gone to church.

* * *

As Monday morning arrived, there were some scattered showers and storms lingering along most of the Eastern United States, while most of the rest of the country to the west was enjoying clear, but still dark skies. An armada of aircraft had already lifted off at the stroke of six, eastern time. The saturation spraying was to start on the East Coast and proceed to the west until the whole of the continental US was covered. Hawaii would be the last state to be sprayed. By seven, a number of radio and television stations had already reported low flying military aircraft which had caused some public concern, not to say alarm.

In preparation for that possibility, the Air Force had put together a response which noted that some extensive aircraft maneuvers were underway all across the country, and there was no cause for any concern. That measure did seem to stem the number of calls to the networks. The reality, however, was that there was only a mere dozen or so people including the president himself who knew the truth.

Alex had wondered when he listened to the proposal at the meeting on Saturday if an operation of such magnitude could be carried out in secrecy. It seemed incredible to him that the entire military capability of the nation could be activated with so few people knowing what was really going on. That, he was thinking, really did belong in a third rate science fiction movie. It was beyond imagination, yet he could give testimony that it was true. That reckoning alone made him more than a little worried. He and the other members of the committee could simply be made to disappear and no one would have any notion why. No one, that is, except Congressman Branch and the president. Such thoughts made Alex's drive to work Monday morning all too memorable.

Alex parked his car and started up to his office, all the while trying to think of how he was to pretend it was just another day at work. It would only have been in his fantasy life that he could have imagined he would be trusted with secrets that affected national security. He was thinking that even Walter Mitty never had day dreams as bizarre as the reality he was experiencing; and if Maria was still around, she would be laughing her ass off.

As he entered his office, Alex found Emily already at her desk, doing whatever she did in the morning before the patients started showing up. She looked up at him somewhat quizzically, but only greeted him with her usual curt "Good morning." Alex returned the greeting and walked into his office. He abruptly turned around and came back, stopping in front of Emily's desk.

"Did anything happen Friday afternoon, Emily?" he asked.

"You mean other than the Rangers winning another one? I think the world might have come to an end, but I'm not sure. Everybody is moving kind of slow this morning," she replied and gave him one of her broad, pasted on, enigmatic smiles. Alex just rolled his eyes and turned toward his office again.

"I should have known better, Emily," he said. "You will let me know, however, if the world really does come to an end, won't you?"

"Oh, yes, sir. You'll be the first to know, sir," she deadpanned. Alex continued on into his office and closed the door behind him. He was thinking that Emily may have had the perfect personality to live in an otherwise crazy world.

* * *

Harold had given her some knowing glances throughout the day, but for Lauren, Monday passed without great distinction at the offices of the FPA. She and Ann Brady had lunch across the street at the small café they frequented; and she also fended off an invitation from Art Loman for a dinner date. Lauren had come close to saying yes, as she really did not know when she would see Alex, or if she would, in fact, ever see him again. She put it off to one of those nutty things smitten people did. Maybe it was a way to keep a fantasy alive; and everybody knew that fantasies were better than reality any day and all the time. Fantasies were a lot easier to live with than real people, too. Lauren liked Art, but she knew he would be wasted time for her. Even Ann had stopped talking to her about him.

Ann did not know anything about Alex, because if she had, Lauren knew she would have been all over her about him. Ann was married with two sons nearing college age, and Lauren suspicioned for some time that Ann took a great deal of vicarious pleasure in her singleness. Ann's husband was a loan officer at a bank, and judging from comments she had made to Lauren over the last few years, the magic had departed from their union long ago. Lauren also suspicioned with some not-so-subtle corroboration from her friend that the disinterested couple would no longer be keeping company when the boys were out of the house.

It was the American way of marriage and divorce for many whose marital bonds had been forged with tentative commitment. It was a well-worn story: when locked in a dead or dying relationship, it seemed that most everyone believed that their happiness lay with someone other than the someone they were with. It was the ultimate irony that made so many people betray their loyalty to one someone while pledging it to another in the universal search for finding that thing that was missing in their lives. And it seemed that the ecstasy they were seeking would soon be in their hands if only they could rid themselves of their current entanglement.

These kinds of notions wandering around her consciousness were precisely what often led Lauren down the path toward an inevitable cynicism regarding the human condition. Despite the events of the last two years, however, she curiously had found herself in a more hopeful frame of mind. It had been so easy for her to keep herself at an uncaring distance from the human race. It was an existence that required no real participation on her part in the affairs of the world. Her cubicle at the FPA building and her townhouse at 1734 Barkley Street was all the world she wanted or seemed to need. Lauren had resigned herself to the numbness of the walking wounded; or worse, the living dead.

Now, when she felt like she could come alive again, the world was about to collapse into chaos. The irony there was not lost on her, but she was helpless to do anything to change it. Eight months ago, Lauren began to feel life stirring inside her again, and when Alex Madison almost knocked her down that day after the committee meeting, she felt positively invigorated. Lauren smiled to herself as she surmised that if the country got any worse, she might find true happiness at last.

* * *

The last visible remnant of the sun was sinking into the Pacific Ocean. The earth had made several more rotations since Monday that were not unlike the millions it had made since it was a ball of cooling rock eons in the past. But, a mere handful of people residing in North America held the hope that these few days in particular would hold great significance for the inhabitants of this small, fragile, and embattled globe. The next two weeks might well be the longest, most crucial fortnight in human history.

16

Jamison Junior High School was generally considered a "rich kids'" school. It was located near several affluent neighborhoods of upscale homes populated by affluent, upscale people who had annual incomes of six figures or better. The school did draw from some nearby neighborhoods of more modest homes inhabited by mostly blue collared working people as well. Although the class system had supposedly vanished from American society several generations ago, some remnants of it were still alive and thriving and likely would be for as long as human beings lived in close proximity to one another.

Because of the financial demographics prevailing at Jamison, it was a surprise to no one that tension existed in the halls of the institution from time to time. It wasn't exactly a case of rich vs. poor, but more like affluent vs. less affluent, or the haves vs. those who didn't have as much. That line of demarcation was all too apparent at times. The kids were much more inclined to ignore those invisible but substantive barriers than were their parents. The teenagers, however, at the junior high stage of development, were not as of yet burdened with a crystallized set of attitudes and beliefs that might or might not have much to do with emotional good health and maturity.

Charlotte and Amy had been close friends since they started school in spite of the fact that they were on opposing sides of the financial demographic line at Jamison. Neither one of them had ever considered that an issue, or at least they had never discussed it or apparently even thought about it much. The fact that Charlotte's father was a physician and Amy's father worked for a janitorial service had never clouded or threatened their fast friendship. But, while Charlotte enjoyed the warmth and security of a sharing, trusting relationship with her parents, Amy was fiercely independent and not close to either her mother or her father. That did not bother Amy, but it bothered her parents a great deal as they tried to find some common ground with their headstrong daughter. Amy was also an only child. She did not have to deal with siblings or compete with them either.

By the time Monday morning arrived and classes resumed at Jamison, there was not one student who had not heard of the confrontation between Amy and Charlotte. What was even more apparent, the majority of kids had already began to choose sides and draw battle lines, as it were. If the social demographic had been blurred between the two girls previously, it was now being brought into clear relief in the halls of Jamison. Many of the teachers took no notice, but given the state of things in the world at the moment, some were seriously worried.

* * *

Charlotte was putting some books in her locker and was about to head for her next class, when she noticed Amy coming down the hall towards her. Amy was two steps ahead of three other girls who Charlotte knew only by sight and barely by name. As Amy approached, Charlotte took a deep breath and turned to face her.

"Amy," she said, "I need to talk to you."

Amy turned her head for a brief look into Charlotte's plaintive eyes and kept walking, making no reply. The coterie of girls behind her just glared at Charlotte as they continued their lockstep down the hall.

"Amy!" Charlotte pleaded as Amy was receding into the crowded hallway, giving no indication she had heard her. Charlotte just stood and watched as her friend disappeared into the mass of students milling about the hallway.

Charlotte sighed and turned to walk the opposite way from Amy's line of march as she haltingly started toward her next class.

Several girls who had witnessed this scene gathered around her as she trudged up the hall.

"Charlotte, are you alright?" one asked.

It was Ginger Allen, a girl she knew only casually at best. Ginger was a bright, perky blond who definitely belonged on the affluent side of the ledger. Her father was an investment banker. Charlotte had heard her dad say he was one of the wealthiest men in the Dallas/Ft. Worth area.

Charlotte could not conceal her surprise that Ginger was talking to her, much less expressing an interest in her welfare. Charlotte just looked blankly at her classmate. The several other girls in Ginger's entourage were all looking at Charlotte intently as though they were desperate to hear what she was to say next.

"Uh... I'm Ok, Ginger. I just didn't want to be late to class," she said in reply and started again to walk up the hall.

"I was just wondering, Charlotte. I know you and Amy are best friends. I heard about that thing last Friday, too. It looks like she's still mad about it all," Ginger said and looked at some of her friends and giggled. "She's definitely a nobody around here, especially after that episode. I'm glad you finally stood up to her. Only the dweebs would talk to her now," Ginger added and laughed with the other girls who joined in on cue. "Why don't you join us for lunch today?" Ginger asked.

Charlotte stopped abruptly. Now she knew she could only be dreaming. The most popular girl in her class had made a gesture of friendship to her. It was something she could only have imagined in a teenaged fairy tale. A sense of exhilaration swept over her body like a million little pin pricks. It couldn't really be happening.

"Sure, Ginger." The words flowed out of her so easily that Charlotte couldn't believe she had actually said anything. Her head was swimming in astonishment and disbelief as her legs began to move her down the hall again.

"Great!" Ginger exulted. "We usually meet over at the corner table close to the doors," she added.

Charlotte knew exactly where Ginger and her friends met. She had seen them there in the cafeteria often. No one would have dared to try to take that table or sit anywhere near it for that matter. The air around it was much too rarified. And now, the lowly Charlotte Madison had been extended an invitation by Ginger the Great herself to join this celebrated coven of teenaged chosen ones. It was an event of untold magnitude at Jamison. She knew that Amy would have laughed in their faces had she been approached by these girls. But Charlotte was not Amy. Maybe it was time for her to make some much needed changes. She couldn't help but think that for a day that started out with the promise of so much dread, she was now feeling like she surely must have died and gone to heaven!

Charlotte's head was spinning and her feet were light as she and the other girls hurried toward the cafeteria.

* * *

Alex made some notations in a file on his desk as he picked up his telephone. "Is that everyone today, Emily?" he asked as he closed the file.

"That's all the patients, but I wanted to talk to you a minute," Emily replied.

A deadly silence fell on the open line. Alex was unaccustomed to the serious tone in Emily's voice. It made any words he might want to speak catch in his throat. Finally, though, he managed to ask her to come into his office.

Scarcely a few seconds later his door opened and his office manager walked in and sat down in one of the large comfortable chairs not far from Alex's desk. Alex got up from behind his desk and sat down on his couch across from her.

"Something on your mind, Emily?" he asked.

Emily was dressed in a dark, navy blue linen suit with a straight skirt and a white starched blouse with a matching navy blue bolero jacket over it. Her dark hair was pulled back from her face and tied in the back of her head in something like a bun affixed with a comb. For the seven years she had worked for Alex, she had always been conservative in her dress which belied her quick wit and buoyant personality. To Alex, she was something like what he imagined a flower child of the sixties and early seventies would be, minus the psychedelic paisley peasant dress over faded blue jeans. But they had always worked together well, and he had never had occasion to be unhappy with her. She was assertive and did many things for him he would have not expected of her such as assertively handling nuisance calls and such. For that he was eternally grateful. It saved him a lot of time and grief. Today, though, he was genuinely baffled as to what she might want to talk to him about.

Emily cleared her throat as she looked down at the carpeted floor.

"My husband called me today over lunch. He told me when he was driving to work this morning about six thirty, there were some huge planes flying over at a very low altitude. It startled him. I wondered, Dr. Madison, if you know anything about that? It scared me when he told me about it. You know, like some military thing, or World War Three or something. If we're about to get bombed or go to war or something, I want to know about it," she said and looked intently at Alex.

The days were getting longer now and the sunlight was still pouring through the large windows of his office, as Alex's eyes were roaming over the buildings across the freeway that reflected the golden hues of the waning daylight.

Damn! he thought. *How much should I tell her?*

Alex knew Emily would know in a few milliseconds if he tried to be cute or glib with her. He felt trapped, but he could not violate his word about national security, either. For one thing, it was a matter of principal to him; and for another, he did not know if he might get a visit from someone in a dark suit and sunglasses if he said something he shouldn't to someone he shouldn't.

"Don't worry, Emily, we're not going to war," Alex replied. "At least as far as I know we're not. I know you're concerned, but I can't say anything about the planes. It's some kind of maneuvers the military is conducting. But, believe me when I say you don't need to be worried." Alex sank back on the couch and gave Emily a rather pasted-on smile he knew was not going to reassure her much.

Emily just looked down at her clenched hands in her lap for a moment.

"I know I make a lot of jokes, Dr. Madison, but I was worried when I talked to David earlier. I know your last trip to Washington was a secret kind of thing. I'm not prying; I'm worried," she said and paused. Before she could continue, Alex leaned forward.

"I know, Emily. I've been worried, too. The world is a crazy place right now. Who could've thought we would be going through something like this? It seems the world might be coming to an end and not with the big bang everyone thought, but with a long sigh and a whimper. It's like no one cares anymore." Alex once again sank back on the couch and took a deep breath before slowly letting it out.

Alex looked out his window again as the golden late afternoon light became even richer and took on a more orange hue. He then looked back at Emily who was still taking an unusual interest in her hands still clasped in her lap.

Alex then noticed something that stunned him.

Emily was crying.

Almost instinctively, Alex leaned forward and extended his hand. Emily put her hand in his as they sat together for a moment. Alex then stood, still holding her hand, and as she stood with him, he folded his arms around her. They had rarely touched in the past, and embracing one another was just never on the menu despite the care and respect they clearly had for each other.

Alex patted her gently on her back as they relaxed their embrace. Emily then got busy dabbing at her eyes with a tissue.

"Just look at me! Making a maudlin spectacle of myself, especially in front of the boss," she said and broke into a self-conscious giggle as she continued to dab at her eyes.

Alex tried not to look at her, thinking it would only add to her discomfort; but he couldn't keep from smiling. Somehow, Emily's momentary loss of composure was reassuring. It was the warm, personal part of her he was well aware of, but had seldom seen in this likeable woman. He reached over and kissed her on the cheek.

"Don't worry, Emily. Be careful going home."

17

The FPA was busier than usual, although no one could say exactly why. The workload was about what it always was. There had been a good bit of talk in the break rooms about something big going down, but it was mostly the usual office brand of fanciful rumors that swelled and grew when somebody caught wind of something, true or not.

Harold Janes was sitting in his transparent office observing the increasing hum of activity, all the while wondering what anybody or everybody knew. Lauren tried to stay in her cubicle, out of sight for the most part. She had fielded a few questions in the corridors and break rooms from some of the others, always deflecting them as best she could. There was a growing appreciation in her now for those who knew things of great importance and far-reaching consequence but were unable to speak freely about them. It was no small burden; and it certainly was not for the faint of heart. Lauren was now thinking she had been awfully hard on some past presidents and other high ranking politicians. It was certainly easy to have opinions, but thoughtful, effective leadership in the face of intense public scrutiny was another matter entirely.

The Saturday morning meeting at which she had last seen Alex, seemed eons ago for Lauren. That span of time had not tempered the aching knot persisting in her gut. She was glad of that though. It was a good kind of ache-the kind that poets and songwriters had celebrated for centuries. The same kind of hurt that doubtless had caused many a human heart to do things it did not understand. It had humbled the haughty and empowered the meek. It was the kind of feeling that consumed a human heart and was only deterred momentarily by life's mundane necessities like working, eating, and slumber-the latter of which Lauren had not had much of lately.

It was wonderful enough when only one person experienced this near universal malady; but when it was shared by two, there were no words in any language that were adequate to explain it. It was something that just was; but that was enough. For Lauren Marsh, it had resurrected what the last seventeen years had been slowly eroding in her: she felt hopeful again.

"What in the world are you doing?" a disembodied voice jolted Lauren from her trance.

She jerked her head around to see the looming visage of Ann standing over her. Ann snapped her fingers a few times in front of Lauren's startled eyes.

"Where are you, girl? Wake up!" she added, waving her hands in front of Lauren's face. Lauren recoiled from her standing friend, but then waved Ann off with a gesture.

"Ann, you ninny! You scared me. Can't a girl have a daydream around here without her best friend harassing her? Don't you have something else to do besides bug me?" Lauren's protest had more than a hint of over-dramatization in it. Ann threw her head back in mock surprise and shock.

"Oh, nobody's supposed to bother the queen when she's in repose, I guess," she replied sarcastically. Lauren just pursed her lips as she gave Ann one of her "don't mess with me" glares. "I'll bet I could guess what's swimming in that empty head of yours, Lauren," Ann added and then continued, "You've met a man." She paused and took a breath. "Did Art finally break the ice, or is it somebody new?" she persisted. "I'm betting it's someone else. What about it, Toots?" Ann just looked at Lauren with a knowing smirk on her face.

Lauren's shoulders relaxed and it seemed her whole body drooped for a moment as she slumped in her chair. "Why Ann, whatever do you mean?" she said in the best Southern drawl she could muster at the moment. "The way you go on. I do declare sometimes I think you've taken leave of your senses," she concluded and batted her eyes at her friend.

Ann just turned her head away and rolled her eyes.

"Oh, brother," she said and began to giggle. "It's worse than I thought." She hesitated a moment before a scowl crept across her face. "How could you keep this from me, your best pal?" she asked in disbelief. Lauren could then see that her deception had been effective. Ann had no clue how far down the tube her best friend had fallen.

"Well, can't a girl have some secrets, Miss Scarlet?" she continued in her feigned drawl.

"Not from your best friend, you can't," Ann answered with feigned disgust. "Just see if I ever tell you anything again," she huffed and stuck her nose into the air, trying not to laugh.

She did not fool Lauren, though. Lauren knew that behind the mirth, Ann was hurt that she had not shared her amorous secret. They were close like sisters, and as such, were susceptible to the same wounds and snares that siblings shared. Lauren then stood and hugged her friend's uncooperative, stiff body.

"We'll talk at lunch today. I promise to tell you everything," Lauren said as Ann's arms slowly circled Lauren's waist.

Ann then gave Lauren a quick squeeze and turned to go back to her desk.

* * *

To people who knew something of critical importance that they just as soon not have known, the passage of time was a burden almost beyond bearing. It was a kind of tension that imbued a person invisibly, but had the distraction of a ball and chain. Whether someone was a practiced possessor of such acquisitions or not, a telling price of ownership was near impossible to escape.

For Alex, it had resulted in his migrating over onto Maria's side of the bed at night, as though some part of her might still be there to give him the comfort he needed. Since her death, he had jealously guarded her place in their bed by avoiding it. Maria's absence from their bed had left a burden for Alex which was invisible but inescapable. He awoke at times and found himself reaching for her, but that was as far as he could go to trespass into her territory. At least that had been true until the last week or so since the meeting in Washington and especially after the planes took flight the Monday afterward.

Alex had awakened more than a few times to find his head on Maria's pillow, stroking the soft sheets on the bed with his hands. And, in his desperate nocturnal search for his absent wife, the face he saw in his imagination and the body he felt in his hands were Lauren's. It was a sacrilege to Maria's memory he could not countenance despite the pleasure he felt from it. It was a clash of emotion that his training, common sense, head, and heart could not rectify. It seemed so wrong; it felt so right.

It also felt so good.

It must have been like the sirens' song that Ulysses heard as he sailed past their island in *The Odyssey,* all the while thinking of his beloved Penelope faithfully waiting for him in Greece. Like the ancient Greek warrior, lost and longing for home, Alex kept looking to Maria. She had always been his true north. Now, his compass was misaligned and he was rudderless in dark, forbidding waters. What was worse, he felt his emotions were betraying him. He wasn't sure what he still needed from Maria, but whatever it was, Alex felt helpless to rid himself of it.

18

It was something like happiness. Everyone wanted it, but no one seemed to know if they had it or not until they stopped and looked backward for a moment and only then realized they were or were not in a state of it. Of all the emotional conditions of the human heart, happiness was the most sought after and the most difficult to appreciate when it was present.

It was no different with the entire country. As the days rolled into weeks after the baptizing of the nation with the anointed mist, the change was slow to evidence itself.

Probably the first to notice anything noticeable were the hospitals. The necessity to house patients in the hallways on makeshift beds and pallets began to disappear. Discharges began to outnumber the admissions. Alex witnessed this daily metamorphosis as he made his rounds in the mornings at the clinic where he worked. All the units now had their patients in regular rooms and were beginning to have vacant rooms much to the chagrin of the administration that was enjoying record profits at the expense of a beleaguered, depressed humanity. An ill wind blowing nobody good must have been one of those rare clichés that resounded with the absolute, clarion ring of truth.

Emily had also noted to Alex that the waiting list for appointments in his office had also disappeared as well. It was a welcome relief, but immediately sent him into another theater of worry. He seemed to be unhappy without some approaching storm threatening some critical area of his life. After forty plus years of living, Alex concluded he was not going to give up that personality quirk so easily. For now, he just put it under the "it's always something" folder in his mental file and went on down the road.

* * *

Almost two months had passed since that Monday morning in which the Air Force armada had swarmed over the ailing nation delivering its invisible cargo. Alex had heard nothing from Washington in the meantime. He was just as glad. His last sojourn to Washington was exciting, but it was all he wanted of governmental cloak and dagger secrecy. He liked all the attention, but he would gladly forego it in favor of getting those kind of kicks from books and movies in the future.

The only remaining interest Alex had in Washington had chestnut hair and pale blue eyes complimenting her mesmerizing presence. He didn't even have her phone number. He supposed he could get it, but there was still the not-so-small problem of the other hurdles he needed to clear before he dared venture into those waters. Yet, he was dying to go there, and wondering if Lauren felt the same. He felt like he was seventeen again. It was that magical mix of emotions that was both wondrous and dreadful. He had been happy with Maria, but her death had sent him spinning back to emotional adolescence. When he had emerged from that murky state of his development into manhood, it was a place he never expected to find himself again.

Twenty years of marriage had not given Alex any more of the evenness of temperament that Maria had in abundance. She had her passions, to be sure, but she could survey most any circumstance or situation that worried Alex and deal with them in ways he never would have considered. The conflicts that brought him serious apprehension usually meant little to her.

Maria was not a manipulator, but her people skills far outdistanced Alex's. That alone bothered him, as he was supposed to be the expert on human relations; but eventually he just accepted it. He looked to her to manage situations that were hard for him, like making conversation at social gatherings. Alex always felt gawky and awkward at those times. Maria came, in time, to recognize those things and simply considered it a part of their marriage contract. Along with her innate warmth and fidelity to their union, Maria was, above all things, a realist.

All that made their marriage a bastion of safety, security, and satisfaction also made her death more mystifying and confusing for Alex. That he would be thinking of another lover after only these few short months, he could only feel as a desecration. It was a wholly untenable, unspeakable, unimaginable aberration; yet there it was, making him crazy like a horny seventeen year old.

* * *

The news from the rest of the country was such that it appeared for the first time in the last three years that there was reason for optimism. Industry reported less absenteeism in the workplace as the wheels of the nation's manufacturing and commerce seemed to be on the move again. Hospitals were discharging patients in great numbers, most of whom had been housed for depression and other emotional ills. The prevailing atmosphere of gloom and despair in an embattled country was showing signs of dissipating. All things considered, it was a time for celebration and the weary nation would soon be doing just that.

* * *

In Washington, the politicians were letting no grass grow under their feet in declaring that America's recent crisis was on its way to being resolved. Peace, prosperity, and improved mental and emotional health were all now at hand for every American citizen. In truth, there were few in Washington who did not hail the resurgence of the country's vigor and potency as near miraculous. Even the jaded veterans of political warfare and intrigue like Congressman Branch were amazed at the change. It almost seemed like there really was a Land of Oz, and a wizard who could make unimaginable things come true. It was an era of unparalleled optimism. Who would have thought or dared to question it?

* * *

"Do you really think we need to do that, Congressman?" Harold Janes spoke into the telephone as he was casually leaning back in his large, leather covered chair. He paused for a moment as he listened to Congressman Branch's reply. "Well, sir, I do think it's a good idea when you put it that way," he intoned and listened again. "Well, just let me know when and Lauren and I will be there, sir," he concluded and put down the handset of his phone in the cradle.

He paused and thought for a moment as his gaze passed over the scattered papers on his desk. It bothered him to see his work area so cluttered, but he knew it was just temporary as he began to gather up the scattered papers and stack them neatly in separate piles. He couldn't help himself. He had always been a neat freak. Untidiness was to Harold Janes among the worst desecrations in the human inventory of unpardonable sins.

After completing his housekeeping, Harold picked up his phone again and punched at the keys in his rapid, staccato fashion. He waited a moment, and said, "Lauren, Congressman Branch wants another meeting of the committee. It's sort of a celebratory thing to let everyone know how pleased the president is with the work of the committee. I also expect he wants to get some considerable political mileage out of this thing, too," he said and paused. "You may get to see your doctor from Texas again, Lauren," he added and smiled to himself as he put down the phone.

Lauren could feel the warm, flushed sensation coursing over her face like a spray of water when she stepped into her bath in the morning.

How did he know? she thought as she sat embarrassed and puzzled.

She had kept Ann in the dark, but not Harold. Perhaps she had badly misjudged him. Maybe there was more to him than just his concern over dotting the "i's" and crossing the "t's" on those zillions of reports passing over his desk every day. Apparently he wasn't just another retired military obsessive in a boring government job whiling away his days until retirement. Lauren hated that she could have been so transparent, especially to a man. It almost seemed a betrayal of her womanhood.

She felt the blush fading away from her face and hoped it would be gone before anyone came by her cubicle to notice. Lauren was beginning to regret baring her soul to Ann at lunch already. She loved Ann dearly, but she also knew she couldn't keep her mouth shut sometimes, even when it imperiled their friendship. Lauren sighed deeply and wrote it off as one of things that friends had to overlook in each other. She knew Ann would never be malicious or petty. Her friend was just excitable and couldn't rein in her tongue when she was out of the starting gate with something irrepressible. Or at least irrepressible to Ann Brady. Lauren wished she could get as excited about things as Ann did. But she decided those kinds of differences were what made them friends.

Lauren also knew that she would be toast around the office once it became known she had set her sights on a man… any man. It was widely presumed by both the men and women alike that she was an unassailable fortress of womanly virtue and self-control. She knew most of her coworkers snickered behind her back that Art would have even tried to breech her ramparts.

That she would have been viewed in such a way made itself felt in Lauren's gut like an aching knot of disgust. She turned her gaze down at the floor and took an unusual interest in her plain black shoes as she sat in her chair with her shoulders arched forward with her arms stiffened and her hands pressing on her knees. All of her ardor to protect herself from she wasn't sure what had only succeeded in leaving her with a hollow disdain for herself. She didn't have a man; she didn't have any children; and now she had no self-respect. Lauren wondered who would embrace such an example of womanhood.

* * *

"It's Congressman Branch on the line, Dr. Madison," Emily's voice came over the intercom with her usual stentorian clarity as Alex was making some notations in a patient file.

"Thank you, Emily," Alex replied, "you can go back to your knitting now."

"Yes, sir, but you must remember, sir, I'm the one who makes the jokes around here."

"Oh, yes, Emily, I almost forgot. I hope you will pardon the oversight," Alex added a rejoinder.

"Only this one time, sir." Alex rolled his eyes and hit a blinking button on his telephone.

"Hello Congressman Branch, I hope you are well, sir," Alex turned his chair to the side as he greeted his caller.

"I can tell you, sir, we are all doing much better now. Everyone is pleased and, to say the least, relieved," he responded.

"I know how you feel, Congressman. Things here have shown a remarkable turnaround. I've never seen anything remotely like this before."

"I don't think any of us have, doctor. That is why I'm calling. I wanted to invite you to a final, I hope, meeting of the committee. The president will have a few words to say to us by telephone. He wanted all of the members of the committee to know how pleased he is." The congressman paused as though waiting for a reply, but he then continued, "I know it may be an inconvenience for you, but I hope you will be able to come. I can send a plane for you if that will help."

"I will be only too glad to come, Congressman. I can get there on my own. No need to come for me. Just let me know when."

"Well, I'm glad you will be able to join us, doctor. I will look forward to seeing you next Thursday. The meeting will be at noon in the usual committee room." The congressman then rang off as Alex turned his chair around and looked out his big window onto the freeway below where the noonday surge of traffic was escalating. He felt a sensation coming over him like a refreshing wave at the beach. He was glad the congressman had called. He was glad there would be another meeting of the committee. He was glad at the prospect of getting out of the office for a day or two. But he was ecstatic at the thought of seeing Lauren again.

19

"Hey, dad, are you going to see the president this time?" John asked as he walked past Alex's chair in the den. "Can you get me an autograph?" the teenager continued. Alex put down his newspaper for a moment and caught a glimpse of his son as he disappeared around the corner into the kitchen.

"I thought you didn't like the president," Alex countered.

"I've changed my mind. He's pretty cool after all. I found out he's a baseball fan...he likes the Atlanta Braves. That's cool since he's from South Carolina," the voice continued from the kitchen.

"The Atlanta Braves are not in South Carolina," Alex answered.

"I know, dad, but they're in the same part of the country."

"Well, I don't think the president gives out autographs, unless you have a bill he's going to sign into law, son," Alex drawled.

"Dad... you're such a dud. Surely you can get him to sign something for me since you're both such pals now," John answered and started to laugh.

"Son, I've never even met him. I don't know where you get such ideas." Alex resumed reading his paper as John poured himself some iced tea. "Have you seen your sister today? Do you know where she is?"

"I think she's out with some of her friends. She's been getting pretty tight with Ginger Allen since she and Amy hit the skids," John replied as he came into the den and sat on the couch. Alex dropped his paper and looked at his son.

"Roger Allen's daughter?" Alex asked.

"Oh, yes, dad. Your daughter is now quite the little social butterfly at Jamison. Or she will be when school starts back up again. She's become one of Ginger's entourage from what I hear. Charlotte seldom talks to me, you know," he finished and took a long gulp of his tea.

Alex continued to stare at John. It occurred to him that since his talk with his daughter on the swing in the back yard several weeks ago, he had not heard much from her. He had been busy, but the gnawing realization that his children were growing up in front of his eyes with his taking little note of it was unsettling to him. John would be in college soon; Amy would be in high school; and before he could turn around, he would be living in an empty nest...just like it was rendered in the books and magazines.

I'm supposed to know how to handle these things, Alex thought as a chill settled over him.

"So, she and Amy didn't get things worked out?" Alex asked.

"I don't think so, dad. She's hardly mentioned her name in over a month." John continued to gulp down his tea. "Amy's a tough nut when she wants to be. I don't think she's ever even talked to Charlotte since that thing at school. Charlotte hasn't said so to me, but I think she's been bothered by it."

Alex turned his attention back to his newspaper, but all he saw was a mass of black and white. Also that odd sensation was coming on that left him with a swirling head. He suspected it wouldn't be long before the little dancing lights would appear. They looked like little check marks lined up in a semi-circle that blinked and shimmered like neon whether his eyes were opened or closed. He would also get a nauseous feeling in his stomach when this phenomenon was accompanied by the blind spot in the center of his visual fields. Fortunately, it didn't usually stay long, but while it was there, it was maddening.

What was even more maddening was the fact he could not will it away. But Alex had learned that if he relaxed and distracted himself from thinking about it, after an hour or so, it was usually gone. It was kind of like he had to fool his unconscious into thinking he didn't care about it. He grinned when he thought about that.

Could a psychiatrist fool his own subconscious mind?

He didn't think so.

* * *

Monday and Tuesday came and went, and by Wednesday of the week of the committee meeting, Lauren was beside herself. She couldn't type a simple sentence without having to start over two or three times. She kept dropping her purse and tripping over her chair every time she got up from her desk. While she was getting dressed for work that morning, she dropped her favorite gold pendant down her bathroom drain as she was nervously trying to affix the clasp behind her neck. She had left the water running in the sink and the gold amulet along with the fine, delicate chain that suspended it were gone forever. Lauren thought she might take the P-trap off underneath the sink, but she didn't have time; and with the water running, she knew it was now history.

Lauren also knew that there was no doubt as to the explanation for her sudden case of the klutz. It was no different than when her husband would walk by and pass his hand softly over her cheek. She could still feel it now. When she was under his spell, she would have done anything he asked and begged for the chance to do it again. With that kind of power over her, she still marveled at how she could have ever mustered the strength to leave him. As she thought about it, she doubted she could ever give herself a satisfying answer.

Will he even look in my direction? Lauren thought.

She was not absolutely sure he would be coming at all. As she pondered the possibility that Alex would ignore her, she took in a short breath that caught in her throat. Lauren knew he would not ignore her, as he was always polite and gentlemanly; but the notion that he would not return her tender regard was worse than tragic. It would be unspeakable.

What's the matter with you? she said to herself. *He's a grown man. He has his own feelings. He's probably still grieving over his wife. Why would he care for you?*

Lauren was thinking of every likely and unlikely possibility about this man she hardly knew at all. There was nothing wrong with being in love, but this was bordering on craziness.

But, then again, love usually was.

The only bright spot at work was that Ann had surprisingly kept her mouth closed about Lauren's infatuation with Alex, for which she would be eternally grateful. There had been a few unguarded cracks a time or two, but nothing damaging. By lunchtime Wednesday, Lauren was unsure she could cross the street to the little café she and Ann frequented without falling down or getting run over. Somehow she managed, however, and as she and Ann sat down at their favorite table in the corner, Ann could see that Lauren was in a hopeless state.

"Will you relax, for heaven's sake! He's just a man and he's probably more nervous than you are," Ann said as she put her hand over and touched Lauren's arm. All Lauren could do was just look back at her friend and shake her head.

"I feel like I'm going to fly into pieces," Lauren finally said. "I wish I would and just get it over with." She looked down at her sandwich which she knew she was going to have to take home. She couldn't have eaten if she had been threatened with the guillotine.

"He may not even come. Have you thought about that?" Ann looked into Lauren's eyes.

"About a million times. And then I prayed that God would not be that cruel to me," Lauren answered as she picked up a potato chip. "Then I prayed that He would not subject me to this misery any longer...maybe I should enter a convent."

"If you did that, you'd just have to leave and break your vows," Ann replied and started to laugh. "You'd be the horniest nun in history." Lauren pursed her lips as Ann's laughter had lapsed into an episode of coughing.

"You're always so helpful and supportive, Ann, and just

when I need it most." Lauren was frowning and trying not to laugh at the same time.

"And speaking of THAT," Ann continued, "how long has it been since you've done the dirty deed?" Lauren looked at her comrade with a glare that she reserved for her most severe responses to insensitive questions. "Ok, Ok, so I was out of line. What are best friends for if not to ask embarrassing, insensitive questions?"

"NOT to ask embarrassing, insensitive questions," Lauren shot back. "Good grief, Ann!" Ann immediately knew she had pushed the envelope too far. Her face flushed as repentance crept into her voice.

"I'm sorry, baby, I was just trying to lighten things up. I'm sorry." Lauren's laser sharp glare faded as she looked down at the floor.

"I'm afraid it's been much too long, Ann. I don't know what I've been waiting for, though. Prince Charming, I guess. I've been so stupid!" Lauren's voice trailed off and she looked as if she might cry. But, she didn't. "Now, I've seen a man who I think is worth the trouble, and I don't know if he will even look my direction. I might be crazy, Ann, but I haven't felt this good *and* bad since I was married." She paused for a moment. "I certainly don't want another philandering husband who will make me give up my own identity because I love him so much. But I'm afraid I might do it again." Ann just looked at Lauren without blinking. She had no idea their conversation would be plumbing these kinds of depths.

"Lauren, all any of us can do is follow our hearts. Sometimes it leads us astray, but all of our choices when it comes to love are half chance at best, honey. I'm afraid none of us has a lock on it. If that doctor has half a brain and half a heart, he will grab you like the pearl of great price you are if you give him a chance."

The two women looked at each other without speaking. Lauren's pale blue eyes were beginning to moisten. "Now look what you made me do," she said. "Everybody in the office will know I've been blubbering," she blurted out and began to dab at her eyes.

"Join the rest of the world, Lauren," Ann said as they both stood up and started out the door of the café.

* * *

"Are you sure, Ginger? Are you sure that's what she said?" Charlotte asked anxiously as her pulse began to quicken and her breathing became more rapid and shallow. "I can't believe it. How could she be so lame?"

"Well, Trudy heard it with her own two ears, Charlotte. You know she never lies," Ginger Allen answered to a bewildered Charlotte. "She said that having you for a best friend just wasted the last several years of her life and you were probably too stupid to understand why."

There was a prolonged silent pause on the line as Charlotte swallowed hard and her throat became something like a desert. Her heart was beginning to slowly ascend from her chest up into her mouth.

She was thankful that Ginger was on the other side of a telephone line as she delivered this stinging revelation. Charlotte doubled over from the dull, merciless ache suddenly opening an unseen gash in her stomach. It was the kind of assault that could not be measured in terms of mere pain. It was the kind of pain that no physical blow could have produced. Only human emotion could deliver something with such agonizing destructiveness.

Despite the congealed mix of feelings in her gut, Charlotte did her best teenaged impression of someone who could not have cared less.

"She's a piece of work, isn't she?" Charlotte replied with as much offhand teen sneer as she could manage. "I only wish I could have seen this sooner before I wasted so much of MY time," she added smearing as much sarcasm onto the statement as possible.

"Well, we all make mistakes. I'm just glad you've seen the

light before it was really too late. Just imagine wasting your adolescent years on a loser like Amy," Ginger said gleefully. "I'm so glad you've come into the fold, Charlotte. It looks like it was just in time, too."

"I'm just glad you, Trudy, and the others welcomed me in, Ginger. I'd hate to think of what might have happened otherwise. It scares me when I think about it," Charlotte added. "My life could have taken a wrong turn and I'd have been nowhere. I'm glad I have friends like you, Ginger."

Charlotte felt strangely detached as she was speaking, like she might have been dreaming. It had that odd, surreal moodiness about it like when she was not quite asleep and not quite awake and couldn't tell the difference. She fell back on her bed and stared at her ceiling. For some reason, it wouldn't stay still but kept dancing above her like an earthquake might have been shaking the house.

"My dad is calling me, Ginger," she managed to say after a longer than comfortable silence ensued between her and her newfound friend. "I think he wants me to go somewhere with him. He promised we would spend some time together today."

"I feel sorry for you, honey," Ginger offered. "What a drag. My dad's such a doofus. I'm glad he doesn't subject me to such punishment. Let's get together tomorrow for a movie or something. Ok? I'll call you."

"Sounds great!" Charlotte replied as she hit the "end" button on her phone.

She continued to stare at the ceiling. It, at least, had stopped jerking around like it had been only a few seconds ago. Charlotte now was left with the desperate hope that her stomach would do the same thing and let her rest. She then rolled over onto her side, closed her eyes, and buried her face in her soft pillow. Charlotte lay motionless for a time, but soon her soft sobbing began to rock her bed.

20

Alex's flight had been delayed due to air traffic congestion at Dulles. He had hurried to get a taxi as he hoped he could get to the committee meeting on time. Alex despised being late for anything, and today he had other things on his mind as well. Thoughts of Lauren had assumed control of his waking hours to the point where he had simply given up the mind games he often played when he was faced with an especially important or anxiety-provoking issue. Alex had become a master at fooling himself into believing that whatever it was that was so important really wasn't —or that he didn't care if it was important or not.

Those neurotic ruses were not working today.

Alex could have cared less about the meeting, the politics, the other members of the committee (except for one), or the hoopla that was bound to surround the festivities of the day.

He just wanted to see Lauren.

Actually, Alex wanted to do more than that. He wanted to talk to her, to kiss her, to have his hands roam over her inviting body. To tell her how much he had missed her and how often he thought of her would also be wonderful. The great pressure of emotion pushing from inside him was now beyond his control. He also knew that when he saw her, he feared he would be helpless to prevent making a colossal fool of himself. Somehow, though, that didn't matter. He had done the same thing when he first met Maria. Alex had never doubted that his nose dive to the floor at her feet all those years ago cemented their fate. Or at least that's what he told himself. Maria never actually said anything about it. When the subject arose, she just smiled and changed the subject.

Alex told himself that if he thought about it too much, he was likely to screw this thing up. He often lectured himself in such a way. Basically, he felt that most things were better left unsaid and unthought about. The really good things in life just happened and you needed to just let them happen—not contrive to make them happen. Right then as he was getting out of the taxicab, he had no idea if any of those religiously held axioms about human behavior held any credence at all. He was in love and he was nervous. That's all he knew for sure as he ascended the steps to the Capitol Building.

* * *

The gathering at the meeting room was considerably larger than at previous meetings of the Healthcare Committee. Alex needn't have worried about being late as it was nearly 12:45 before Congressman Branch called the meeting to order. The political wheels were turning as there were numerous reporters present along with cameramen and an ample supply of microphones. It took the congressman close to a half hour to have all his comments duly recorded for posterity and the six o'clock news.

When Alex arrived at about five minutes after noon, he immediately recognized some of the reporters he often saw on the evening news reports. He also noticed that Congressman Branch was careful to speak to all of them before he herded them out of the meeting room before he opened the meeting. Alex was thinking that all this unusual activity surrounding the meeting was actually having a calming effect on his otherwise excited emotional state. He kept looking around the room for Lauren, but had not seen her as of yet. There was quite a crowd in the room, so he thought he may just have missed her, but as he began to look more in earnest, she was nowhere in sight. A dull ache was beginning to settle in his gut.

Alex caught himself before he was too far along in his self-flagellating angst. The rationalization he came up with was that not everything we want or hope for in life comes about. Just because Lauren had succeeded in getting his attention and his hormones circulating at full tilt, didn't mean anything was going to happen. She was just one woman; he was just one man; blah, blah, blah; yaddah, yaddah, yaddah. He sighed deeply and started making his way toward one of the chairs around the long conference table. After he maneuvered his way through the crowd and sat down, he started to think that it was nice while it lasted. Then he cursed Maria for putting him in this conundrum.

In the meantime, Congressman Branch was at his most skillful as he hustled the media types out of the room so he could start the meeting. Alex was looking wistfully out the window at sun drenched Washington and wishing he was somewhere else. It was as though someone had sucked all the air out of him and left his deflated remains just sitting at the table.

He wished like hell he was at home.

When the meeting was at last commenced, Congressman Branch went into a long, windy rendition of the past few months' events and the revitalization of the country. It was clear he was relieved at how the devastating downturn of the past several years had been reversed in such a short time. He expressed gracious thanks to everyone on the committee and their efforts. Alex was thinking that although the congressman was a seasoned veteran of hardnosed politics, he was also a good man who wanted to do the right thing. He did not begrudge him his moment in the spotlight, he just wished he would get on with it.

Alex had chosen a chair near the head of the table, owing to the crowd in the room at the time he was looking for a place to sit down. He was trying to give the congressman some measure of attention and did not notice the door near the far end of the meeting room slowly open and two latecomers ease through it and sit down at the opposite end of the table from the congressman. Alex was still facing front as the congressman spoke.

"I hope you will forgive these meanderings of a happy politician today, folks. In my years of public service, I haven't had occasion before to take such pride in an association with such a wonderful group of people as you are," Congressman

Branch went on. "When we started this venture several months ago, the country was in one of the worst plights in its entire history. But today, our nation has hope because all of you did not give up and gave your best when we needed it."

There was a spontaneous eruption of applause and some cheers around the room as the congressman spoke. He raised his hands and smiled broadly to quiet the outpouring of celebratory elation in the room. Alex felt a smile coming across his face as he turned to look at the joyful gathering around the long table. It was then that he was stricken with the sight of Lauren sitting next to Harold Janes at the back of the room. The sunlight coursing through the large window was dancing off her reddish brown hair as she turned her gaze toward him. An eager smile parted her lips and enlivened her pale blue eyes. Her dark blue dress contrasted with her light toned skin as she nodded her head and broadened her smile.

Alex managed to nod back and return her smile. He was glad he was seated as he wasn't sure his legs could have held him if he were standing. All he could do was stare at her. He was beginning to feel foolish, but he couldn't move his head as the cheers began to subside. A warm, flushed sensation flooded over him as he at last turned his attention back to the congressman, but, didn't hear another word he had to say.

* * *

"I thought you might not be coming," Alex said as he finally was able to get to Lauren as she stood by her chair after the meeting was adjourned and everyone had gotten up and started to wander around.

"Dr. Madison, I don't think you have met my supervisor, Mr. Harold Janes," Lauren said as she turned toward Harold. Alex looked at Harold and extended his hand.

"I'm pleased to meet you, sir," Alex replied.

"Likewise, Dr. Madison," Harold answered. "Lauren had mentioned you're from Texas, I believe."

"Yes, sir, I'm afraid so. It's hot down there this time of year, but it's hot here, too, today."

"Yes, the summer is hot and balmy here. Have you seen much of Washington? Today would be a good day to see some sights if you don't have to get back home," Harold added.

"I was thinking of doing just that, sir. I've not seen much of the Capitol as many times as I have been here," Alex continued participating in the social pleasantries as he rocked side to side from one foot to the other.

"Well, I hope you will enjoy your stay, sir," Harold replied. "I need to talk to the congressman, so I'll ask you to excuse me." Harold then smiled and walked toward the front of the room leaving Alex and Lauren standing by themselves.

Lauren had a death grip on some folders she was holding, and Alex had both hands in the pockets of his suit pants as he studied the pattern of the carpet on the floor. He did manage an uncomfortable looking smile as he looked into her eyes.

"I was hoping you would be here today, Lauren. I was looking forward to seeing you again," Alex said as he fumbled with the silver dollar he always carried in his pocket. "I thought about calling you several times, but I didn't know how you would feel about that. I didn't have your number, either." Lauren held her bundle of papers close to her breast as she looked at him blankly. Alex didn't know for sure if she was listening or not. He stood for a moment before a grin started across his face.

"Are you as nervous as I am, Lauren?" he asked.

They both gazed at each other for a few pregnant moments when Lauren looked down at her shoes and began to giggle. That was all it took for Alex. Soon they were both blushing and laughing together. It was as if the two of them had just discovered the other and everybody else in the room had vanished.

"You're not supposed to ask me questions like that," Lauren replied as her eyes kept darting between the floor and Alex's face, "but, I'm glad you did." Alex just smiled as they both sat down in two vacant chairs by the long table.

It would be an hour before they got up again.

* * *

Things were uncomfortably quiet when John and Charlotte sat down for supper Thursday night. Grace was in her usual state of perpetual motion as she was setting the table and generally fussing over anything related to mealtime that needed fussing over. She stopped to cross herself when John offered a perfunctory prayer before he hungrily dived into the pot roast and potato salad Grace had prepared. Charlotte slowly picked up her napkin and put it in her lap as she looked at her plate and frowned.

"Eat your supper, sweetheart," Grace said to Charlotte who had made no effort up to that point to put any food on her plate. "You look like you've lost some weight, baby," Grace added with a frown of motherly concern and disapproval. Charlotte did not mount a rebuttal, but only turned to look out the window into the back yard. It was still bright and sunny outside even though it was after seven.

"She wants to become one of those models in the fashion magazines, Aunt Grace. You know the ones that are so skinny it looks like they're on a hunger strike," John quipped and giggled. That remark seemed to energize Charlotte from her doldrums. Her eyes began to glisten as her head snapped up and turned toward her brother who was still laughing.

"Where do you come up with all that sprite, sophisticated insight?" she offered and glared at him. "You're such a dweeb, John. No wonder Mary Brim won't go out with you."

Now it was John's head that snapped up and it was his turn to glare. Charlotte felt a pang of guilt at his reaction. She knew she had drawn blood. Hurting John was not her intention, but she was in no mood for a round of sarcastic fencing with him at the table. She had been feeling like crap ever since her conversation with Ginger about Amy. Charlotte was only approaching fifteen, but it was her fervent hope that she would never experience anything as painful again. If wounding her brother would make her feel better, so be it. He didn't seem to mind shooting painful arrows at her.

"Now, now, you two," Grace admonished them both. "One day you'll both regret those hurtful things you say to each other today. You think I'm just an old woman talking, but one day you'll know," her voice took on a tone that both of the warring siblings had never heard from her before. Almost simultaneously they both turned to look at her with unblinking stares. "And what would your mother think?...you talking like you hated each other?" The heavy silence that followed Grace's comments froze all of them. "She would die all over again," Grace added and quickly crossed herself.

With her comments still hanging in the thick air, Grace beat a hasty path to the kitchen sink where she turned on the water like something was on fire under the tap. John looked down at his plate and feebly stirred his potato salad with his fork, while Charlotte sat motionless. The tears that were forming in Charlotte's eyes began flowing down her cheeks and sprinkling the front of her blouse. She raised her head and peered across the table at her brother. His glare had softened to the sheepish seriousness his face took on when he had been caught committing some social or personal misdemeanor.

Pushing her chair back from the table, Charlotte then stood up and walked over to the sink where Grace was busying herself. The teenager placed her hands on her aunt's shoulders and kissed her on the cheek. She then slowly walked out of the kitchen and toward her room.

21

It was nearing eight and the sun was hanging in the afternoon sky as it bathed Washington in gold. Alex was standing in front of his hotel rocking from one foot to the other in a nervous rhythm. He had chosen his most elegant dark blue suit and a burgundy patterned tie along with his most expensive black wing-tips for the occasion. Along with the myriad other matters he and Lauren discussed that afternoon, they had made a date for dinner.

As Alex continued his animated dance under the covered driveway of the hotel, it occurred to him that he had not been on a date with a woman not his wife in over twenty years. It was one of those realizations that had not as yet penetrated his mind. He really had no cause for such a thing to invade his thoughts until Maria died, that is. Even then, it was not as though he was anxious to think about the possibility. Now, all manner of emotional winds were blowing at him in ways he never expected.

Alex knew, and had told himself many times, that Maria would never have visited such a burden on him had she not been in the grasp of something that had overwhelmed her. The ultimate irony was that it had deprived her of her life while those who loved her looked on with unseeing eyes. Despite knowing all this, Alex also realized he could not just cast her memory aside. If he knew nothing else about people and loss, he knew that one way or the other, the piper was going to be paid. No one suffered loss without cost. It was the cost that people feared the most. It often made them sick and useless.

It was just at that moment that Alex saw a dark red compact car come winding up the semicircular drive. It came to a sudden stop as Lauren waved at him. Despite his misgivings, Lauren suggested that she pick him up since it was convenient. And it was, after all, the twenty first century and women had achieved some measure of liberation from the social restrictions of the past. Being an old fashioned guy, this did give Alex some pause, but he didn't make an issue of it. His desire to spend some time with Lauren was a powerful moderator of his otherwise ingrained beliefs about the socially acceptable behavior of men and women. He waved and climbed into the passenger side of Lauren's car.

"Would you like to drive, Alex?" she asked and looked at him. Alex just looked back for a moment as he was thinking.

"Well, I will if you want me to, but since you know where we're going and I don't, maybe it would be better if you drove," he answered. Lauren just looked at him and smiled.

"Ok, that will work fine. Just don't say I didn't warn you," she added and began to giggle. "Ann tells me I am the worst driver in the District of Columbia," she continued, laughing as she spoke.

"You can't be that bad, Lauren. If I get worried, I'll take over," Alex replied with a smile. "Where are we going?"

"It's a small Italian place I know. It's quiet and the food is outstanding. I hope you'll like it."

"Sounds great. Italian is one of my favorites," Alex answered as he was watching the traffic.

"It's Thursday, so it shouldn't be crowded," Lauren added as she drove on.

The rest of the way to the restaurant passed quietly between the two who were little more than strangers. Lauren was dressed in a light blue sleeveless dress that hugged her body but was not tight or binding. It accented her small waist where it was drawn in by a patent leather belt. The fullness of her breasts was evident against the bodice; Alex tried his best not to be too obvious as he stole a number of furtive glances at them. Her long dark auburn tinted hair flowed down over her shoulders. Her understated allure was completed by a single strand of pearls that circled her delicate neck. She busied herself watching the traffic and being alert for the turns she needed to make, while Alex did his best to act calm and casual. He was also thinking how wonderful a glass of Chardonnay would be at that moment.

After Lauren parked the car, they walked into the restaurant which was in a smallish, free standing brick building located on a rather quiet side street off a busy thoroughfare. There was a small, noticeable but unobtrusive sign in dark letters arching over the door that read, *Emiliano's*. There was a smattering of other cars in the parking area.

"It looks like they're not too busy tonight," Alex said as they reached the pristine, white door with ornate gold handles. He grabbed one of them and opened the door that led into a small foyer where a somewhat portly man with an apron wrapped around his waist greeted them with friendliness.

"Good evening. Just the two of you?" he asked.

"Yes," Lauren answered. "I have a reservation. Marsh is the name."

"Ah, yes, Ms. Marsh. Please come this way." The man then led them to a table in one corner of the restaurant which was secluded from the others. The dining area was quiet and had a simply stated elegance. The tables were all covered with crisp, white tablecloths and fresh flowers in the center. The chairs all had curved armrests with cloth seats. There were several other couples present and soft violins accompanied the diners' muted conversations.

Alex and Lauren sat down at their table and ordered some wine. As the waiter left and made his way toward the small bar off the entry, Lauren turned to face Alex.

"You're a long way from home, Alex," she said as her eyes met his directly. Alex just looked back for a moment as he studied her face.

"Yes, Lauren, but there's no place I'd rather be right now. I must confess I was hoping to see you again. It was quite a letdown when I arrived at the meeting room today and did not see you there." Alex reached across the table and put his hand on top of hers. Lauren smiled as she looked away for a moment.

"Harold and I got away from the office later than we wanted to. He got stuck on the phone. I was on pins and needles waiting for him. I was anxious to see you, too, Alex," Lauren replied as her gaze lingered on his face. "I was relieved to see you when we arrived." Alex smiled when she finished. They just looked into each other's eyes.

Neither of them noticed the waiter as he arrived with the wine.

* * *

Lauren had some trouble getting her key into the lock of her townhouse door. She wasn't sure if her invitation to Alex to come home with her was wise. If he had picked her up, she told herself, the same thing would have happened anyway. She didn't know why she was concerned about it because at that moment she was so nervous she could hardly breathe. Every fantasy she had about this man had led up to this very moment, and it would have been futile to try to stop the train now. Even though it felt so right, the thumping of her heart was shaking her whole body. She was sure Alex could feel it, too.

Alex placed his hand over hers and took the key gently from her grasp. Lauren ceased fighting with the lock and turned her face up and looked into Alex's clear eyes. He leaned forward and their lips met at first gently, but then with increasing, passionate ardor. His arms encircled her small body, nearly lifting her off her feet as they pressed themselves closer together in a rapid succession of clinging, expressive kisses. Alex let go of her only long enough to unlock the door as they both stumbled through it in their excited, lustful dance. He then pressed her against the inside of the door, closing it before they continued their journey through the entryway, clinging to and groping at each other hungrily as they went.

After negotiating the two small steps down to the living room, they stopped for a long, lingering embrace as Alex kissed her lips and moved his head down to her small, soft neck, biting it tenderly. He reached up and found the zipper on the back of her dress and parted it down to where it stopped below her waist. Lauren had already unbuckled her belt and dropped her arms which allowed her dress to fall to the carpet. She stepped out of her shoes and her full length slip followed her dress to the floor, tumbling in a soft heap on top of it. Her mouth found Alex's neck as her arms encircled him. He inhaled the scent of her hair's fragrance as he pressed his lips against her cheek.

Alex then took her by the shoulders and slowly turned her around until she was standing with her back to him as his hands moved down to the black, silky garment that remained above her waist. He had not been challenged with a brassiere hook since before he and Maria were married. They were the tiny little marvels of mechanical engineering that so effectively supported a woman's assets and teased every man's manual dexterity. This time, however, they parted with his deft touch and released their burden as the lacy encumbrance fell to the floor along with Lauren's other shed garments.

Lauren then turned and began to loosen Alex's tie as he removed his coat and unbuckled his belt. She knelt down at his feet and untied his shoes as he stepped out of them along with his trousers. They both began unfastening the buttons of his shirt and it was soon cast aside along with his shorts and tie. Lauren peeled her panty hose down and kicked them away. The two excited, soon to be lovers finally ceased their fevered groping and grabbing and faced each other as their bodies gently melded together into a long anticipated embrace.

A dim glow emanating from a kitchen appliance was all the light cast on the room where the couple now stood. Alex reached around Lauren savoring the softness of her light skin as his hands encircled her body. He looked into the dark recesses of her eyes as he pulled their bodies even closer together. They stood for lingering moments enfolded in each other's arms, until Alex gently but firmly laid her backward until they were lying on the welcoming carpet. It was then that he kissed and caressed her and their bodies meshed together. Whatever they both fantasized about this moment's coming to pass, it was a fantasy no longer.

* * *

Alex awakened to the muted glow of the morning light filling the room. Nothing looked familiar; he was disoriented and suddenly alarmed. His body lurched upward from the bed as he looked around the room. It was then he felt a hand on his shoulder. He jerked his head around to see Lauren looking both sleepy and startled.

"What is it, Alex?" she asked. Before he could reply, she went on, "It's alright, you're with me." Alex suddenly felt sweat on his face and body as he began to assess his surroundings. Lauren pulled him back down onto the bed and stroked his shoulder with her hand. He put his hand on his face and rubbed his eyes and then turned toward her.

"Whoa! I lost it there for a minute. I didn't know where I was," he said and paused. "Where am I?" he asked as a smile started over his face. "Who are you?" he continued. "I haven't awakened to a strange woman in my bed for, oh, I'd say at least a week or two."

Lauren pulled her hand away in feigned irritation. "That's not funny, Alex," she said and tried not to laugh. "I knew you were quite the ladies' man all along. Boy, was I dumb!" she added and popped herself on the head with the flat of her hand.

"But you love me anyway, don't you, Lauren? Go ahead and admit it. You couldn't help yourself, I know." They both laughed together and Alex rolled over next to her nuzzling and kissing her. Lauren put her arms around him and squeezed him tightly.

"Oh, Alex, I've wanted you so much. I've laid awake so many nights wishing you were here with me, not knowing if you knew if I was alive, or if you even cared."

"It must have been preordained, Lauren. I've thought of little else but you," he replied as his face changed expression. "I don't remember getting into bed last night. I guess you bewitched me, madam."

"I'll never tell," she answered and batted her eyes.

The two lay in silence for a few minutes. The light was getting brighter in the room as the first rays of the sun found their way through a crack in the curtains. There was an old fashioned grandfather clock standing in one corner of the bedroom whose swaying pendulum Alex was following with his eyes. As the silence between them became more prolonged, the relentless ticking only got louder.

"What do we do now, Alex?" Lauren asked.

"I don't know, Lauren. Is one of our options to live happily ever after?" he asked. "God knows I would love that."

"If that could only be true, Alex. But, this is all so fast...and I mean...we don't even know each other. And what about your wife? Maybe the cards are stacked against us to start with," Lauren replied and turned her face away towards the wall.

There was another long silence until Alex said, "I have no wife, Lauren. She's dead. We were married almost twenty years and we were truly happy, but she's gone. Believe me, I've been wrestling with this for a while now."

"I know, Alex. I'm sorry if I hurt you, but if we care for each other at all and this was not just a hormone drenched one night stand, these things will come up again," she said drawing short, staccato like breaths. "I was married for three years and I loved him dearly, but he just used me, so I left him. That was seventeen years ago. Since then, I've been absent from the living world. This is my first foray back into it. When I saw you, talked to you, and then couldn't get you off my mind, it made me want to try again. And now I think I love you, Alex. I know that sounds crazy, but I do."

Alex rolled over on his side to face her back. He put his hand on her shoulder and squeezed as he kissed the back of her neck.

"I know, Lauren. It IS all too fast and I know we don't know each other. But, I've had a wonderful feeling about you for months now. Maria was the best of women and I know she would want me to be happy. I've been the one with the reservations. I've been blown away by the guilt. I've seen this in so many people in my office but, believe me, it's different when it happens to you. I need to get on with it. I can't just fester the rest of my days, yet that's what I seem to want to do at times—like I don't have the right to go on and live. I know that's crap, but it's real crap and it bothers me."

Alex spoke these things softly and steadily into her ear. Lauren turned abruptly and thrust her arms around his neck.

"Oh, Alex!" she exclaimed as she pressed her arms tighter around him. "I've dreamed of holding you like this. I know modern women aren't supposed to need a man for their fulfillment, but that's not comforting to me when I'm here all alone. I've starved myself emotionally for so long because I thought I was being strong, but all I've been is miserable and lonely. Everyone around me snickers behind my back and thinks I'm some fossilized monument to misguided femininity." Lauren paused and continued. "I'm so stupid!" She buried her head into his neck and started sobbing. Alex pulled her to him, engulfing her body in his own.

"You're anything but stupid, Lauren. You sound lonely and tired of being that way. It's hard to live without people in your life. I know, I've tried. Maria kept pulling me back to reality and showing me how much we all need others, but then she left me. She left me; she left the children; she left the world. I'm a psychiatrist for Heaven's sake, and I didn't even know she was depressed. Do you know how much that hurts?...I can't begin to tell you, Lauren." Alex paused and breathed deeply. "That's how out of it I was."

It was then that Alex realized that he had not really talked to anyone since Maria's death. He'd talked at it, around it, about it, but he hadn't let anyone know how he felt. There was no closeness with his parents, or his younger brother who lived in California. He kept telling himself they wouldn't understand anyway. That bold-faced lie that passed for rationalization had served him well most of his life.

His best friend Ray Meyer, a plumber, was bright and sensitive but had the same restrictive emotional makeup Alex did. Their friendship was real enough, but was mostly based on shared looks and glances unhindered by the spoken word. It appeared that was all the closeness they could tolerate with any degree of comfort. Although he hated it to the core of his being, Alex realized his fears imprisoned him. The calm he was feeling just a few moments ago had given way to a growing disquiet.

"Don't you have to work today?" Alex asked.

"I took a vacation day. I guess I was hoping lightning would strike, and I guess it did. My body feels kind of scorched," Lauren said as she started to laugh.

Alex joined in as they coiled themselves around each other again on Lauren's big bed.

22

The summer days in Texas were endless, monotonous, and stifling. An occasional rain shower provided some welcome relief, but they were seldom predictable and always too brief. The natives complained; the tourists complained; the transplants from the north complained; but somehow these supplications had no effect on the mercury readings. It was as if there was some expectation that this summer would be different than the one last year or the year before that. Sometimes it was. There were summers that were ushered in by devastating tornadoes and ushered out again by hurricanes that were born and grew to adulthood in the Gulf of Mexico and then meandered their way northward until they landed at some unfortunate spot on the coast, leaving their mark in unforgettable ways.

Those kind of phenomena were expected, but unpredictable. Mostly people didn't think about them until they were on the doorstep. Alex was thinking it was probably best that way. If mortal man had no way of putting the possibility of unexpected catastrophe out of his consciousness, he would be in a state of psychosis most of his life. Some people were anyway, but most had the capacity and the desire to see things more hopefully.

As America's fortunes improved, the strident clamoring of the naysayers and prophets of ultimate doom began to wane. Or at least most people didn't pay them any more heed than if nothing had happened at all in the last several years. Alex marveled at the fact that people recovered so quickly from the attacks of the "slings and arrows of outrageous fortune," as Shakespeare had put it several centuries ago.

Some expected the inevitable storms of living like they expected the dawn of every new day; some tried to ignore them; some feared them; some pretended not to care. Like the ancient Stoics, Alex thought that every man needed to arm himself against "outrageous fortune," and not just passively await it. But, after all, Shakespeare had written comedies as well as tragedies. The tragic in life was obvious enough, but Alex often felt that it was the comedic that cut closest to the bone and to the heart of truth.

Alex remembered one of the doctors he trained under trying to explain how jokes sometimes contained painful revelations about people. People could often laugh at something and not understand the underlying seriousness of it, such as making jokes about death which helped most people to fend off their fear of it. The same doctor also observed that looking into one's own character was next to impossible. Alex smiled as he thought that of all the things he had forgotten in his training, he had never forgotten that. On those rare occasions when he felt he was favored with a glimpse into his own inner workings, he appreciated the truth of it. But those fleeting glimpses left him with only a vague feeling, nothing he could have written down or articulated to anyone. It was almost like a dream in which an illuminating revelation appeared obvious only to vanish when he awoke. He concluded from this that a man's character was so private, that it defied explanation, though some foolhardy souls continued to search for one.

* * *

As the summer began to melt into fall, it would have taken an exceptionally negative minded observer to find anything untoward in the lives of the Madisons. Alex was feeling that giddiness that accompanied a new love affair. He and Lauren talked on the phone almost daily. Although Alex was not a phone person, he looked forward to calling her. Lauren made several trips to Texas to see Alex, while John and Charlotte initially looked on with that unblinking reservation that only the offspring of a single parent

167

are capable. They seemed to like Lauren and tried to make her feel welcome, although their father had been scrupulous in his efforts not to influence them. That would have been the kiss of death, and Alex knew it. Lauren and John began to hit it off more with each visit, while Charlotte was quieter. Alex noticed, however, that the two often shared momentary glances and knowing smiles. Despite that, the two females maintained their wariness.

Charlotte had been quiet all summer, though. She was spending a lot of time with Ginger and her friends, but not talking much about it. At least she was not talking to her dad and John. There was no one else in whom she felt she could confide. She had not seen Amy since the school year ended, although she had been tempted to call her at times. Charlotte knew Amy only too well and reasoned that she would likely be opening herself up to some serious personal punishment if Amy would even speak to her, which was doubtful. Amy didn't do things by halves, and she would have frozen to death before she asked to come in out of the cold. So, Charlotte endured in silence. She remembered that her dad had told her that losing a friend was a terrible thing. Up until now, that observation had only been theoretical and rhetorical. Since that day in school a few months ago, its painful reality had slowly burned into her teenaged consciousness.

John's summer had been what summers had been for most of his life since he was ten or twelve—fielding ground balls at shortstop, trying to master hitting sharply breaking curve balls, and hanging out with his friends. Despite the angry confrontation at the supper table earlier in the summer, he and Charlotte seemed somehow to be growing closer. At least he felt they had a shared respect for one another. She had come to him and apologized for the remark about Mary Brim. He just smiled and told her to forget it. To tell the truth, he was more interested in whether he would get a baseball scholarship to Texas A&M after his senior year in high school. He liked Mary Brim but had decided she was a second tier consideration right now.

So it was with the Madisons. School started again, the weather in Texas got cooler, and Alex and Lauren were in love. To Alex, it was beginning to look like the living happily ever after option for him and Lauren might be a winner. The leaves on the trees were beginning to show their magical kaleidoscope of color, and the fall wind began to chill as it turned out of the north. As people were so fond of saying, if you don't like the weather in Texas, just wait a minute.

It will change.

23

"Well, when are you moving to Texas?"

Ann was scraping the pickles off her sandwich as she spoke to Lauren. She was not smiling either. Their friendship was one of the things Ann held inviolate for more than one reason. Things with her and her husband had not changed much. Their marriage was now like a slowly-decaying, one hundred year old tree in which the rot and other signs of impending death were difficult to detect from month to month, but were present nonetheless. The once robust new growth that each spring brought to pass had lost its vibrant sheen. The once vivid greens in the newly minted leaves had turned pale and wan as if from fatigue or loss of interest. Some branches and limbs were now devoid of foliage altogether. The bloom of its existence had drained away leaving an outer bark of pale gray that looked like old concrete. There could be no mistaking that death was imminent and inevitable.

Now, the only person Ann could call a friend and mean it would soon be leaving. Even the pleasure of seeing Lauren happy could not make up for the gnawing unrest she was feeling. Lauren had downplayed it, but Ann knew the score. Her friend would soon be gone... as in, gone for good.

"Oh, for Heaven's sake! You won't even miss me. Neither will anybody else. Maybe Harold will a little bit. I think he depends on me more than he'd like to admit," Lauren replied as she dived into her French fries.

"Oh, really! And what was your first clue, Sherlock?" Ann riposted without bothering to mask her sarcasm. "You certainly beg the obvious sometimes, kiddo." Lauren just looked across the table and made a face.

"You're not going to get me in a bad mood. I won't let you... not today."

"What's so special about today?" Ann asked.

"As of today, Alex and I have been dating for two months," Lauren answered with obvious glee.

"Good grief! You sound like some airheaded teenager. Get a hold of yourself, girl!" Ann exclaimed and sighed deeply. "Did you also exchange your senior rings, too?"

"I told you, Ann. You can't make me mad today." Lauren then stuck her tongue out at her friend as she threw her head back and laughed.

"I see you're beyond repair at this point," Ann barked. "Are you ever going to answer my question?"

"Jesus, Ann, I don't know. We haven't talked about anything permanent yet. It's just kind of been in the background, I guess," Lauren's eyes narrowed a bit. "I think we both don't want to go too far, too fast."

A brief silence changed the mood at the table as both of the women took a keen interest in their lunches. Lauren looked up from her plate.

"Damn it! Ann. I've let you do it again. You're not happy unless there's misery coming out of all the pores. Some people really are happy, you know. Like, it *is* possible. I wish you'd get over that soap opera mentality of yours," Lauren went on. "Ahhhhhhhh! If you weren't my best friend in the world, I'd like to kick your ass when this happens." Lauren then leaned back in her chair and glowered at Ann across the small table.

Ann made a pouty face by pooching out her lips.

"I'm sorry. I'm really not trying to rain on your parade, Lauren," she offered and looked away. "I just can't imagine what I'll do without you." Ann paused a bit, then added, "I guess that's the long and the short of it, baby." Ann looked out the large window onto the busy street outside. "How long have we been friends? How long have we worked together? Now you're going to up and get on your horse and go to Texas for Christ's sake. Lauren, you can't do this to me...not for a man you can't."

Lauren looked across the table and managed a half smile.

"The only reason I would do it at all is for a man, you ninny!" she exclaimed. "Did you think you and I were going to move in together when you and Bill decided to throw in the towel? Huh?" Lauren stopped to take a breath. "Everybody would be convinced we were Lesbians for sure."

They both looked at each other and started to laugh.

"You really think anybody would notice?" Ann asked. The two women just looked at each other and continued to laugh as they got up from the table and started to walk back to the office.

* * *

Aaron Black was sitting on an examining table in his doctor's office drumming his fingers on his thigh. He was not a patient person, and being at a doctor's office only made it more obvious and uncomfortable. It was one of those things he considered an unnecessary nuisance and a waste of time. To his way of thinking, doctors didn't have a clue what they were doing most of the time. All you ever got was a few inane questions, a lot of poking and prodding, and an expensive prescription of pills for your trouble as the great healer went flying out the door.

But, Aaron was worried. His forty-fifth birthday had just been observed and up until lately, he had always been healthy. At least he had never had any kind of health issue that made him slow down to notice. People who complained of every little ache and pain he viewed with contempt to put it charitably. He suffered fools unwillingly or not at all. The door to the small room suddenly opened and a tall, slender man with graying hair and a neatly trimmed mustache strode in. He had on the long white coat that all doctors on TV wore, apparently so everyone could tell they were doctors.

"Hello, Mr. Black. I haven't seen you in forever and then some," the doctor said as he folded his arms and leaned back against the small counter across from the examining table. "I hope you've been well. What brings you in?"

"I've had some numbness in my legs, doctor. I noticed it about two weeks ago, and now I'm having some unsteadiness on my feet, like my legs are weak," the worried man said and looked at the doctor with unblinking attention. The pleasant expression on the doctor's face faded into seriousness as he came toward the patient and took hold of one of his legs.

"Have you had any pain, Mr. Black?" he asked.

"No, sir. Just some tingling and numbness. Maybe a little stiffness, too," he continued. "I do a little running every day, and I've stumbled several times lately. I almost fell down a few times. I mean, I didn't trip or anything. It was like my leg just gave way. It scared me." The physician continued to hold the patient's leg in his hands as he moved it about.

"This movement doesn't hurt, does it?"

"No, sir. Just kind of feels funny."

The doctor finished his pushing and prodding, and true to Aaron Black's prognostication, wrote out a prescription before leaving the small room. As he closed the door behind him, the physician stopped and looked down the hall as though he was viewing something of interest through the glass door that led to the outside of the clinic.

"What is it, Dr. Thompson?" one of the nurses asked after almost a minute passed and he had not moved.

"Linda, that's the third patient I've seen today with those exact same symptoms. You think it's the moon? Maybe the water?"

He didn't wait for an answer, but only smiled to himself as he continued on to the next examining room.

* * *

He never really stopped to think about it before, but Alex didn't feel like he was single. There had been some kind of unrealness to it all since Maria died. It wasn't like it was a new concept or anything. He had heard similar things from patients and friends alike. Women had a harder time with it. But, maybe that was because they actually talked about it. It was a rare man who talked to another man about his feelings on such matters.

When a woman became single, especially a middle aged woman who had had a lengthy marriage, it seemed she would cling to it, like the fact that her husband or significant other was no longer physically there carried no emotional importance. She was still married to him and was destined to live her life as such. It didn't matter if the spouse was alive or dead, she was still a married woman. To see herself any other way was the same as being unfaithful.

When he and Lauren made love, Alex couldn't help but feel at times like someone was going to report him for it. He was doing something he shouldn't and there must be a price to pay. Maybe it was an absolute truth that people were allowed one spouse or one true love per lifetime and when it was over, it was over. There were no "do-overs" and no second bite at the apple.

That's the most neurotic crock of shit I've ever heard, he thought. *Man, your punitive superego is working overtime today.*

The unending parade of traffic on I 30 outside his office window appeared to have him mesmerized as he was sitting in his chair behind his desk watching. He had had a light afternoon in the office. The thought of doing something constructive or something that would actually count as productive was about as appealing as having a root canal. As much as it aggravated his inbred Germanic work ethic, sometimes just doing nothing was like the ultimate tonic of satisfaction. If he were to win the lottery, he could easily see himself morphing into a worthless derelict as far as any kind of valuable productivity was concerned.

I'd love to have that chance, he thought.

Just then some kid wearing a bright red helmet and a red and white jacket went careening down the interstate on a motorcycle weaving gracefully from one lane to another, each crowded with cars and trucks. He was astride a small crotch rocket whose engine was radiating a high-pitched whine as he flew on toward Ft. Worth.

Despite the chill he felt in his gut, Alex smiled as the sound of the bike slowly died away in the distance. Since he was a teen, he had lusted for a two wheeled vehicle. First, he wanted a motor scooter, and later a big Harley street cruiser. He got neither though, either because of lack of funds or his father's disapproval or both. Alex put it down in his book of unfulfilled dreams. A few of his doctor friends rode motorcycles and some of them were avid. But most of them looked at him with glares of incredulity when he brought it up. Then, he would get all sorts of stories about the death, injury, and mayhem surrounding the victims of motorcycle accidents that they had seen while working in emergency rooms. Those who rode, though, invariably said it was one of the most exhilarating and enjoyable things they had ever done.

Crazy world, he thought as he walked over to the window to follow the quickly disappearing image of the bike and its pilot.

Alex's motorcycle fantasies were interrupted by the staccato beeping of his phone. He walked over to answer it and was greeted by Emily's voice.

"Dr. Madison, there is a Dr. Thompson on the phone. He says he knows you," she said.

"He does, Emily, and I know him, too. Put him on."

"Well, isn't that special," Emily intoned in a high, squeaky voice that she used when she wanted to irritate Alex.

There was a momentary silence and a clacking sound in Alex's ear. "Is that you, Ray?" Alex asked.

"Sure is, Alex, how goes it man?"

"Can't complain, how's Marilyn?"

"Oh, everybody's Ok. I haven't seen you in forever and I never told you how sorry I was about Maria. I've thought about you many times, though, Alex," he said in his usual flat intonation. Alex knew Ray Thompson to be a rather quiet, stoic man who he did not know well, but liked a lot. He wished they were better friends.

"Thanks, Ray. I appreciate it, man. There is just nothing anyone can do. I still miss her every day," he said with a twinge of guilt as he thought of Lauren.

"I know you must, Alex." There was then a pause as Ray Thompson cleared his throat. "Do you have a minute?" he asked.

"Sure, Ray, go ahead."

"Had a patient today complaining of some weakness and parasthesias in his legs. I can't find anything else. He's active and in good shape; works out regularly...you know the kind."

"I know. I wish I was that way," Alex interrupted and started to laugh.

"Me, too, son. Seems like all the exercise I get is walking over to my recliner," he replied and joined in the laughter. "Well, anyway, he's taking this new wonder drug, Dynasane, that you shrinks are so high on. Doesn't take anything else. Are the weakness and the funny feelings in his legs coming from the drug? Are those side effects?" The line was then filled with silence as Alex searched his mind.

"Those are not the most reported side effects, Ray," Alex answered. "I haven't heard that from anyone else." More than a twinge of unease swept through Alex as a frown developed on his face. "Let me see what I can find out. The drug's just been out a few months now. Sometimes it takes a while for some side effects to show up. I've heard nothing but great things about this medication so far. I was afraid it was going to put me out of business," Alex added with a nervous laugh.

"It's the only thing this man's taking. I thought I'd better call," Ray replied. "Let me know what you find out, Alex."

"No problem, Ray. I'll call when I have something."

Alex put down the phone and just stood at his desk for a moment as he turned his gaze to the traffic on the freeway. This time, though, he didn't notice any cars, trucks, or motorcycles. All he was aware of that moment was a vague but disturbing uneasiness in his mind.

24

The screen was glowing with bright, colorful images of habitations each of which were under intense scrutiny at the moment. Lauren was using her mouse to flip from one to the next while she checked the square footage, location, and finally the values of the passing parade of homes on her computer monitor. She had not lied to Ann when she told her that she did not know when she would move to Texas, but she wanted to be ready when it was time. Nailing down the value of her home would be one of the biggies if and when she became Mrs. Alex Madison. It would be the only thing she would bring to the union that would constitute a dowry of sorts.

Lauren really had no other assets of real value other than a modest savings account that only amounted to several thousand dollars and the antique clock in her bedroom. When she had it appraised, she was told that it was made in the 1700s and would likely bring about $20,000 in today's market. Her grandmother had bequeathed it to her, much to the chagrin of Lauren's younger sister, Angela. Her sister had exacted her revenge, however, by marrying into a family from Boston who claimed they could trace their ancestry to the 1600s and were thoroughly endowed with "old money". The two siblings saw each other only at Thanksgiving each year which amounted to a few hours too many for both of them.

But Lauren was not going to waste any of her precious time on such familial nonsense. She knew the tenuous bond between her and her sister was just that, tenuous, and consisted of only the fact that they were family. They shared some of the same DNA but little else in the area of life's purpose or goals.

To put it in another, more meaningful way, Lauren considered her sister to be both shallow AND stupid. The fact that their mother doted on the younger of the two irritated Lauren, but she had long ago written that off to her mother's frustration at being trapped in a lower middle class marriage to a man of modest goals and like ambition. Lauren's father's idea of success was an inexhaustible supply of Budweiser in the refrigerator, a television that would faithfully transmit the activities of the Red Sox, Celtics, and Patriots, and all the pasta he could want. He was a good hearted man who loved his family but who would never completely understand why he could never seem to do enough to please his wife. When Angela married her blue blood, her mother's dreams took flight. However, on takeoff, there were no seats available for Lauren and her father.

Lauren was now experiencing that tingly sensation all over as she continued to make her preparations for being a bride once again. This newfound energy and excitement had taken her by surprise. She had resigned herself to being a spinster, or at least an unmarried woman of a certain age. The computer screen just winked back at her as she shook her head while wondering how she could have become so ossified and hopeless about her life. For the first time in a long time she was happy.

In between mouse clicks as the images continued to parade by her wondering eyes, Lauren stopped when her phone began to pulsate with those irritating beeps she hated, but could not change. All the employees of the FPA had the same phones with the same irksome noises built in.

"Lauren, could you please come down to my office for a moment?" Harold's voice had that intonation that usually meant it was an order and not a request. It surprised her a bit in that she had not heard much from her boss in the recent weeks. Lauren certainly liked Harold, but she was just as glad when he was in his office playing with his reports and leaving her alone.

"Yes, sir, I'll be right there," she said and left clicked her mouse. The real estate website on her screen disappeared as she got up from her desk.

* * *

Harold was sitting at his desk frowning as Lauren pecked on his glass door. At first, he seemed to ignore her, but he finally raised his hand and motioned for her to enter without looking up from whatever was so intensely interesting him. As she walked slowly into his office, her boss suddenly jerked his head up and gave her a rather perfunctory half smile.

"Oh, come on in and sit down, Lauren. I was somewhere else for a minute," he said. "But, this is something that could put a person somewhere else."

Lauren cautiously sat down in one of the chairs in front of his desk. Now she was frowning, too.

"What's going on, Harold?" she asked. "Things are going too well for you to look so glum," she added.

"That's what I was thinking, Lauren, until I began reading this," he said as he pointed down to a document in front of him.

Harold was not an alarmist and that was what bothered Lauren most. If he was worried about something, it was important. She shifted in her chair and folded her arms across her breasts as if she was attempting to cover herself. Harold just looked at her in that way he always did when he was puzzled or frustrated. Lauren wanted to say something, but had no clue as to what it might be. Furthermore, her boss was not illuminating the situation for her. In fact, it was almost like she wasn't there. This Mexican standoff continued uncomfortably for Lauren until Harold suddenly drew a breath.

"I've been getting reports just recently that have me worried."

He aimed this remark in Lauren's direction, but didn't seem to be speaking precisely to her. It seemed more like he was making some editorial comment intended for all the employees under his command. Lauren did her best imitation of someone who was hanging on his every word, which in a way she was. "There has been no question that Dynasane is the most effective antidepressant we've ever approved. Nobody is challenging that," Harold finally offered up.

"Is there a 'but' in there, Harold?" Lauren asked. It was then that Harold turned and looked at Lauren like she was actually in the same room with him.

"I'm afraid there is, Lauren," he answered and sighed at the same time. "We've been getting an increasing number of reports from emergency rooms and doctor's offices of people coming in with some consistently similar complaints. And, not all of them are taking the drug."

He pursed his lips a bit as he looked across at Lauren. Their minds were on the same track almost at once. If there was any possibility that what they were thinking had any merit, it might be the cruelest turn of events in world history. Lauren's mind went back to the meeting that Saturday morning at the compound in which one Alex Madison, MD, had brought up the caution regarding doing no harm before the committee did anything at all. The ensuing months had all but erased any notion of anything negative coming to pass, however. Now, it was beginning to look like the blue bird of happiness may have been shot out of the sky by somebody with a 12 gauge.

"What kind of symptoms, Harold?" Lauren asked.

"Mostly weakness and numbness in the legs. Some people have reported paralysis in their lower limbs. The symptoms looked somewhat like multiple sclerosis, but most of the doctors have ruled that out with so many people reporting the same thing. It would have to be the worst epidemic of MS in the history of the world," he said as he steepled his hands up under his chin. "There have been no deaths yet, and I guess we can be thankful for that." He then turned his chair sideways to his desk and looked out the expansive window that made up one wall of his office.

"What are you thinking about doing, Harold, if anything?" Lauren asked. He turned back to face Lauren as he looked down at the reports on his desk.

"I was wondering if I needed to talk to Congressman Branch

about reconvening the committee," he answered haltingly. "What do you think?" Lauren was rather stunned that Harold would ask her opinion on such a matter. "Please tell me what you think, Lauren. I respect your judgment on these things."

Lauren hesitated a moment and cleared her throat. "Well, I was wondering if it would be a bit soon to jump at conclusions. Maybe it doesn't have anything to do with the Dynasane, Harold," she offered without much conviction.

Harold cut his eyes over toward Lauren for a moment. She knew then he had already formed his conclusion and Harold Janes was not a patient man.

"Well, it's just a thought, I guess," she said and looked at her hands which were now folded in her lap.

"I'll give it another week," he said.

* * *

Alex had not had much time to be concerned with introspective issues like whether he really felt like a single man or not, as he had been spending a great deal of time in the local emergency rooms doing consultations when he wasn't in his office. It had only been a few weeks after he talked to Ray Thompson that he began to get calls to see patients in the EOR for things very similar to what Ray had described. The salient feature among these consults was that they all were taking Dynasane. At least all the ones he was asked to see. However, the emergency rooms were reporting a number of patients having similar maladies who were not taking Dynasane.

The emergency room doctors along with the family practitioners were beginning to pick up on this phenomenon. Many of the sufferers took various medications, but a number of them took none. It also seemed that age was not a factor. Doctors knew that certain illnesses usually appeared in certain age groups. For example, you didn't usually see arthritis in twenty year olds. The leg weakness and numbness seemed to defy that, however, and spanned all age groups from teens to the elderly and even some children. Medical science appeared to be facing challenges in the recent years that had never shown themselves before.

It was close on the heels of this puzzling medical phenomena that it finally happened. A forty five year old man who had first reported complaints of leg weakness and numbness to his family doctor died of respiratory arrest.

His name was Aaron Black.

* * *

The history of medicine and medical practice parallels the history of mankind itself. As humans evolved and developed and became civilized, doing something about the ills that befell them took on greater significance. From the time man first appeared in a form considered by anthropologists to be "human," he had been hurting himself and falling prey to sickness. This was also true of the "lower" forms of life, but if nature did not take care of them, they were just plain out of luck.

Except for some primitive cave art, there was no recorded evidence of what these early people did in the way of treating the ailments that befell them. Some artifacts left behind in early man's dim past may have given some clues as to what constituted treatment for injuries and ills; however, that was for paleontologists and anthropologists to argue about, and after all, would only be guesses.

Throughout history, the treatment of physical and mental disease made its appearance in every culture of mankind. In some cases, the healers were shrouded in mystery and mystique and often under the nebulous auspices of religion. It is also true that among other attitudes toward them, healers had been revered, reviled, and even worshipped in some cultural settings. They also took on the mantle of religious and/or political leadership in some instances which gave them considerable power and influence that could be used for good or ill and fortunately or unfortunately often were.

But, from whatever philosophy, culture, belief system, or

branch of human civilization the healing arts were derived, the purpose was singular. Healing the patient or casting out the offending illness or injury was always the spoken and unspoken goal. It was and is the seminal ethic upon which the practice of medicine was based. That one directive which had been articulated by Hippocrates several thousand years ago, and doubtless had been in the heart of every caring healer for millennia, still rested today on the shoulders of every physician who had taken the sacred oath and set out to do battle with the physical and emotional ills of mankind. It was no small task; and it was a worthy calling to be sure. Those who had down through history been called healers were a society of men and women that spanned the existence of the human race.

Alex could only marvel when he thought of the incredible mass of medical knowledge that now existed. The last two hundred years or so had ushered in an exponentially growing amount of data about and understanding of human physiology and functioning. No one took issue with that. His brow began to furrow, however, when he thought that despite the state of current medical knowledge and understanding, the challenges of medical practice continued to escalate as well.

As recently as the 1940s, as one of his teachers pointed out when he was in medical school, there was no way to cure a simple bacterial infection that entered a patient's bloodstream. The advent of antibiotics revolutionized that, but even today, new and more virulent bugs had developed that were resistant to the latest wonder drugs. It was like when medicine took a giant step forward, illness and disease took an even bigger one.

Viruses and virally derived diseases began to cast an ominous shadow over the medical landscape. AIDS took a heavy toll and continued to do so. Cancer, which had always been around, still was and there was no cure yet. Emotional ills were often relegated to the second tier of medical issues, but the lesson of the last few years had tempered that attitude for many. Still, there were the multitudes, in and out of the medical field, that felt that clinical depression was a condition that could and should be controlled by taking a drug and having a more positive outlook on life; or, better yet, reading a self-help treatise by one of the latest gurus of the school of the quick fix. The road to Xanadu was as simple as presenting your credit or debit card to the cashier at the bookstore. Self-help enterprises had become a billion dollar business and an American obsession.

* * *

"What the hell is this, Alex?" a disbelieving Ray Thompson growled at Alex as they met in the hall at the emergency room.

It was clear Ray was upset. More upset than Alex had ever seen him. He looked like the classic deer in the headlights as he stared at the psychiatrist.

"Remember the guy I told you about on the phone?" Not waiting for a response, he went on, "Well, he died last week. Never been sick a day in his life; and he hated doctors, too. Can't say I blame him much. I know I didn't help him any."

Wow! Ray is on a tear, Alex thought as he listened.

Ray was angry, but Alex also saw hurt in his eyes. Despite his stone-faced stoicism, Alex knew him to be a caring man, but it was unlike him to be so demonstrative.

"I wish I had something profound or intelligent to say, Ray," was all Alex could answer at the moment. "I don't have a clue".

Alex also knew he had just told a lie, which caused him to swallow unexpectedly. This generally happened when he was flustered or embarrassed. He did have a clue; in fact he knew what this whole thing was about, even if he didn't understand why it was showing itself in this way. He had been thinking in the last few days that he might get a call from Congressman Branch. Now, he was sure he would. The incredible irony of it all was that he felt just as hopeless now as he did when he was first invited to serve on the congressman's committee; maybe even more so. If this thing was caused by Dynasane, it was going to take pharmacologists and researchers to explain it, not psychiatrists. He also suspected that right at that very moment, Gardner Pharmaceuticals, the producer of Dynasane, was a buzzing beehive of activity looking at the likelihood that this latest development had anything to do with their drug.

"We had better get some clues, Alex," the family practitioner continued. "I think this thing is just beginning. You know, tip of the iceberg kind of deal. I've got otherwise perfectly healthy sixteen year olds walking on crutches. It's difficult to watch."

He was shaking his head as he was talking and Alex was getting more restless and uncomfortable. Ray was not the kind of man to be unnerved and unbalanced by things he saw as a doctor. Alex just stared at the floor.

"I know, Ray. I think all of us are feeling kind of helpless again."

"Kind of! There's not a damn thing we can do so far to reverse this thing. Nothing we've tried has made a dent."

Alex was fingering the change in his pocket. He wanted to blurt out everything he knew right then, but he knew it would do no good and likely would only complicate things for him and Ray. How could he be in this position? Of all the physicians in the country, Alex felt he was the least likely to be entrusted with some kind of secret knowledge of this magnitude. It was not an honor or a privilege; it was almost as bad as a death sentence. If his colleagues, patients, and friends knew he was complicit in anything that may have brought about these latest happenings, they would be calling for his head. There would be no mercy or clemency. His name would be spoken with the same contempt and disdain as any of the worst traitors in the history of America.

These thoughts, set in motion by his chance meeting with Ray, sent chilling waves through his body. Sheer terror began to grip him like a tightening band around his chest which made breathing a struggle. He began to cough and clear his throat, hoping he could get some air into his lungs.

"You, Ok, Alex?" Ray asked as he put his hand on Alex's shoulder.

"Ok...it's Ok, Ray," Alex sputtered as he continued to try to clear his throat. "I've been fighting a cough lately."

"Well, I guess I've bent your ear long enough. This thing makes me think I may need to see a psychiatrist," Ray said with a half-smile. "No offense, buddy."

"None taken, Ray. I only wish I could be of some real help, here."

"You always are, Alex. You're not some flake that fills the room with Freudian smoke and clichés like some of your colleagues. I always know you'll keep it simple and honest. I appreciate that." Ray looked directly into Alex's eyes as he spoke. Alex could feel the warmth of a blush cover his face as he looked away.

"Thank you, Ray. It means a lot to me to hear you say that." Alex blinked and looked away again as an uncomfortable smile appeared on Ray's face.

"Well, it's true, my friend... Uh, I need to get back to the office... Later," Ray finished and turned to head for the door.

Alex couldn't seem to say anything, but only stood and looked as his colleague made his way through the glass door and onto the sidewalk outside the hospital. Alex just stared after him for a long moment. He then started to think that some days he was glad, indeed, that he became a psychiatrist.

25

Just as he knew it would, the call from Congressman Branch came and Alex found himself on a plane to Washington again. Not that he was unhappy about that; Lauren would soon be in his arms and that made up for any of the downside of the trip. Alex also knew it was time for him and Lauren to start talking about forever like Alan Jackson so simply and profoundly had put it in his song, *I'll Try.* It always amazed him how contemplating such simply stated words like "love" or "forever" could make someone do and say things he didn't know he could or might not even want to if he was not under the spell of the timeless condition that covered people like an unseen, enchanted blanket. But, here he was, in it right up to his eyebrows. Then again, he reasoned there were a lot worse places he could be. And, after arriving at the Capitol Building, he was even more convinced.

The taxi pulled up and stopped at the usual place in front of the huge cascade of steps leading up to the building that was the universally recognized icon for the government of the United States of America. Instead of the usual scattered individuals traversing this hallowed portal, there was a group of reporters gathered around a man in a business suit. They held numerous microphones and cameras and looked intensely interested in what the man was saying. As Alex got out of the cab and began to walk up the steps, he noticed that the man was Congressman Branch. Alex could not hear everything that was said, but he was close enough to tell that the congressman sounded somber and reflective in his remarks. This was far removed from the gushing rhetoric the last time Alex had seen the politician in front of the cameras and reporters.

Alex stopped a moment and drew nearer where he could hear.

"Isn't it true, congressman, that last spring, without the knowledge of the American public, your committee Ok'd the use of an unknown drug in an attempt to stop the epidemic of depression? Isn't that true, sir?"

"Janet, where on earth would you have heard anything like that?" he countered. "We considered any number of drugs to try and stop a deadly medical crisis that had rendered this nation and much of the rest of the world helpless. We found that Dynasane was by far the most likely to stop the epidemic and that proved to be the case, as you know."

"But, congressman, what about this latest onslaught of medical issues? Are they related to the drug, Dynasane?" another reporter asked.

"People, there is no evidence that is the case. I'm just as concerned as the rest of the country about these new events. Our committee reconvenes today to try to answer these concerns," Mr. Branch intoned.

"But, congressman, wasn't there some kind of nationwide distribution of Dynasane last spring without any information given to the American people? Could you and your committee have caused this current catastrophe?" The reporter asking the question pushed his microphone up closer to the congressman and waited for an answer.

Congressman Branch took a moment to consider the question and put his fist up to his mouth and coughed.

"Ladies and gentlemen...the President's Committee on Healthcare Emergency is charged with the enormous responsibility of dealing with medical crises. As you all know, we only recently emerged from the worst crisis in the history of our country, maybe in the history of the entire world. With that said, I can assure you that the committee took no action of a frivolous or ill advised nature in the case of Dynasane. That is all I can say about the issue at the moment... Thank you."

As the congressman turned and began to climb the steps, the reporters followed along after him attempting to ask for additional comments. He did his best to ignore them, but finally stopped when he reached the entryway to the Capitol.

Turning to face the shouting news people, he said, "I will likely have some further comment after the committee has met. Good day to you all."

Alex had been following this swarm of humanity as it ascended the stairs and tried to listen as well. He was impressed that the congressman had so deftly handled the incisive questions; but, after all, he was a veteran politician. It also bothered Alex that the congressman had really not answered the question about the distribution of Dynasane at all. He had fallen back into political rhetoric and draped himself with the flag of government responsibility. Alex had seen countless politicians on the national stage do exactly the same thing countless times. It may have not been particularly admirable, but it was at least consistent.

How on earth could you be a politician and still tell the truth? he thought.

It seemed to be an oxymoron.

* * *

It was a bright day and the wind was having its way with the multicolored leaves as they fluttered and swirled through the air only to be borne up again by the next gust that buoyed them along until they finally settled down to the ground and waited for the next windy assault. Charlotte had never liked fall and winter. Never in all her life. It was cold; it was uncomfortable; it was drab; it was bleak; it made her think of unhappy things for reasons she did not understand.

Her mother had died in the winter. That was true enough, but she had hated fall and winter long before that. It had only made it all the more bitter tasting for her. It seemed that fall and winter had…what was the word her English teacher used to describe the tone of a short story the class had read recently?

189

Pathos!

That was it. A sort of pervasive feeling of sorrow and anguish. It was a feeling with which she was well acquainted. Charlotte was thinking if she didn't watch herself, she was in danger of thinking tragedy was the only thing life had to offer. Or perhaps the only real thing there was in life. Happiness seemed to be fleeting and unsubstantial. Maybe some people were destined to be happy and some were not. What was that called?

Predestination!

That was it. It was like you didn't have a say in the matter. Somebody or something else like fate decided it for you.

Pretty cosmic stuff for a fifteen year old tenth grader, Charlotte was thinking as she walked along the hall with her new coterie of friends.

As usual, Ginger was in the lead, holding forth with some kind of treatise on the unfairness of something that was also cosmically unsubstantial in the course of world events. Trudy, Rachel, and Melinda were as always hanging on every syllable.

Charlotte smiled to herself as she walked. She was fond of these girls. That was true. Ginger probably could not help herself. Her parents were so preppy, pompous, shallow, and insufferably smug that it would have been surprising if she had become something other than what she was. The other girls, Trudy, Rachel, and Melinda were likeable enough, but Charlotte had never seen even the seed of an original thought in any of them. They seemed to be on earth and at Ridgefield High School to echo everything that Ginger said and did. Still, Charlotte liked them all. She was remembering a movie, *Tequila Sunrise*, in which Raul Julia said to Mel Gibson that friends were one of the few things in life we could choose for ourselves. She was beginning to appreciate that. But she was also beginning to wonder why she had chosen these girls. Charlotte had to be honest, though; they had actually chosen her in the beginning, even if she had consented—so here she was.

Charlotte and Amy, on the other hand, had virtually grown up together. They melded together in the unseen, unspoken ways that soul mates always did. They could read each other's minds. Their thoughts and desires and expectations, along with their illusions about life, were in harmony. They were just...friends. There was no other way to understand it or put it. When she thought of Amy, Charlotte began to get that ache in the pit of her stomach that was becoming a familiar but unwelcome companion lately. Just when she thought Amy had vacated her mind for good, she would see her down the hall or in the cafeteria. Their eyes had actually met on one occasion as they passed in the hallway. Almost unconsciously, Charlotte had stopped as though she would speak to her former friend, but Amy's gaze raked over her dismissively as she walked on past in silence.

Charlotte's pace had slowed to the point where she was now several steps behind the others in the small caravan making their way toward the cafeteria. Ginger glanced back at her and frowned as she interrupted her lecture.

"Don't fall behind, Charlotte, and slow us down, or someone else will get our regular table," Ginger admonished her like a benevolent parent.

The other girls turned to look at Charlotte with the requisite teenage anguish pasted across their faces.

Not very likely, Charlotte was thinking as she continued to watch the gliding, fluttering leaves outside the windows whose only concern was where the swirling fall winds would take them next.

How she envied them.

26

Each swing of the old pendulum was laborious and deliberate in its purpose. It made its way to and fro, forward and back, never leaving the confined space it was allowed to travel in its wood and glass-enclosed case. It was relentless and inexorable in carrying out its unending duty to chronicle the passing of that one commodity that was irreplaceable:

Time.

It reminded Alex of the clock in the entryway of his grandmother's house. It was always there and the huge medallion at the end of the pendulum never stopped moving as it made its appointed rounds, day and night. It seemed to Alex that the heavy sounding ticks and tocks gave the old wood-framed house its very essence. It was the heartbeat of the home —like it was a living being. Besides his grandmother whom he loved, it was what he remembered most about her home.

As Lauren lay sleeping, Alex could see over her shoulder the movement of the old clock as it stood in the corner of her bedroom. He was pressed up against her back as he lay on his left side with his right arm around her waist. His face was next to her cheek and the rhythm of her breathing was almost in concert with the clock.

It had been almost a month since he had seen her, so after they arrived at her place after the committee meeting, they wasted precious little time with an early dinner which they brought home with them along with a bottle of Chardonnay. They then adjourned to Lauren's bedchamber and the delights that awaited them both there.

After their passions were sated and their bodies were spent, they both fell into mesmerizing unconsciousness. There were no ghosts, apparitions, or unseen voices from the past that interfered. They were simply two happy lovers that were, well...in love.

Alex seemed content at that moment to just watch the movement of the old clock and breathe in the scented fragrance of Lauren's hair. But suddenly he pushed his face down to her neck and started kissing and biting her gently as he let out a low growl that he hoped would awaken her. As he had gotten older, he was beginning to realize that he was his most amorous in the morning. That's when his blood pressure would be highest, which would be an unmistakable aid to his tumescence. He was beginning to feel the irrepressible urges coming on...again.

Lauren began to stir as she turned her face toward him and a smile crept across her features although she still had her eyes closed.

"You are insatiable! Are all the men from Texas like this?" she asked just before she kissed him and began biting his neck.

"I guess you'll just have to come back to Texas with me and find out, little girl," he replied and grinned.

"I don't think I could handle more than one of you," she said as she started laughing.

"I certainly hope not," Alex riposted and continued to nuzzle and kiss her with more fervor. They would shortly be returning to paradise once again.

* * *

Alex was crouching behind a big rock as the thunderous roar of the huge black aircraft was getting louder. He poked his head out to look as the round nose cone of the plane was almost upon him. The pilots in the cockpit wore helmets with dark visors that prevented anyone from seeing their eyes. He dived back behind the rock just as he began to feel the earth around him shake and shudder...

"Alex! Alex!" Lauren was shoving the still-sleeping man's shoulder. He abruptly sat up and pushed Lauren's hand away from him as he looked at her with wide eyed alarm. For a moment he just stared. He then blinked his eyes, put his head in his hands, and dragged his fingers back through his hair. He shook his head.

"Oh, man! I guess I was dreaming. Did I hurt you, baby?" he asked.

Lauren looked back as if she might have been in her bed with a stranger. She finally relaxed and began breathing again.

"No, Alex, but you scared me. What happened? Were you dreaming?" she asked. Alex just sat up and tried to breathe slowly.

"Big airplanes. The sky was full of them and one was headed straight for me. I mean it was like ten feet away!" he finally offered. It just scared me, Lauren. Damn! It felt so real!"

"Well, next time, I guess we shouldn't be so, ah...active. Maybe you can just handle so much and no more."

"Very amusing. I didn't hear too many complaints."

"And you won't, either," Lauren answered and kissed him on the cheek. "I was just funnin', doctor."

Alex managed a marginal smile as he threw back the bed covers and got up to head for the bathroom.

* * *

"What time is your flight, Alex?" Lauren asked as they were sitting at the kitchen table drinking coffee.

"It's not until four this afternoon. I wasn't sure if you might want to do something today, or not."

"Well, it's past noon now. What could we do?"

"I guess we've pretty much dedicated this day to a single pursuit, wouldn't you say?" Alex replied and smiled more genuinely this time.

"I'm still not complaining," Lauren answered. Alex just laughed out loud as he put his hand on top of hers.

* * *

It was cold and raining as the big jet took off from Washington taking Alex back to Texas and away from Lauren again. He cursed under his breath after the plane had leveled off for not talking to Lauren about his plans for forever, like he wanted to. It seemed they were too busy with carnal matters and in the throes of passion to discuss anything so sensible and mundane as marriage. Alex then thought of that old joke that asks:

What is the cure for sexual desire?

The answer being:

Wedding cake.

It had not been that way with Maria.

Alex wanted her just as much the day she died as the day he fell in love with her. In fact, he still wanted her. Part of him always would. But he needed to move on, and he knew Maria would have told him that as well. Lauren said the same thing. Of course, she may have had her own selfish reasons, but Alex also knew she had integrity too. She was not just out to snare him. Although he did not know everything about Lauren's psyche and her battles with herself over love, he knew enough to know that her reasons for getting involved with him were not a boatload of neuroses but that she wanted something real with him. She wanted something they could share and grow old with together. Lauren wanted to join the land of the living again. The bitter irony now was that the land they lived in looked like it was starting to die all over again.

* * *

The committee meeting had been somber in tone and substance. It was like an unseen pall had been thrown over this group of handpicked people who were charged once again with extricating an ailing country from another unexplainable assault on its health and wellbeing. There was no joy in Mudville as Congressman Branch convened the mirthless meeting.

As Alex replayed it in his mind, he could almost feel the

burdensome heaviness in the air around the table. Congressman Branch was less animated than before; he now looked old and tired. The other faces were the same, with one exception. The research doctor from Gardner Pharmaceuticals had brought with him an assistant, a young-looking woman in her thirties with short brown hair and bangs. She was dressed in a dark red suit with a skirt that stopped just above her knees and had a ready smile that enlivened her whole face when it was turned on. Her eyes were circled with perfectly round, dark rimmed glasses which gave her a rather academic, but girlish appearance.

Another egg head with fifteen degrees, Alex thought as she was introduced by Dr. Harris. *She's probably a Rhoades' Scholar with an IQ of 400 but doesn't know how to make coffee.*

Alex pushed himself back into his chair and smiled wickedly. Sometimes he took great delight in his own unbridled cynicism. Despite her superficial trappings of saccharine friendliness, his mother was the same way. It stung him whenever he thought of it. That he would be anything like his mother stung him even worse.

"Lord," he said quietly under his breath. "Why now, for Heaven's sake?"

The country was facing down a deadly crisis, and he was noodling about his relationship with his mother. His own unconscious was taunting him again to show him it was still there. He was not the paragon of psychological perfection after all. At least not the one he had envisioned when he had finished his residency in psychiatry. His highly evolved and specialized brain was playing a devilish trick on him. Despite all he knew about everything from synapses in the brain to obscure movies and baseball players along with a million other worthless minutiae, he could be reduced in an instant to a few basic, crude urges. That he found particularly annoying, not to mention pathetic. Maybe mankind, especially Dr. Alex Madison, was not worthy of saving.

Dr. Harris, true to Alex's prognostication, droned on about Gardner Pharmaceutical's tireless efforts to determine if the tidal wave of lower limb symptoms could be related to Dynasane. Thus far, they had come up with zip—nada—zero.

How convenient, Alex thought.

If Dynasane was the culprit in this thing, Gardner Pharmaceuticals would soon be only a memory instead of the international conglomerate it had become since the introduction of the "drug that saved the world," as they were so fond of repeating. Their record profits would soon be completely eaten up by massive lawsuits if there was anyone left on earth to sue them. There would not be anywhere near enough lawyers in the country, or the world for that matter, to handle the litigation against the United States Government for visiting such a devastating catastrophe on the American people without their knowledge or consent. The ultimate irony would be that there would be nobody around to collect the damages.

Alex knew that it was almost impossible to remember how something felt at any time in the past, no matter how recent or distant. Human emotion was experienced in the here and now. Past joys and sorrows could be recalled, but the emotions themselves were always felt in the present. He remembered the pessimism he had felt when he attended the first of these committee meetings which had commenced over a year ago. Somehow, that was a pale shadow compared to what he felt now. Back then, people were slow to take the crisis seriously. After all, it was only "depression." Everybody got depressed sometimes, and everybody knew that. The fact that it crippled the country and brought the world to a virtual halt did not seem to matter. People just needed to get over it.

But, there was a different load of wash to do this time. People were REALLY sick. They couldn't walk; they couldn't work; and they were beginning to die. And, like Ray Thompson had said, this might only be the tip of the iceberg.

* * *

It was also raining and cold at DFW as the big jet came lumbering down through the dark clouds with its nose pointing toward the long, lighted runway that was a drab gray but shiny with the reflections from the water that covered it. It wasn't raining hard, just steady enough to create a miserably dreary end of the day. Alex shifted in his seat and yawned as he sat erect and looked out his window at the distant buildings that housed the gates where the plane would eventually end up. It would be then that everyone on the aircraft would hurriedly stand up in expectation of getting out of this fragile cocoon that had only minutes before been some thirty thousand feet above the earth. It was little more than a glorified flying kid's toy as it glided along in the thin air of the atmosphere. To Alex, it almost seemed like a miracle every time one of these behemoths came down safely to mother earth. Yet, it was supposedly the safest way to travel; yet another of life's poorly appreciated ironies.

It was Saturday, and John and Charlotte would likely be home when Alex got there. Grace would be there too, fussing about the house and acting the role of mother which she had never really given up since her own children had gone from her home long ago. Alex was glad she was there to help, but worried what might happen when he married Lauren and Grace would be displaced once more. She was one of those who would never be able to shed her maternal calling and assume a new identity in middle age. Grace was a wonderful woman who would be forever trapped in an identity that was no longer her own. She was a living anachronism.

Congressman Branch had set another meeting to be held in two weeks. It would be *déjà vu* all over again for Alex. But seeing Lauren would be reward enough, even if the real purpose of the trip was likely to be a waste. Alex didn't spend much time in prayer, but he was thinking that some Divine Intervention would now be helpful.

27

Divine Intervention could be viewed and interpreted in different ways depending on who was doing the viewing and interpreting. There was always that constellation of the populace that piously iterated and reiterated that God was just waiting to drop the hammer on a sinful world that was already Hell bound and beyond any hope of redemption. How they had come by such certain knowledge was a little less than crystal clear to those whose minds were broader. Especially those who viewed the God of Christianity as loving and giving. The elitist and entitled attitude of those who draped themselves in such certainty about God's plans as they spewed forth their gospel of hate and retribution had always struck Alex as irrational and repulsive. This new wave of calamity that had been visited on the country had given them reason to gleefully retune their violins and begin playing their old familiar songs again.

Not that anyone had any other, or better, explanations of what was happening across the nation. The medical community was thinking, and maybe hoping, that some kind of unknown virus had been loosed on the land. At least that was something for which there might be a solution. The epidemics of Legionnaire's Disease and AIDS had taught medicine a great deal about the action of viruses and how to deal with them.

It was much more problematic to deal with sinister plagues that were supposedly unleashed by a God that hated mankind. Despite what had developed from the application of scientific knowledge over the last few hundred years, people were only too ready to abandon it in favor of fantastic explanations of things they did not understand and, therefore, feared. Science itself was a god to some, but it was often not a comforting one and, furthermore, did not have all the answers.

Despite these philosophic concerns, people were frightened. One would have had to be insensitive in the extreme to not feel the unrest that was everywhere in America. What was worse, it could easily break through the surface as full-blown panic with little warning. It appeared that no one, old or young, was safe. Absenteeism in the workplace began to escalate. The memory of the near-total collapse of their businesses was still fresh in the minds of employers from events of the recent years. Only now, people were not staying away from work because they were too depressed to go; they stayed away from work because they could not get up to go. The paralysis was spreading and it looked like soon America would not be able to walk at all.

* * *

Most everyone sitting around the large, oblong table in the conference room was looking at the agenda or quietly talking to the person next to them. None of them were registering any evidence on their faces or through their body language that they were glad to be there. This was true of everyone except Dr. Harris of Gardner Pharmaceuticals and his assistant. Today, Dr. Harris was in his usual nondescript dark suit and equally nondescript dark tie, while his assistant (Alex had learned that her name was Dr. Ellen Grant) was dressed in a white silk blouse and a blue skirt. She still had on the circular dark rimmed glasses that almost touched the bangs hanging down from her forehead. These two were in animated conversation punctuated with an occasional outburst of laughter. There were more than a few glances in their direction by the other members of the committee. Whatever the business to be taken up at the meeting that day, no one on the committee would likely think it humorous.

The door at the far end of the room clattered open and

Congressman Branch came trudging in and took his chair at the head of the table. The already muffled buzz of conversation became quieter still as the chairman fussed with his briefcase and removed a sheaf of papers. He did not stand up, but simply leaned forward in his large chair and looked around the table.

"Well, folks, let's get this show on the road. We do have some important things to discuss today," he said in a rather offhand manner that was less formal and more detached than usual. "I think most of you have met Dr. Ellen Grant, Dr. Harris's assistant at Gardner. Today, we will be hearing from both of them on a matter of some critical importance. So, please give them your attention now."

Mr. Branch then turned his gaze toward the two Gardner employees who were sitting to his left.

"I believe I will remain seated, if you don't mind," Dr. Harris said and gave a perfunctory smile that quickly disappeared from his face.

He then launched into a laborious recounting of Gardner Pharmaceutical's tireless, unfettered efforts to clarify any possible link to the rash of reported symptoms of weakness and paralysis that had become evident in recent months.

"We have thus far found no causal link," he added. "But, we do have some ideas about what might be happening."

Those around the table, most of whom had been less than eagerly attentive, suddenly became quiet as they looked intently at the plump, bespectacled doctor who, since he started speaking, had clearly become more uncomfortable.

"At this point," he coughed and cleared his throat, "I will have Dr. Grant explain some of the details."

He then pushed himself back a bit from the table and gestured to the young woman on his left who rather slowly stood up still sporting the smile that seldom left her face.

"Thank you, Dr. Harris," she said and nodded toward Congressman Branch who nodded back. "When Dynasane was developed in our labs less than a year ago, most of us at Gardner were surprised because it did not work like most of the currently used antidepressant medications do. As I'm sure all of you know by now, most of them act at the synapse—the little space between nerve cell connections. It's how nerve impulses get from one nerve cell to another. It's a chemical process. Dynasane does not work that way; in fact, we still do not know for certain how it exerts its therapeutic effects. There is still a great deal that is not known about clinical depression—what causes it and why it happens, and what happens in people's brains when they get depressed."

At last, this woman is speaking to the heart of it, Alex thought. *Maybe she does know how to make coffee after all.*

"What we think might be happening regarding these terrible paralyses we're seeing is that somehow the Dynasane molecule changes when it enters the bloodstream. This could happen in a number of ways. It could be affected by some of the naturally occurring chemicals in the blood, or maybe it attaches itself to some other circulating molecule, like an antigen or antibody. So, instead of being metabolized by the body and excreted through the urinary or GI tract, it stays in the circulating bloodstream. All we know so far is that it looks like it is acting on the motor nerve connections to the muscles of the lower limbs. How it does that, we don't know." A hand went up at the far end of the table. "Yes, sir?" she asked as she directed her gaze toward the questioner.

"But, many of the victims of these symptoms have not taken Dynasane, Dr. Grant. What about them?"

It was one of the non- physician members of the committee who was asking the question. A chill went through Alex and doubtless through other members of the group who were present at that fateful Saturday meeting that now seemed a century ago. Alex looked across the table at Harold and Lauren who were sitting together. Harold remained poker faced while Lauren had closed her eyes and leaned her head back like she was looking at the ceiling.

Dr. Grant looked like she had just been told she was going to be executed at the conclusion of the meeting. Before she could speak, Dr. Harris suddenly stood up.

"Maybe I can help with that, sir," he said. "As we mentioned at the outset, we are not completely sure that these symptoms are related to Dynasane, but since a good number of people taking the drug had complained of them, we have been looking strongly at that possibility." He paused and issued a little cough. "We're just not sure at this point about the others. It could be that some of those people had taken Dynasane but did not admit to it. If they had never taken it, though, I'm afraid we're still somewhat in the dark as to why they would be having the symptoms."

Dr. Harris then sat down as abruptly as he had stood up.

The young Dr. Grant looked like she did not know if she was to fish or cut bait at that point, so she cleared her throat and continued to smile as she pushed her glasses back up the bridge of her nose.

"I'm afraid that is the sum and substance of our knowledge at this point, but we are pursuing other avenues of investigation as well. We are not sure why some of the sufferers have gone on to develop paralysis of the muscles that control breathing and some have not. As you probably know, there have been an alarming number of deaths thus far due to breathing problems, but we don't have a handle on why some people just stop being able to breathe. It's tragic and frightening, I know, for all of us."

As she concluded her comments and sat down, Dr. Grant looked rather sheepishly at her colleague, Dr. Harris, who was busy making eye contact with his shoes.

This woman really does give a damn, Alex thought as he began to feel more hopeful. *She's not just here to cover Gardner Pharmaceutical's ass.*

"It just seems like an overwhelming coincidence," the man who had asked the previous question remarked further. "If Dynasane is not the common denominator, what is?" he asked. Dr. Harris slowly brought up his head and looked at the questioning man.

"I'm afraid at this point, sir, we just don't know."

Everyone around the long table then appeared as though they themselves had been paralyzed. The sound level in the large room would have had to be measured in decibels with a minus in front of the number. The air in the room now had the consistency of molasses and it appeared that no one there had the strength or inclination to breathe any.

It seemed that this symphony of silence would play on endlessly when Congressman Branch suddenly came to life again.

"It's difficult to find the words that would or could convey the seriousness of this situation. We could hope that this is just something that passes us on by without leaving anymore casualties; but I doubt we have the luxury of considering such a possibility. What we don't understand, we fear; and it looks like we have a good many reasons to fear these unfortunate events of late. Let's hope that we can muster the energy and courage to find the answers we need."

Intoning these words appeared to have drained the congressman of any vigor or vitality that may have remained in him. He adjourned the meeting and suggested that everyone keep their calendars clear for the foreseeable future. He stood and started for the door. His usual sprightly gait had turned into a reluctant, labored march.

* * *

"Branch looks like he's aged about a hundred years in the last two weeks," Alex said as he and Lauren lay together in her big bed. He was lying on his back with his left arm gathering her head next to his chest. She was lying on her side facing him.

"I know, Alex. He looks so lonely and distracted. He's usually leading the parade, no matter what the cause, as long as he believes in it. He's one of the few men I can tell you that has the trust of his colleagues of both parties in the legislature. They know he can't be bought off or pressured to back things he thinks are crap," she said with her cheek on Alex's chest. "He's one of the few who gives politicians a good name."

"I just wonder how he's going to handle the thing about the spraying last spring. That's bound to come out now. I don't see how it can be avoided any longer. No more free ride on that." They both lay quietly as the movement of Lauren's big grandfather clock was the only betrayal of the silence in the room.

"Well, he had to roll the dice, Alex. He didn't have any other choice. And remember, it was the president who made the final decision," Lauren reminded him.

"I know, but he's not the one who's going to take the heat for it," Alex sighed. "He'll run for cover when the press starts asking the questions he doesn't want to answer."

"I guess we'll know for sure before too long," Lauren's voice trailed off as welcome sleep fell over both of them.

* * *

John did not like winter much either. He just saw it as a time of year he needed to endure before spring when baseball season arrived. It was also clear in his mind that this, his senior year, was going to be critical for him. He knew there would be scouts in the stands most every game. And he knew they would be watching him. That didn't make him particularly nervous; he knew he could play. But, could he play when all the marbles were on the line? There were some troubling memories from last year; like when he couldn't complete a double play on an easy ground ball that he couldn't get out of his glove to make the relay to his second baseman. Or the time he struck out on a juicy fastball right down the gut with the winning run on third. Baseball was the kind of game that would insert those things in your mind at just the wrong moment—just when you needed all your confidence—just when you needed to be your best.

John was only eighteen, but he had already learned what athletics were all about in today's world of junior high and now high school. It was no longer the casual, lighthearted fun that he had heard about from his dad and his friends that was supposed to teach life lessons about loyalty, camaraderie, and sportsmanship. Now it was unending practice, never-ending seasons, "select teams," and the unspoken rule that winning was everything. Coaches lived and died strictly on their win/loss records. And they faced angry, impatient parents and so-called fans when they didn't win. John wasn't stupid; he knew that winning was better than losing, but he felt that the focus of athletics had become so blurred, he couldn't be sure if he wanted to be a part of it anymore.

Professional sports were big business to be sure; and how many high school athletes had a chance to be a pro? One percent? Two percent? It was a long shot. But John knew that the rewards could be great. As in twenty million dollar contracts for just a few years of playing a game. That's all it was —playing a game. Like the coach had said in the movie, *Bull Durham,* "You catch the ball; you throw the ball; you hit the ball. It's a simple game." John laughed every time he thought about that scene.

John also knew that a baseball scholarship to a major university would not only pay his way through school, but take some pressure off his dad. It might also give him a shot at the big show—the majors. Maybe it was worth that after all.

There was a less than robust knock on John's bedroom door. He was startled out of his philosophic mode as he couldn't imagine who it would be. His dad was gone, Aunt Grace was at the grocery store, and Charlotte would only think of darkening the door of his man-cave if she was at the point of dying.

"Come on in," he said with no idea who might appear from the other side of the door. He saw the handle slowly turn and the door open toward him.

"John, are you in there?" Charlotte asked.

"Now just who did you think invited you in?" he replied.

"I thought you might have one of your friends with you," she answered softly. "I want to ask you something, Ok?" John was taken aback by the unexpected honor of having his sister make such a request. He pushed his chair back from his desk.

"Sure, sis, come on in. What is it?" Charlotte slowly walked in and sat down on his bed. She put her hands on her knees and rubbed them back and forth on her jeans as she looked down into her lap.

"You remember that time we talked just after mom died?" She looked at him and blinked her eyes several times and looked away again.

"Yes, I remember. You were really upset as I recall."

"Well, I don't think I ever told you how good that was, John. I was really feeling low." Charlotte paused and looked out the window. It was getting dark and it was cold outdoors. John shifted in his chair, still puzzled as to what she wanted.

"You feeling that way now, sis?" he asked.

"No, just kind of wondering about some things. I was wondering if you were too."

"What things?"

"What about Lauren, John?" Charlotte looked at him and furrowed her brow. "I think dad really likes her."

"Well, duh," John said as he dragged out the sound. "You really think so, Charlotte?" He knew he risked her anger with that last question, but he couldn't help himself.

"Oh, John, you know what I mean. I can't seem to make up my mind about her."

"I think she's great!" John said with some emphasis. "I really like her and I think she likes dad a lot."

"I know she does, but it hasn't even been a year since mom died, John. Not even a year!" Charlotte was now looking at her brother more intently than ever. "How can he be in love with someone else? Has he already forgotten about mom?"

John breathed deeply and leaned forward in his chair.

"Charlotte, dad could never forget about mom in a million years. You and I both know how much they loved each other. Just think how hard this has been for him. I know he blames himself for not being able to prevent it. None of us knew how bad she must have been feeling," John said and sighed. "He's had a lot on his mind. He worries about us, and I know he wants us to like Lauren. She's a good person, sis, and I think she's good for dad. Maybe you feel differently, but I like her. Lauren knows she cannot replace mom. She doesn't want to. She told me so."

"She's just saying that so you'll like her and she wants me to like her too. I'll bet she just wants dad's money!" With that, Charlotte grabbed her knees and started rubbing them rapidly with her hands. John just looked down at the floor. He knew that when Charlotte made up her mind about something, he was not going to convince her otherwise.

"I don't think so, sis. I really don't. She's not that way."

"How do you know?" Charlotte looked up and glared at him. "You don't know how women are, John."

"Well, you've got me there, sis. You're always reminding me of that."

Charlotte looked down and blushed.

"I'm sorry, John. I didn't mean that. I just get mad sometimes and say things I wish I hadn't."

"Charlotte, you told me that the last time we talked like this. Remember?" She looked back at her knees again and started shaking her head.

"Yes, I'm afraid I do...I guess I haven't learned much in the meantime."

"Have you talked to dad about Lauren?" John asked. Charlotte just shook her head. She sat quietly for a moment and then stood up suddenly like she was energized from an unknown source.

"I saw Mary Brim the other day. She asked me why you weren't speaking to her."

Charlotte then turned and walked out of the bedroom, closing the door softly behind her. John just sat there with his mouth agape. He then pulled his chair up to his desk and turned on his computer.

"Women!" he said.

28

Congressman Branch had been all too prescient in concluding that the waves of patients appearing in the country's hospitals and emergency rooms with lower limb weakness or paralysis were not just some passing happenstance. Indeed, the luxury of being able to rest assured in such a conclusion would have been just that, a luxury not borne out by the evidence of current events.

What was also painfully evident was that there was no treatment for those who were stricken. Consequently, the hospitals, again, began to swell to capacity, and there was also the specter of death that hung over every new admission. Some patients went into respiratory arrest and others did not; and there seemed to be no way of predicting who would and who wouldn't. All any physician could really do was try to make his patients as comfortable as possible and hope for the best. Doctors called that kind of treatment palliative.

It simply meant they couldn't do much to help.

As seemed inevitable when an unexplained leviathan stalked the land, there was an ever increasing clamor for some kind of explanation of these alarming circumstances. This was hardly unexpected and certainly understandable in a beleaguered nation, but along with it came the obvious question of who or what was to blame. To the ten people who attended the fateful Saturday conference of the special committee the previous spring in Washington, there could be no possible doubt of the culpable party or parties, even if they did not completely understand how or why these things happened. It was a done deal, and no one who was present that day believed there was any other likely conclusion but that the distribution of the Dynasane had wrought this calamity. The other inescapable conclusion was that no one who was present and took part in the decision to spray the nation with this largely unknown chemical was going to stand up and publically admit it. And the President of the United States of America was unlikely to stand at a microphone and acknowledge to the world that he had ordered an action that resulted in the worst medical calamity ever to befall our great nation. He was, in fact, about as likely to do that as he was to also proclaim that the Internal Revenue Service had been abolished and the citizens of America would no longer be burdened with any further taxation. If one was to indulge in Disneyesque fairy tales, one might as well stay for the entire movie.

As Alex thought about these things, he was just as sure that there would be plenty of scapegoats for the nation, the press, and the world The chilling conclusion that pierced his entire being at the moment was that once it became known that he was on this special committee and participated in this fiasco, he, too, would be relegated to history along with the likes of Benedict Arnold or maybe even Josef Mengele. There could be no amount of rationalization or explanation that anyone would believe or consider. It almost seemed that the best possible outcome would be that the human race would be obliterated and there would be no one left to remember any of these things. So much for living happily ever after with Lauren and his children. Even if they survived, John and Charlotte would live with a mantle of disgrace endowed them by their father. Any direction he looked for consolation, the options were clear; it was lose, lose, lose, and lose again.

* * *

Lauren was not going to be able to get away from Washington, as all vacation time was cancelled at the FPA. She would have to wait until Alex came to see her when the committee met. Fortunately for them both, there was a called meeting about every ten days, so they weren't without face to face time, so to speak. She was glad for that.

They had still not talked seriously about forever, but had touched on it a few times. It seemed odd to her that both of them were so timid about taking that step. There was really no hindrance to either of them to moving ahead. That is, if one did not count a nationwide medical catastrophe to be considered a hindrance.

God only knows how a mind works when it's in love, she was thinking and laughed to herself.

The phone on her desk barked out its irritating beeps as she quickly reached for it.

"We having lunch today?" Ann asked. There was a silence that followed as Lauren listened but did not readily answer. By this time in their relationship, she had something like a sixth sense about her friend no matter what came out of her mouth.

"I'm kind of behind, but I guess so. Everything Ok?" Lauren asked. There were just those few milliseconds of hesitation to her question that gave credence to her suspicions.

"I'll tell you at lunch," Ann said and hung up the phone.

Lauren was left looking at her handset as though it held some critical truth that it would not reveal. She slowly put it down in the cradle and looked at the time down in the lower right hand corner of her computer screen. It read 11:15 in its pristine white numbers. They usually left at about 11:45 when they lunched together. Her pulse began to quicken a bit as she thought about her friend. Ann had seemed nothing but her old self lately. There was no drama going on that she had mentioned. Lauren contented herself with the fact that as Hercule Poirot would say, "Soon, all will be revealed."

* * *

The walk to Jarrod's Café usually took Lauren and Ann about ten minutes. Today, it seemed like an hour or so to Lauren. Ann wouldn't look at her even for a moment as they walked together.

Whatever was going on with Ann, Lauren now knew it was not casual. She had never seen her like this before.

Jarrod's was one of those places where you waited in line to place an order at the counter and were given a number. Today, there were fewer people in line and most of the tables and booths were empty. Usually Lauren and Ann would then sit down at one of the tables or booths. The staff at Jarrod's knew the two women well by now and generally would just bring their food to them when it was ready. Lauren was thinking they might as well have been waiting for the next appearance of Haley's Comet as they settled into their booth. Ann's face had turned a ruddy, brownish red and looked like a mask. She still avoided any eye contact with her best friend as they waited in an uncomfortable silence.

A young man in a white apron came sauntering over to the booth and placed two baskets down in front of them. "Ladies," he said, and then went gliding away silently. Lauren wanted to say something, but knew better. Whatever was going on in Ann's mind, she wanted to respect it along with their friendship, but her own impatience was becoming unsupportable. Finally, Ann took a breath and let it out slowly.

"The son of a bitch left me."

The words weren't so much spoken as they just escaped her lips. Lauren could see Ann's face darken and redden more as she continued to stare at the nothingness of the white wall that made up the inside confines of the booth. Lauren wanted to let out a cheer, but thought better of it if she and Ann were to remain friends. Instead, she opted to just continue listening like she thought a best friend should. She looked down at her sandwich and just waited.

"I know what you're thinking, Lauren. You're thinking I should be glad. Maybe even count my blessings. Consider myself lucky. I wish I could. I REALLY wish I could, but goddamn it, it hurts! It hurts like hell. I didn't expect that when this thing finally happened."

Ann now turned her face down as though she was talking into the little basket in front of her. She then put her hands up to her head as her whole body began to shudder in wracking sobs.

Lauren remained motionless and chided herself silently for being so cavalier about Ann's feelings. Or at least what she anticipated would be Ann's feelings about the impending demise of her marriage. It was always so easy to think that a leaden, dead relationship could be cast aside without so much as a backward glance. That untold lie lay harbored in everyone who sought escape from a union that had lost its luster and vitality. But it was only when the deed was done and the moorings were severed that every personal need and neurotic weakness that had been served by the liaison was laid painfully bare. The expected free ride to jubilant freedom suddenly disappeared.

"You know what's funny?" Ann asked as she raised her reddened eyes and looked at Lauren. "I thought I was the one holding us together. I thought I was the 'strong one,'" Ann deepened her voice for emphasis on the last two words. "I thought if I walked away, he would fall apart and be paralyzed. What a dumbass I am!"

Ann shook her head side to side as she tried to wipe the tears away with a napkin she had picked up out of the basket in front of her. "Turns out he's had a little cutie for a while now. How do I know, you ask?" Ann paused as she took a deep breath. "He left me a note...he told me he knew we were done a long time ago, and he thought I would be glad to see him gone. Jesus, how right and wrong he is!" Ann continued to dab at her eyes and wipe her face. "I'd like to wring his neck for being so right. What on earth did I ever need from him?"

"That's always the hardest part to see, Ann. It's hard to see the needs that make you stay when you know you should've left long ago. It takes a lot of guts and grit to make changes. But, you can do it. I know you probably don't feel you can right now since you're so disoriented and scared. It will get better, baby. You'll have to trust me on that."

Lauren reached across the table and took her friend's hand and squeezed. Their eyes finally met for more than just a moment, but

Ann began to sob again and looked away. Just for the briefest few seconds, Lauren felt that gnawing, yearning pain of loneliness and abandonment inside herself. She loved Ann, but was glad she was not going through what her friend was feeling right now...and hoped she never would again.

"Try to eat something, Ann. You'll feel better."

Ann smiled.

"Now, you're sounding like my mother."

"Oh, God! What a low blow, but what's a best friend for?" Lauren countered.

"You're supposed to save me from myself, so I don't have to go talk to my therapist about all this."

"That's who you need to be talking to about it, you ninny!"

"I know, but I'm not your common, every day, garden variety ninny. I'm a special kind of ninny. I'm a scared ninny and I hate feeling like this."

"I know...I know, baby. It hurts like hell. Anybody who says it doesn't is lying their ass off." Lauren paused as Ann continued to sob. "It will go away, though. It will."

Ann said nothing, but continued to cry as Lauren just sat being her friend. It would be a long walk back to work.

* * *

There was no mirth in the land. The malady that had started as a curious trickle just a few months ago was now marching relentlessly through emergency rooms and hospitals over America with no indication that there was anything to slow it down or stop it. There were more cases of paralysis and an increasing number of deaths day by day. Despite Sherman Branch's eloquence before the press, there was an ever increasing clamor for some explanation about the "military exercise" that had been carried out the previous spring. Most importantly, did it have anything to do with the current medical crisis?

There were no explanations or answers forthcoming from the seats of power in Washington. The president and other high ranking officials maintained that the military exercises of the preceding spring were just that—military exercises, and nothing more. It would have been foolish and unrealistic in the extreme, however, to think that such a massive effort by the military could be kept totally secret. It was not long before the tabloids and soon afterward the legitimate press began to hammer down on the issue with increasing intensity. Some veterans of the Washington political scene were put in mind of Watergate, now some forty years in the past, but certainly not forgotten.

That particularly distasteful episode of American History, however, was not accompanied by a nationwide medical epidemic of an extent never before experienced. That fact in particular allowed the current administration to continue to dodge and feint on the issue while continuing to declare that the primary goal was now the solution of this emergency that threatened the entire planet. No one but the hardiest supporters of various conspiracy theories could take much issue with that view.

But, as the crisis deepened and more people were dying, there was a growing impatience along with the burgeoning specter of intolerance of the government's meaningless and insubstantial rhetoric. America was dying and doctors were helpless to save it.

29

Alex felt guilty. The crisis in the country was deepening. He and every other physician he knew was working long hours without seeing any stemming of the tide of humanity assaulting the emergency rooms across the land. It was discouraging to see and heartbreaking to feel. He took refuge in the arms of Lauren, which was the source of his unwarranted guilt. Why should he be enjoying himself when so many were suffering? Reminding himself that life was unfair only made him feel worse. When it was unfair in his favor, it stoked the fires of the guilt he was already feeling. It seemed there was no way to win. It also sounded masochistic.

Life is a bitch and then you die, he thought as the well-worn adage would not vacate his mind.

The committee meetings had proven to be thus far largely meaningless as all that was being done was going over the latest from Gardner regarding how to reverse or stop the weakness and paralysis and death. Dr. Harris and his assistant kept giving upbeat reports with smiles pasted on their faces which amounted to nothing of substance. Dr. Grant, the young assistant to Dr. Harris, gave a rather long, obtuse (to Alex anyway) explanation of nanotechnology which might hold some promise when it came to finding a way to get some kind of effective medication to the areas in the brain and spinal cord where the problem lay. She said it had something to do with the blood brain barrier which prevents some molecules and chemicals from penetrating the brain and spinal cord. Alex was aware of it and tried to remember what he could from medical school, but it was not something he dealt with every day in his work. He was just hopeful that the biochemists could come up with something to help. The ship was sinking and it looked like no one could bail fast enough to prevent it.

On top of that, the press was clamoring for somebody's head with greater vigor. There was mounting suspicion that the president, the Congress, and Congressman Branch were not giving them the whole truth. While that in itself was not unheard of in the Nation's Capital, the nature of current events made the issue more painfully acute. As had been true only a few brief years in the past, this was not just some political football to toss around at press conferences. But Washington being Washington, politics was the name of the game whether in peace or in war. This, however, was a special kind of war that people were beginning to believe was unlikely to be won. That was reason enough for many to believe that optimism was foolhardy.

* * *

"I miss John and Charlotte," Lauren was saying as she was pouring two glasses of wine at her kitchen counter. "It seems like it's been ages since I've seen them."

Alex had taken off his coat and shoes and was half lying down on Lauren's sofa. He was blankly staring at her TV set which was turned off. Lauren was in a beige pants outfit with a light green silk blouse. She had removed the jacket when they came through the door and hung it on one of the chairs at her dining table. She had also taken off her shoes and was in her stocking feet.

"Uh...what was that, Lauren?" Alex asked rather lazily.

Lauren arrived at the couch with the wine and gave Alex one of the glasses. It was a Chardonnay, which she now knew was his favorite.

"Are you tired?" she asked. "You looked like you were having a hard time staying awake at the meeting this afternoon."

Alex just looked at her as he thrust his glass toward hers.

"Happy days," he said as their glasses clinked together. They both took a sip and looked at each other.

"I said, I miss John and Charlotte. Haven't seen them in

ages."

"Oh, they're both Ok, I think. Hard to tell sometimes. John usually tells me what's going on, but Charlotte not so much. She still misses Maria. They were close."

"She lost her mother, Alex. How on earth do you get over that? No wonder she's been so slow to warm up to me. I want to know her better, but I didn't want to push her and maybe ruin any chance we could ever be friends."

"I know, baby. But Charlotte's a resilient kid. I think there are some other things going on. She also lost her best friend last spring before school ended after they had a fight." Alex took a drink of his wine. "I mean they had a physical fight. I think it scared Charlotte. She attacked her friend Amy and hit her several times. Now Amy won't talk to her." Alex looked into his glass as he swirled the wine. "She's made some new friends, but I can tell she's not the same."

"I don't see how she could be. How long was she friends with Amy?"

"Since they were both in kindergarten, I guess. They've been more like sisters." Alex drank more of his wine. "Amy is a good kid, but she's intense. Charlotte's been more of a follower...she goes with the flow most of the time. But she drew the line with Amy over something that happened between them. I think it was more of a slowly developing kind of thing." He drank more wine. "And, when it happened, it was like something just went off inside of her. Charlotte tried to apologize, but Amy has been adamant. She's rejected Charlotte completely."

Alex began to make circles around the top on his wine glass with his finger until it made a ringing sound.

"Poor thing. I wish I could help, Alex, but that's more your department. I wouldn't know what to say. I'd probably only alienate her. I'm not sure she likes me anyway...I've never had kids, or really wanted any. It scares me...the thought of being a parent."

Alex looked at Lauren over the top of his wine glass.

"It's usually the ones that are so confident about the kind of parent they will be that do the most damage, Lauren. If you're a thoughtful parent who cares about your kids, you know how scary it is. Sometimes you know the answers and sometimes you don't have a clue, but you suck it up and make a choice. It's when the kids know that you're unsure about something that they're the most nervous. Whether they understand it or not, they want decisive parents who care about them enough to set limits."

Lauren found herself looking at Alex while he was talking like she was in some kind of trance.

"I never thought of it like that." She spun her glass in her fingers by the stem. "Thank you, Dr. Freud," she said and sipped her wine.

"Was I giving a lecture again?"

"Uh-huh, but it's Ok. I need to learn if we're going to be in the same rowboat, don't you think?"

Alex stopped drinking and put his glass down on the coffee table.

"Why, Ms. Marsh, are you proposing to me?"

Lauren's glass looked like it was balanced on her lower lip while she held it there for a long moment as she looked into Alex's blue eyes. As Alex looked at her, he was thinking she looked a bit like Ingrid Bergman in *Casablanca,* only Lauren was more striking with her long, rich reddish brown hair that hung down around her face and fell over her shoulders. She was not classically pretty like a lot of women, but Alex noticed that she had been attending to her makeup and grooming more than she used to, which had given her whole presence an irresistible allure. The dark red tint of her lipstick contrasted with her light skin, which gave her the look of a woman unrestricted by time or fashion.

"Dr. Madison, I believe I did, sir. It was thoughtful of you to notice. You're so wonderfully observant."

"Well, I'm a trained professional, you know."

Lauren leaned forward and put her glass on the coffee table next to Alex's. She then turned her body toward him as he gracefully folded her into his embrace. Their lips touched and brushed in a rhythm that only lovers could hear and know.

"Thank goodness for that," she whispered. "Do you have other talents as well?"

"I'm so glad you asked."

* * *

Georg J. Luger was Austrian by birth. His name was known and celebrated by many for the fact that he designed and brought to the world a pistol. As it turned out, it was to be no ordinary pistol, but would become widely known and appreciated by the militaries of a number of nations. It was usually just called the Luger although its proper name was the Pistole Parabellum-1908. It was the sidearm of many German soldiers in both World War I and World War II. Various manufacturers produced it from 1905 until 1945. It has been produced in replica by a number of companies until the present day.

Those who appreciated firearms in general, and pistols in particular, had been collecting Lugers for some time. After the Second World War, Lugers were to become avidly sought after by gun collectors. One of the reasons for this love affair with the Luger was that those who had them and fired them reported that when you held one, it felt like a part of the hand and not just an extension of it. The parts that made up the gun were carefully machined as only the Germans could seem to do; so, consequently, Lugers became more valuable as the years went by to collectors and various other enthusiasts as well as war buffs.

Congressman Sherman Branch was not a war buff or a gun collector, but one of his most prized possessions was a Luger that had been brought home from World War II by his father. It happened to have been carried by a member of the *Luftwaffe* which made it more valuable and rarer still. That was because many of the Lugers carried by the pilots of the German Air Force were destroyed along with their owners over the skies of Europe. Not many survived the war.

Congressman Branch's father had, however, managed to bring one home from Europe and had given it to his son. Mr. Branch kept it in a locked drawer in his study at home and would only rarely remove it from its resting place. It reminded him of his father who had died of cancer shortly after he returned home from the conflict in Europe. Mr. Branch had taken it to the range once and fired it a few times, but he was more comfortable with it resting in its place at home. Shooting was really not his thing, and he had little time for it. Along with the pistol itself, a magazine filled with 9mm cartridges lay beside it in the drawer.

It was Saturday and Congressman Branch had seen all the football he cared to see for one afternoon. He was by himself since his wife was in Maryland visiting with their daughter for a day of shopping and seeing the grandchildren. He was in casual attire, which consisted of a pair of his most comfortable pressed jeans and a long sleeved, dark maroon rugby shirt that was both soft and warm. He finished off this outfit with a pair of dark brown Wellington boots. The day was cold, drab, and colorless which was not unusual for wintertime in the Washington area. There was a smattering of snow on the ground and the promise of more over the course of the weekend which made the snapping sounds of the wood in the fireplace as it burned all the more inviting.

The study was his and it was rarely visited by Mr. Branch's wife or any other family member who might have been in the house at any given time. Although he was gregarious by nature, the congressman enjoyed the time he could spend sitting alone in his leather covered, overstuffed chair with the wide armrests and listening to a symphony or some country and western if he was so inclined. He was pretty eclectic in his musical tastes; if he liked it, he liked it—Alan Jackson or Beethoven.

Today, it was Beethoven—the *Allegretto* from the Seventh Symphony. It was his favorite classical piece and he thought it to be the most beautiful passage of all music of any kind. Well, the Sonata Number Fourteen for piano, or *Moonlight Sonata* as it is known, might have been just as beautiful and mesmerizing. He was glad Beethoven had written both of them.

Outside, the weather forecast was proving prophetic as a light snowfall was beginning to show itself almost like a white mist in the air. It was coming up on three in the afternoon and his wife would not be home until eight or so. The fingers of his right hand encircled a glass filled with ice cubes and the dark caramel tint of a single malt scotch. There might be better combinations of things to enjoy than scotch and Beethoven on a day such as this, but right now he didn't know what they might be.

He let go of his glass for a moment as he stood and walked over toward the bookcase on the far wall of the room. He then took a key from his pocket and slid it into the lock of one of the drawers built into the cabinets at the base of the bookcase. The drawer slid out with ease and the congressman looked down at the Luger in the drawer for a second before he reached and took it out with his left hand. He then took the loaded magazine in his right hand and put it in the slot at the base of the grip and slid it home with a click aided by a tap with the heel of his hand. Holding the gun pointed straight down at the floor in his left hand, he took the toggle on the top between his right thumb and forefinger and snapped it back in one quick motion. When the congressman released the toggle, it slid forward quickly with a metallic sound and closed the breech. There was now a loaded round in the chamber. The congressman only needed to release the safety to fire the weapon if he so desired.

It took about four strides for him to get back to his chair and sit down. He moved the glass of scotch to the left armrest and carefully placed the pistol down on the right where the glass had been. The barrel of the pistol was pointed into the fireplace in front of him. Placing his right hand over the grip of the gun, he pushed himself back in his favorite chair, breathed in slowly and listened to Beethoven.

30

Despite the slowdowns, flight cancellations, and the many other distractions and inconveniences that go along with human calamity on a grand scale, Lauren was able, at last, to get a weekend off to come to Texas and see Alex. She was fiddling with the clasp on her purse as the plane was descending toward the runway at DFW. The thought of having a whole, readymade family to suddenly appear in her life was beginning to settle uneasily into her mind as a real possibility and not just some fanciful daydream. It was one of those things that she wanted, but as the reality grew nearer, the more it bothered her. It thrilled her to be sure, but it also scared and confused her.

Was she family material? What kind of mother could she be? Did John and Charlotte really want another mother? Or at least someone to act like one in the family? Lauren knew it would never be the same for either of them. Their mother was gone—dead forever and there was no replacing her. And the thought that they might look to her for some direction in their lives made her whole body quiver. Perhaps she was more afraid that they might actually accept her. That idea had never occurred to her before. Somehow the thought of something working out never had the same emotional punch in the gut that the possibility of failure carried with it.

What did punch her in the gut at that moment was the sudden lurching of the plane as the wheels hit the runway a bit too abruptly as it landed. Lauren felt like her stomach had taken a nose dive down to her feet. The big aircraft tilted to the side for a brief moment until the pilot righted the behemoth as it began to roll straight down the long runway and struggle to come to a taxi speed slow enough for the pilot to turn it onto one of the lanes that lead across another runway on its way to the arrival gate. The brakes wailed in protest at having to stop, but the huge conveyance with wings that was now just a big bus finally came to rest as it waited for another plane to depart before starting again toward the terminal.

The flight was nearly full and there was the ever present buzz of conversation as most everyone began to fidget with their briefcases, purses, bags, and other accoutrements that attended their journey as the plane neared the gate. Invariably, some stood up to open the overhead bins to retrieve things, despite the entreaties of the flight attendants and the captain to remain seated. Lauren thought it to be one of the strangest and most infuriating facets of air travel-- at least air travel involving human beings. Herding cats could have been accomplished in much less time and with a great deal less effort she thought. And then there was the daunting task of actually getting out of this huge contraption she had been sitting in for the last several hours. If Alex had not been waiting for her at the gate, she would just as soon have been home with a glass of wine.

* * *

"Daddy, when is she getting here?" Charlotte droned in her best Valley Girl whine she had learned from her new entourage at school.

She had resisted it as incredibly pretentious and lame, but somehow it just rubbed off on her without her conscious permission. Like some virus maybe. What it said to her was shallowness and insincerity, but she was now into it, and Ginger's lifestyle, right up to her eyebrows. She frowned when she thought about it, but she figured that maybe it was just one of those teenage things that wouldn't leave her permanently scarred.

What was it that was supposed to be so great about being a teenager? she was wondering.

Somehow, no ready answer came to her mind.

"Her flight gets here about three, honey. Do you want to go with me to pick her up?" Alex asked. "Lauren would like that, you know."

"Daddy, please, I've got about a million IMPORTANT things to do today. I'll see her tonight," Charlotte said with a scarcely disguised sigh of near disgust.

Alex knew he had overstepped the mark.

"Well, excuse me!" Alex said and made a face, shaking his head side to side.

"Don't be a dweeb, Dad."

With that, Charlotte took marching steps off in the direction of her room. Although he was smiling, Alex felt rising anger inside him as he just stood and watched her sassy retreat. Her penny loafers made a clacking sound on the marble entry as she strutted across it and then down the hall toward her room. Alex took a breath to call after her, but stopped. This was not the time to get into some kind of squabble with Charlotte. He took another long, deep breath and turned toward the kitchen to pick up his car keys off the counter. He opened the back door of the house and closed it behind him.

Standing for a minute, Alex paused to look at the small lake behind his house and the mostly bare-limbed trees in the backyard. It was a gray, colorless day that reminded him of his childhood and how those kind of days always reeked of sadness. There was no joy in them. He wasn't sure why; it just felt that way on days like these. His mind went back to the old gas space heaters in his grandmother's house and their distinctive odor on cold days that always seemed to give him a headache. If he didn't get right up next to them, he was always cold in the house; and if he did, the smell of the gas made him sick.

Alex smiled as his melancholy thoughts transported him back to another time that he would have liked to forget for the most part. His childhood was not particularly unhappy, but he tended to remember the unhappy times the most vividly. As his eyes swept across the dark gray water of the little lake, he was reminded of one of Ben Hogan's golf books in which the famous golfer said that somehow it was easier to remember the notably bad shots he had hit in his career rather than the really great ones. It was a concept with which Alex could easily identify. With life's successes, there was nothing to regret or obsess over. Failures were a different matter, however. Sometimes he just wished his restless mind would leave him alone.

As if he was suddenly lit up by an electrical charge, Alex turned and walked to his car and got in it. He put the key in the ignition and started the engine, giving the accelerator a few taps to liven the cold, lazy motor. The thought of Lauren settling into his embrace at the airport made him want to drive a little faster as he darted out his driveway and down the street.

* * *

Alex hated airports almost as much as he hated flying. Getting there was a hassle; parking was a hassle; getting through the security checks was a hassle; everything about it was a hassle. There was hurrying; there was waiting. It was mostly waiting. The flights were never on time, coming or going, which always meant more waiting.

People were moving in all different directions at the same time. It was a great sea of humanity in which, for the most part, each individual was unfamiliar to the other and possessed of a zillion different agendas and final destinations known only to them. Despite the crowds of people, it always struck Alex as an incredibly lonely place. Those with a layover would wait for another flight to another place. Those whose destination was DFW would gather their bags and leave by car, taxi, limousine, or whatever to some place for some purpose. Some would go to warm, friendly domiciles where they would be joyfully welcomed while others would put their keys into the doors of lonely apartments or homes occupied by familiar people living with them in dysfunction and unhappiness. But, somehow the world kept turning and the sun kept rising. Whether someone was happy or miserable did not affect that. All Alex knew was that he was anxious to see Lauren. She would be the perfect antidote to the funk that had been hanging over him all day.

* * *

It was nearing the time for Lauren's flight to arrive, so Alex sauntered over to the gate and leaned up against one of the pillars with his hands in his pockets. It wasn't long before some uniformed men came walking up to the gate. They began to talk to one another in animated conversation. Alex assumed it must have been the pilots who would fly Lauren's plane to its next scheduled destination. They both had small bags with the pull handles that slid out from the sides and small wheels on the bottom that made it easy to move them around. They were soon joined by several attractive, uniformed young women along with one young man of about thirty who stood next to the pilots as they began to talk together.

The din of conversation was overwhelmed by the glass-shaking whine of jet engines as the arriving plane pulled slowly up to the gate as the jet way reeled out like the folded hallway it was and came to rest on the side of the plane. A man at the desk made the announcement that the flight from Washington DC had arrived.

Alex's pulse began to quicken. He watched anxiously as the agent threw open the doors leading to the jet way.

I guess I'm more nervous than I thought, fluttered through his mind.

It wasn't long before arriving passengers began to pour from the jet way into the gate area. Alex knew that if Lauren was toward the back of the plane, it would take a while for her to emerge. So he resigned himself to having to wait a while longer than he hoped.

The large plane must have been full as the steady flow of arriving passengers did not slow for some time. After a few minutes, however, the parade of humanity began to thin to a trickle and Lauren had still not made an appearance.

Alex was shifting his weight from one foot to the other almost like he might have been dancing.

The exit from the gangway was now empty and still Lauren had not come out. Alex suddenly stopped his dance-like gyrations and stood rigid.

He then walked over to the ticket counter and got the attention of one of the agents.

"Have all the passengers on the Washington flight come out yet?" he asked.

The agent just looked at Alex blankly as though the question was absurd. The man turned his attention back to his computer screen as he clacked away at the keyboard for a few seconds as Alex just looked on.

"Just a moment, sir, and I'll check. Just wait here if you will," the man said.

He then started over to the double doors of the gangway where he stopped a moment to speak with the woman stationed there. She and the agent exchanged some words and she pointed down the jet way. The man then started down the hallway toward the plane.

Alex's eyes were glued on the gangway entrance which was still unoccupied. He resumed his jerky dance step routine from one foot to the other as he eyed the doorway.

What on earth am I so upset about? he asked himself. *She's probably just taking her time. I know she doesn't like to fly.*

Alex looked at the entry to the gangway again. Still nothing.

What could she be doing? he asked himself again.

No answer.

The agent who had disappeared down the jet way had not returned.

Some of the waiting crew for the next flight were looking down the corridor leading to the plane.

The hallway was still empty.

Alex walked over to where he could see down the companionway. Still nothing. Finally, he saw the agent round the corner down the hall and come walking up toward the door. There was no one behind him.

It seemed to Alex like it took a lifetime, but the agent finally came through the door and walked toward him.

"Sir, is the passenger you're expecting Ms. Marsh?" he asked.

"Yes, yes she is."

Alex looked at the man anxiously.

"You'll need to wait just a minute, sir. I'm afraid there's been an accident."

"An accident? What kind of an accident?" Alex's anxiety was escalating; his words were clipped and demanding.

"It's not serious, sir, she just had a fall as she was getting off the plane. The staff is helping her up the jet way now."

Alex's attention went immediately to the hallway again which was still empty. He started toward the double doors of the gate when the agent took him by the arm.

"I'm sorry, sir. You cannot go past the doors of the gate. Please, sir. She will be along in a moment," the man's grip grew tighter.

Alex reluctantly acquiesced to the entreaty of the agent as his eyes kept sweeping the empty hall that led down to the plane.

It seemed to Alex like time had stopped completely. The group of pilots and flight attendants standing next to the gate doorway continued their banter as though nothing was happening.

Alex was feeling like a guitar string that had been stretched too taut by the tuning pegs. He couldn't remember the last time he felt so helpless.

Just then, a middle aged woman in a blue skirt and white blouse came rushing past him pushing a wheel chair. She took no notice of anyone else as she swept passed the doors of the gate and into the jet way. The woman walked briskly down the hall and disappeared around the corner.

There was more anxious waiting for Alex. His eyes were still riveted on the empty jet way.

Although it seemed much longer, it was only a minute or two later that Lauren came into view. She was sitting in the wheelchair pushed by the lady who had rushed it down the hall a few minutes earlier. Alex rushed forward to meet her as she sat in the chair looking embarrassed. Her skin was so light normally that it was always easy for him to tell when she was blushing.

Alex put his arms around her as best he could. The familiar fragrance of her perfume welcomed him into her embrace. She finally pulled away from him after a moment and kissed him on the cheek.

"Oh, Alex, they made such a big deal of this. I just tripped on the threshold as I was getting off the plane. I'm alright, but they made me wait until they could get a chair. I guess they're worried about lawsuits or something," Lauren said half disgustedly as she was trying to manage a smile. "I think I may have cut my knee." Lauren continued to blush. "But, I think all my brains are intact—such as they are."

"I was worried. I didn't know what could have happened. You know I always expect the worst," Alex said and squeezed her face close to his. "I hadn't realized that you had this flair for the dramatic, though. I learn something new about you every day."

"I guess I owe that to my drama class in high school. The teacher begged me to become an actress. She said I could become the next Elizabeth Taylor. I told her she must have been on acid and also had terrible eyesight."

Alex smiled and they both managed to laugh as he stood up and the lady behind the chair began pushing Lauren toward the baggage area.

There was the usual wait for the carousel to start up and the bags to start spilling out of the opening at the top of the ramp. The two lovers did not mind the wait as they watched for Lauren's suitcase to make its appearance. The wheelchair lady insisted that Lauren stay in the chair until she could be loaded into Alex's car in front of the building. The woman politely told Lauren it was a policy of the airline and the airport management when someone might possibly have injured themselves while in the terminal.

Alex had parked close by and it wasn't long before his car stopped in front of the arrival area and Lauren was deposited gently into the front seat beside him. The wheel chair lady closed the door and the two just looked at each other for a moment.

"I don't fall down at airports for just any man, you know," Lauren said and began to bat her eyes.

Alex just grinned and turned the key to start the car. The engine came to life as he moved the shift lever into drive. He pulled away from the curb and accelerated toward the nearest exit.

He just wanted to get home.

31

If people were depressed, as recent history had so vividly revealed, that was one thing; debilitating to be sure, but at least people felt like it could be managed even if recent experience suggested otherwise. However, if people were depressed and could not walk —or if they were depressed, could not walk, and were dying in increasing numbers—what then would be the fate of the country, or possibly of mankind itself?

These questions were now not just the abstract concerns of philosophers and intellectuals sitting in armchairs by the fireplace as they expostulated their theories. America was on its knees, almost literally now, and looking for rescue that appeared to be notably remote. The best medical minds in the nation and the world had been loosed on these pending matters. Nothing of substance had emerged in the way of a possible solution. Whereas the mood of the country several years earlier had been one of malaise, now the overriding temperament of the nation was a rising sense of impending panic. People were afraid. The thought of being in a wheelchair was grotesque to most. Yet, it had become the grim reality for many. And it looked to be the fate of many more to come. The specter of becoming permanently immobilized began to hang over the country like a thick, dreary cloud that would not clear.

Once again, in the space of just over a short year, the hospitals of the country were filling up with a never ending tide of new patients. Age was not a consideration. The pediatric wards were full right on up to and including the geriatric floors of every hospital in the land. Whatever might have been perpetrating this

232

nightmare showed no partiality in selecting its victims. Everyone was at risk without exception. And death pointed its boney finger at sufferers without consideration of race, religion, cultural background, or anything else that anyone observing could determine.

Physicians were concerned that if the entire population was susceptible, then it was only a matter of time before virtually every man, woman, and child would be taken down. It was a concept no physician could imagine or even conceive, yet it seemed to be a prospect that was now not only possible, but perhaps inescapable. Those preaching that the end of the world was at hand seemed to be nearing their promised land and whatever reward that held for them. But there was no celebration evident at that proposed reckoning. The nation was filled with fear. The winds blowing across America carried with it only hopelessness.

* * *

"Things in Washington any better than here, Lauren?" John asked as the two sat quietly on the couch in the den. The TV was on, but nobody was paying it much attention. The news was on and all of it was bad, to no one's surprise. The news anchor was droning on about the latest statistics regarding the epidemic and how it was affecting business and the American people.

"Pretty much the same, John. Debilitated people and gloom and doom everywhere, I'm afraid." Lauren tried to smile as she talked, but she was not having much success. "Will you be playing baseball again soon?"

Lauren had changed into some jeans, a cotton blouse, and a pullover sweater of dark blue along with a pair of white running shoes. In fact, John was wearing almost the same thing, only his sweater was red.

"We start practice in about two weeks if this cold, rainy weather will let up. Two of our really good players are down with the paralysis. One is serious now and they're not sure if he'll live." John looked away at the TV as he spoke.

A lingering, unsettling silence fell over them.

"I'm sorry, John. Is he one of your good friends?" Lauren asked.

The teen slowly turned his head to look at Lauren again.

"We're just buds, like most of the guys on the team. My best friend is Ray Applewhite. He's a football player and will probably be valedictorian of my graduating class. Smart dude." He paused and his eyes became dark. "That is, if we make it to graduation this year." The teenager turned his gaze back to the flickering TV screen and the two reporters trying to make some jokes that only those truly dislodged from reality might have found amusing.

"I know. It's discouraging, John. I wish I could say we were at a breakthrough point or something that was more optimistic, but it's a blank right now." Lauren was looking straight at John who kept blinking his eyes and looking away. He was taking a great deal of interest in his sneakers at that moment. Suddenly, he turned and looked at her.

"What about you? Were you hurt today? Dad said you fell."

Lauren started to blush.

"Oh, it was nothing. I tripped getting off the plane and they made it out to be an emergency, like I needed brain surgery or something. Come to think of it, that might actually help." Lauren did manage a genuine smile this time. "I'm fine...just embarrassed." She then took a drink of the iced tea Alex had made for her earlier. "Of course, my dress flew up and now everybody who was standing behind me at the time had a front row view of my round, colorful, derriere. I'm only glad I wasn't wearing a thong." Lauren smiled while she blushed.

Now it was John's turn to blush, which he did, but said nothing.

"I heard that, Lauren. You didn't tell me that part. Are you sure you weren't just flirting with some guy?" Alex said as he walked into the room from the kitchen with a broad grin on his face. He had on his favorite velour beige jogging outfit along with dark red sneakers. He had on a long sleeved rugby shirt under the jacket.

"Well, for your information, sir, the onlookers were mostly women and they tried to help me in my state of, uh... embarrassment."

"Well, I should hope so. You gals need to stick together. Especially at a time like that," Alex riposted and laughed good naturedly. John smiled and started laughing, too. "What about your knee? You said you might have cut it."

"It was just a scratch. No surgery necessary."

"That's lucky for you. If you had needed it, you fell in love with the wrong kind of doctor." Alex looked at John and laughed again.

John smiled self-consciously.

Lauren blushed again.

"Well, next time, I'll be on the lookout for a surgeon, I guess," she said as she stuck out her tongue at Alex just before she kissed him on the cheek as he sat down next to her.

John was still smiling, but this time it settled more naturally on his face.

"Do you know where your sister is, John?" Alex asked.

John hesitated a moment as though he needed to think about it.

"I think she's with that bunch she's running around with now. I thought she said they were going to a movie."

"Oh, that must have been the terribly important thing she had to do this afternoon, then. Did she say when she would be home? I was hoping we could go out for some dinner if Lauren feels up to it," Alex continued.

Lauren then perked up as though someone had prodded her.

"Oh, don't do anything special on my account. I'd just as soon we stayed in. I'm feeling Ok, but the weather is dreary."

"Well, you'll have to settle for whatever we have in the fridge for supper," Alex reported.

Lauren smiled.

"I had never heard that term when I was growing up in Boston...supper. You mean dinner, don't you, Alex?"

"Well, ma'am, sometimes here in the land of cotton, we say

supper instead, Miss Scarlet," Alex drawled. "I know you girls from up north probably have not heard how really gentrified, civilized people are supposed to talk."

"Well, kiss my grits, Colonel...or is it General Madison, sir?" Lauren came back at him. "I can never remember."

"And here I thought you could learn Southern ways. You'll have to put those Yankee customs behind you, dear."

"Oh, brother! How long are you two going to keep this up?" John asked and rolled his eyes. "I'm getting hungry."

Alex and Lauren looked at each other and began to laugh.

"The teenager's lament," Alex said. "You can never fill one up. See what you're getting into, Lauren?"

Lauren took a sudden interest in the TV and did not respond to Alex's question. John remained silent as well.

They were all saved any further awkwardness at that moment by the opening of the front door. Charlotte closed the door behind her and walked into the den.

* * *

Charlotte had to walk by the entrance to the hall that led to the bedrooms in order to get into the den. Her steps were tentative, but she continued forward. Everyone had fixed their eyes on her as she continued into the family room. A stranger might have concluded she had not been in this house before and now confronted a group of people she did not know. Charlotte looked at everyone in the room except Lauren. If the air in the room was heavy before, it was now solid lead.

"Hi, sweetheart," Alex said cheerily. "You girls see a movie?"

Dressed in jeans and a light blue windbreaker with penny loafers and white socks, Charlotte looked as though she couldn't make up her mind if she wanted to answer or not. She looked out the back window of the den at the darkening skies and then down at the carpet as she shifted her weight from one foot to the other.

"We went out to the mall, but there was nothing playing that any of us wanted to see, so we just hung out. It was kind of a drag," she offered with a sneering sigh that only seemed natural to a teenager.

"I'm afraid most movies are a drag these days, Charlotte," Lauren said. "Not many of them are memorable anymore." Lauren hesitated a second, "At least the ones I've seen the last few years."

Charlotte looked at Lauren for the first time since she entered the room. The look was not exactly disdainful, but more like the teen thought Lauren might have been speaking some foreign language she had never heard before. Then, suddenly, she spoke.

"You like movies, Ms. Marsh?"

Lauren was caught short, but recovered quickly.

"I love movies, Charlotte. I really like the old films like with Bette Davis or Humphrey Bogart...Clark Gable and Elizabeth Taylor. It just seems like they don't make then like that anymore." She paused. "Please, call me Lauren."

John and Alex then turned to look at Charlotte like they were watching a tennis match and the ball just went back into her court.

A tense silence lingered.

"Yeah, I like that guy on that old movie channel who talks about the movies and what was going on at the time with all the stars when the movie was made, like who hated who, or who was having an affair with who," Charlotte giggled as she talked.

"I know who you're talking about. I like him, too. Sometimes I just turn on that channel so I can hear what he says about the movie they're about to show, even if I really didn't want to see it."

Lauren started to giggle along with her.

John and his father were watching now as though they were hypnotized. Charlotte and Lauren had exchanged more conversation in the last minute or two than they had on all Lauren's previous visits to the Madison household. Father and son sat motionless and speechless.

"Why don't you come back to my room and I'll show you a book I found on the Internet. It's got a lot of pictures and stuff about Hollywood in the fifties. Maybe you can tell me about some of the ones I don't know about, like Marlon Brando or Joseph Cotten. I really like reading about that stuff."

Lauren now looked like she was hypnotized along with Alex and John. It took her a long moment, but she was finally able to answer.

"Sure, Charlotte. I would like that. We can let these guys watch a ball game or something boring like that," Lauren said and made a face at Alex as she got up from the couch and started toward Charlotte. The teenager just smiled as they both turned and headed back toward the hall and her bedroom.

"You girls don't go too far, now. We're going to have supper in a little while," Alex called after them.

"Right, dad," Charlotte said as the two rounded the corner and walked down the hall.

Alex just looked at John and both of them shrugged almost in unison.

"Dad, sometime I want you to tell me about girls," John said as a smile began to lighten his face.

"Son," Alex said as he took in a long, deep breath, "it would be a very short sermon."

It was quiet for a moment and then they both started laughing.

* * *

A man in a dark overcoat and fedora parked his car in the park next to the Potomac. The night was black with no moon and a bitter wind that was not strong, but biting. There were bare trees scattered on the expanse of snow covered ground next to the river. A long, more or less straight walkway stretched out and followed the course of the water. There was no one on it. That was likely due to the hour and the uninviting weather. It was almost ten thirty. It was also Sunday and most people would be home or elsewhere sitting by something to warm them. The traffic was light across the bridge over the river.

The man turned off the ignition and put the keys in his coat pocket as he stepped from the car and closed the door. There was a gazebo with benches just off the water. He looked at it, but walked slowly toward the nearby bridge and took the sidewalk up to the pedestrian walkway across the expanse of dark water. DC was well lighted at night, but it was still dark where he was walking.

The man walked about fifty yards or so onto the bridge and stopped with both hands in his pockets. There was no one else on the walkway on either side as far as he could see. The north wind bit at his face in little waves of discomfort. He stood motionless for a time as his gaze took in the city skyline with its familiar landmarks. For over two hundred years now, it was the symbol and citadel of the worst form of government in history, except for every other one created and put into practical use by mankind. Just thinking about that fact still caught in his throat and gave him a chill not related to the weather.

The man turned his eyes down to the rippling water below and took something from his right coat pocket. The dark metal of the pistol reflected only the barest bit of light in the cold night. He looked at the gun as he held it in his hand for a lingering moment, and then heaved it into the air. It tumbled through the blackness to the water below. He heard the sound as it hit the surface of the water. Then except for the nipping wind, it was quiet.

"I'm sorry, dad. I couldn't keep it any longer," he said as the wind subsided leaving everything deathly quiet for a few moments.

He then walked back to his car, got in, and drove home.

* * *

Lauren had stayed with Alex until Monday afternoon when he took her to catch her flight from DFW Airport. They had sat down on Sunday afternoon and dutifully informed John and Charlotte of their intent to marry. John was all smiles, while Charlotte just listened without much animation or comment. However, on Monday morning before she left for school, Charlotte took Lauren aside, hugged her warmly, and asked when she would be coming back. Lauren just looked at the teenager and smiled, but inside she felt like her heart might suddenly fly off to the moon or some other distant destination. There were some good things that came with having children, she thought, even if she would only be a step parent. Lauren didn't know how she could wait till the next day, at work, to tell Ann. When they arrived at the airport, Lauren kissed Alex tenderly at first and then pressed her lips against his as hard as she could. She squeezed him and put her cheek next to his and took in the lingering aroma of his cologne.

"I love you, doctor, I can't deny it," she said and smiled.

"I thought maybe you might, but then again, I'm a trained professional in these matters."

They both laughed like only those in love laugh when they're together. Lauren then headed for the metal detectors.

32

There was a scheduled meeting of the Healthcare Emergency Committee on Thursday of that week at ten in the morning. Most of the members were assembled at the appointed time, including Doctors Harris and Grant of Gardner Pharmaceuticals. By ten twenty, however, Congressman Branch had not made his appearance.

The meeting was held in the usual place and everyone in attendance was sitting around the large oblong table drinking coffee, talking quietly, or simply waiting. The gaiety of the celebratory meeting of a few months ago had vanished. It was replaced by anxiety and fear. The buzz of conversation was muted and the enthusiasm level of the attendees was hovering around zero on the Richter Scale. It was gray and raining outside and the leafless trees in view only added to the dismal tone of the occasion. Alex looked across the table at Lauren and Harold Janes and made a face that said he would rather be somewhere else—anywhere else. Even the two doctors from Gardner were uncharacteristically long faced.

Alex was about to get up when the door nearest the head of the table broke open with a cracking sound and Congressman Branch came striding into the room. The world-weary shuffle that had characterized his gait in recent weeks was not in evidence this day. He was standing tall, smiling, and looking every bit the confident politician he had been all his career. Taking his chair with his right hand, he pulled it back away from the table and sat down.

"Sorry, folks, I was delayed by a pesky reporter. Couldn't shake him." He surveyed those in attendance with a sweeping glance around the table and opened the floor for discussion.

There was none.

The solemn faced assembly just looked back at him wordlessly. Dr. Harris, whose face was usually animated with a ready plastic smile, was busy attending to one of his fingernails, while his associate, Dr. Grant, was engaged at that moment cleaning the lenses of her round framed eyeglasses with a tissue.

The congressman leaned back in his chair and sighed.

"I need some help here, folks. What do I tell the president?" he asked as his piercing glare swept around the table. The room continued in dull silence for a long, awkward time.

"Why don't you tell him to tell the American people the truth, sir? Tell them that we did this thing to ourselves."

The voice came from the far end of the table. Alex turned and looked, but couldn't tell who made the comment. He knew that it didn't really matter who said it; it was the truth and it was also what everybody around the table was thinking. By now, the meeting on that Saturday morning last spring was no longer a secret. Everyone including the press now knew, or had to know, what had really happened. There was no "military exercise" last June. That was now abundantly clear.

Congressman Branch glowered at the speaker and then looked down at his briefcase lying on the table in front of him. All eyes in the room had turned to him. He continued to stare at the tabletop in front of him as he made little circles with his forefinger on the black surface.

"People, I can't tell you how many nights these last few months I have pondered that very thing. I have spoken candidly to the president about it. I've come up with a million reasons and rationalizations about what was done and why it had to be done. We are now at a point where this thing is beyond the scope of careers and legal and moral culpability. The nation is going to be lost, and maybe the world with it, if we do not do something. My God, we must do something!"

Alex was stunned, along with everyone else at the table. Sherman Branch was no longer only a politician with immense power and well-earned and deserved respect; he was now just a man begging for some help from any quarter. He looked like a man who didn't know what else to do. There were no reporters, cameras, or any other audience to play to now, and it wouldn't have done any good if there were. There were only twenty or so souls in the room along with an abundance of deafening silence.

Then, there was a voice:

"We haven't heard from Gardner, sir. Is there anything that appears to be promising as far as an antidote?" Alex asked.

Alex's question seemed to break the tension in the room like brittle glass. There was suddenly the sound of shuffling feet and murmuring.

The congressman looked to his left at Dr. Harris who had stopped paring his fingernails, but now looked to be in a trance. Finally, Dr. Harris swallowed with some difficulty and tried to clear his throat. He then managed to begin speaking.

"We think we might have something that could be effective. We've only begun to do some testing. It's an unusual compound that likely would be lethal to humans if administered in its naturally occurring state. We're thinking that if it can be administered in another form and metabolized by the body into an isomer of the active compound, it could possibly reverse the paralysis and not harm the patient. Thus far, it's only a theoretical possibility, but it's all we've come up with at this point, sir. We've tried it with lab animals, and the compound shows promise."

The doctor fell back in his chair like he was out of breath from vigorous physical exercise.

The congressman just looked back at him for a moment before he spoke.

"Any other complicating factors, doctor?" Branch asked.

"None that we have encountered, sir, but our experience with this compound is limited to say the least."

The bespectacled Dr. Grant now came alive suddenly.

"It's a chemical that was identified from research on cancer-treating compounds. As you may know, cancer drugs are designed to kill cancer cells, or prevent them from growing. But it's hard to find a drug that just kills the abnormal cells. Often healthy cells are destroyed along with the malignant ones. The compound we're talking about now was discarded from cancer research because it proved to be fatal to most of those who took it. The initial research was hopeful, but then people began to die."

The big eyed, little girlish demeanor previously characteristic of this woman had disappeared, and she now appeared every bit the serious scientist she was.

"We've been trying a slightly different form of the molecule that we hope will be safe for people to take. We think this may work, sir."

She stopped speaking as suddenly as she had started and was now looking intently at the congressman whose stern glare had not changed.

"Then why the devil didn't you say something earlier when I asked for input? Were you going to keep it a secret?"

The congressman's voice got louder and more insistent when it finally got to "secret." He slammed his hand on the table as he finished his questions.

Dr. Grant leaned forward to speak, but Dr. Harris put his hand on her arm and looked at the congressman.

"That's my fault, Mr. Branch. We had discussed before the meeting whether or not to bring it up. We just didn't want to be premature, especially owing to the events of the past year. It was my decision, sir. We wanted to have more substantial data to bring to the committee."

Dr. Harris spoke out forthrightly in a manner not seen before in the meetings. There was none of the fawning tentativeness in his manner now.

Congressman Branch continued to sit motionless. He did not take his eyes off the two doctors from Gardner. No one in the room had seen in the congressman anything in the last year that would have qualified as an outburst of temper. He was often direct; he spoke his mind; but he had never approached volatility. It appeared like the congregation around the table had ceased breathing.

Congressman Branch then sat up straighter in his chair and took a breath.

"We're going to meet again next Thursday. By then I want some detailed information on this new drug and anything else you have going on over at Gardner. And I want some input from the rest of you as well. You're all here for a reason. That reason is that you are prominent in your fields. We cannot just sit by while this thing...this malady...destroys us all. We may have done it to ourselves. That's true. But if we did, we're going to do everything we can to undo it. Our country, our families, and yes, even our world, demand no less."

The congressman's words had not had time to die in the air when there was a rustling sound at the far end of the table. A man at the far end of the room had stood up and stepped up onto the table. He put his right hand in the pocket of his coat and took out a pistol which waved above his head. Everyone in the room became statues as the man took two steps forward on the table toward Congressman Branch. Alex recognized him as the psychiatrist who was also a researcher.

"This is all so much crap!" he screamed. "I could have told you long ago that Gardner couldn't come up with the answers to the crisis. You should have come to me!" The "me" rang out as he dragged the word on like the lyric of an angry song. "I could have given them to you! Everyone will die now because of this committee."

The room erupted from around the table as people dived on the floor and started to run for the doors. The man fired two shots into the ceiling which succeeded in freezing everyone once again. He then took another step forward and pointed the gun at Harold Janes who was still sitting in his chair, leaning forward as though he might get up. The pistol roared again and Harold was thrown back against his chair. The force of his body as it fell then rolled the chair back and he fell to one side on the carpet. Lauren who was sitting next to him was motionless except for the fact she had raised her hands in front of her as though she might be fending off a blow.

Alex was across the table from Harold and Lauren. He had turned away from the shooter as though by reflex, but when he saw that the man had fired at Harold, he sprang up on the table toward him.

The man stepped back as though startled and pointed the pistol as Alex.

"You can't stop me! You'll never stop me!" he screamed as he started to back away from Alex. He then suddenly put the gun to his temple with a gesture that looked like a salute. His eyes widened and he let out a horrific shriek as the pistol blared out again. Blood, bone, and brain matter gushed from his head as he fell over a chair and sprawled on the floor.

There were screams and more scrambling around the table. The pistol, having done its deadly work had fallen from the man's hand, clattered on top of the table, and bounced to the floor.

Alex was left standing on the table as he stared at the man's body which was now lying on the floor motionless. A spreading lake of blood surrounded his head and kept getting larger. Alex then turned and frantically began looking for Lauren. He saw her on the floor next to Harold. After he was shot and landed on the floor, Harold had tried to throw his body over Lauren who had crawled over to help him. Jumping off the table, Alex rushed over and put his hand on Harold's shoulder.

"Harold! Harold! Can you hear me? Where are you hit?" Alex shouted as most everyone else in the room was scrambling toward the doors. As Alex turned Harold over and off of Lauren, he could see the red stains on Harold's shirt high on his left shoulder and just down from his neck. Alex put his hand on the wound and pressed.

"I'm alright, Dr. Madison. I think the bullet went straight on through," Harold said as he was trying to get up.

"Don't try and get up, the medics will be here soon," Alex said as he kept pressure on the wound.

Lauren had recovered enough to throw her arms around Alex's neck as he was tending to Harold.

"Alex! Alex! Are you alright?" she screamed.

"Yes, baby. Yes, I'm fine. The man's dead. He killed himself. He must have been psychotic."

Just then, as members of the committee were furiously trying to get out, several men in dark suits came rushing in with weapons drawn. Most everyone had vacated the room except for Alex, Harold, Lauren, and the dead man. It was then that a host of paramedics dressed in dark blue pants and white shirts hurried in carrying black bags. One of them came briskly over to Harold and knelt down beside him.

"It's a gunshot wound just above his clavicle at the base of his neck. There's not much bleeding, I don't think any major vessels are involved. It may be a through and through wound," Alex reported to the somewhat surprised young man who replaced Alex's hand with his own and began to examine Harold.

"Thank you, sir, I'll take over now," he said as another paramedic arrived. "You've been a great help, sir."

Alex and Lauren then watched as the medics put Harold on a gurney and wheeled him out the door and down the hall. It was then that it occurred to Alex he had not seen Congressman Branch since the melee started. As far as he knew, Harold and the shooter were the only two casualties of the incident, but he might have been mistaken. The man fired several other shots before he turned the gun on himself. Alex also wondered why the man had not shot him, too. At the moment, he was just as glad not to know.

Alex also thought that when he got back home and John asked him if he was on the news, he would have something to tell him.

* * *

Neither one had a really good reason for it, but after the meeting, Alex and Lauren decided to go back to Texas together. Lauren was feeling some guilt about it, but Harold's injuries turned out not to be serious and his wife told her he would only be in the hospital a day or two at most. So, she decided to take some vacation days and planned to be back for the meeting on Thursday of the next week. She wondered if any of the committee members would be returning at all after what had happened. But Lauren also knew that the crisis in the country and, indeed the world had not changed because some lunatic had shot up the conference room and killed himself in the process.

Also, the press was going to have open season on politicians and all the members of the Healthcare Committee especially after this latest array of current events. But she thought it ironic that the press would be calling for blood when the future of the country and the world had fallen in serious doubt. If no one was to survive this creeping degeneration of mankind, who would they blame then?

Congressman Branch tried to calm the waters by stating the events of the last meeting of the committee were orchestrated by a sick, deluded person and did not represent the abilities or the intent of the committee's work. And that the Healthcare Committee would continue and not be deterred from its purpose.

But it seemed to many at least, that the Armageddon foretold millennia in the past was now at hand.

* * *

Lauren was looking forward to spending more time with Charlotte. The change in the climate of their relationship the previous week had caught her by surprise, and Lauren wanted to build on it. She also liked the idea of practicing being a wife and mother for a few days, too. Alex had told her that he was hoping they could be married in the spring or summer, depending on what might happen in their uncertain world at any moment. And the uncertainty was not just in the world; Lauren was excited about it all, but she was not without worry. When relationships that had begun in the flames of love cooled and headed south, she knew that there were few, if any, more painful or unhappy events in life.

But she also knew that when they had the fever, lovers never gave that any meaningful thought.

Ann's barely concealed skepticism when they talked of such things stood out in Lauren's mind, but she also was content to write that off to the recent dissolution of her friend's marriage. Lauren also took solace in the knowledge that her friendship with Ann was one of the never changing, unshakable, unsinkable facets of her life, and perhaps her proudest possession. Whatever happened, good or evil, ecstatic or painful, Ann would be there. Lauren really couldn't say that about anyone else in her life, except now for Alex. Now, she could count herself twice blessed.

Alex had been in her life only a short time, but Lauren knew he was the one. She knew it in the same way she knew Ann was her friend forever; the same way she knew her father loved her even though he rarely said so; the same way she knew that some people were innately good and others were not. She knew it like she knew that the freshening coolness of the September air would soon make the trees start undressing themselves for the fall. These were things she knew with unchallenged certainty that were so much easier to feel than to say.

It was no mystery to her why Maria had fallen in love with Alex and bore him two children. Lauren did not know Maria, but she knew why she had loved Alex. He was just a man, it was true, but he was a man whose compass was fixed on true north. Lauren knew as surely as spring followed winter that she would never have reason to doubt him. Whatever might happen tomorrow, Lauren knew that when she finally repeated, "for better or for worse," it really would be that way. It would be something she would not regret.

As they drove toward home in the cool evening, Lauren's mind was swimming with these thoughts as she put her head on Alex's shoulder. The flight to Texas was tiring, but she was glad to be where she was right then. Tomorrow was Friday, and they would have a whole week together.

33

The contentment some people may feel in their lives at any one moment in time may not be in concert with the goings on in the world around them. The fact is that there might be no connection in reality whatever between them. Whether this was true of anyone else, it was certainly true of Alex and Lauren. While they drank in the joy of the union between them and shared a growing love and respect for one another, the fortunes of the world around them continued a precipitous decline.

Hospitals were now past capacity with debilitated patients who for all intents and purposes could not be helped. More were dying now than before, and there was no indication of any likely change. American society was now at a juncture that was more potentially destructive and tragic than at any time in its two hundred plus year lifespan. The country was not, however, at risk from any political or sociological ideology that threatened to bring it to collapse. It was dying because it could not move. America could not walk, and in some cases could not breathe either. Not being able to walk was severe enough, but like most forms of life, if the country could not breathe, it would die.

Industry was now approaching a standstill. Many companies were working with skeleton crews to provide necessary services and goods. The American economy was subsidized at every level by the government in Washington to avoid complete collapse. Those who could work, worked around the clock with no assurance they would be paid. In the large population centers, lawlessness and looting began to appear which the dwindling law enforcement presence could not begin to engage, much less control. It would only be a matter of time before anarchy would be the prevailing form of government in the United States of America. The president, Congress, and even the military could only look on helplessly. The only solace that was apparent was that if the paralysis felled everyone, there would be no one left to break the law and cause havoc in the streets. That, however, was cold comfort indeed.

* * *

Ironically, Lauren was as happy as she had ever been in her life. Probably more so. She told herself she could not remember a time when she took such sheer joy just in living or knew such contentment. She had never seen herself as domestic, but here she was, getting Alex and the two teenagers up and off to work and school each morning as she cooked and cleaned and shopped and fussed over all of them. If John and Charlotte were uncomfortable with her being there, they didn't show it. And Alex just smiled and helped her any way he could despite the fact that he was away from home most of the time.

Lauren sat with Charlotte on the swing by the lake in the late afternoons talking about whatever drifted into their minds —which was usually plenty and varied. The frightening, conflicting, emotionally imprisoning reality of her mother's death that had stifled her silently for the past year now found its way into words. Somehow in being with Lauren, her internal resistances had been overridden. She wasn't sure how or why, but it was now safe for her feelings to find their way out of her heart. This stranger she had seen as only trying to steal away her father was now becoming an ally. What surprised her most of all, though, was that she felt her mother would see Lauren that way, too. It would be Ok. There would be no betrayal of her memory. Charlotte knew she needed to let her mother go, but she was also beginning to understand she did not have to somehow fool herself into pretending that she had never existed.

Lauren was not sure when she and Charlotte had crossed that unseen line, but she knew they had. Sometimes she felt as though her growing love for this girl would burst from her breast. It was a feeling she had long abandoned any hope of experiencing. To Lauren, it was what she imagined a woman must feel when she had given birth.

John had always enjoyed Lauren's company and continued to do so. They seldom talked of weighty matters; the unspoken bond between them was sufficient for both.

The dismal state of affairs in the country had no bearing on the comings and goings at the Madison household as far as any outside observer could tell. Their world was insular; their lives were real; but they were still connected.

The mayhem outside the residence was another matter, however. They did not speak it aloud, but they were all afraid.

* * *

Although it would only be a week between meetings of the Healthcare Emergency Committee, it was beginning to look like the country would not survive even that short time span. More and more were falling prey to the paralysis as the wheels of the nation were slowing, and it would not be long before they squealed to a stop altogether. It was a state of emergency the president could only talk about on TV. There was no solution he could offer. To his credit, he tried to be reassuring, but he could offer nothing of substance. The country knew his words were hollow, although well intended, but no one could present any alternatives. By this time, the vice president had been felled by the paralysis, as had about half the members of congress. The only wheels of government that were turning were the ones on the chairs of some of the nation's lawmakers who now needed them for mobility. The military was not spared. The number of able bodied personnel was dwindling daily. The titan that had been the beacon of the free world was being reduced to a helpless invalid.

* * *

It was Tuesday and Lauren and Alex would be leaving for Washington on Wednesday afternoon. Lauren had been up early even after she and Alex had spent half the night rolling in the hay in ecstasy. She was officially ensconced in the guest bedroom, but usually made an entrance into Alex's bed around midnight each night. They both knew they were fooling no one, but somehow it seemed the only proper thing they could really do. Lauren was always up before everyone in the morning and made sure her bed looked slept in. She knew that some aspects of her moral code of conduct were difficult to simply abandon no matter the circumstances. If you had to create an illusion to maintain it, so be it. At least it felt better that way and she could live with it. Despite the mores of a liberated world, it still seemed an unpardonable transgression to simply throw everything she valued to the wind.

Everyone was gone now to work or school. It was about nine thirty and Lauren was sitting in the swing by the lake which had become the favored meeting place for her and Charlotte. She was in her favorite cotton jogging suit and sneakers. Under the jacket which was now zipped, she had on a long sleeved jersey. The whole ensemble, to her, was the embodiment of comfort. Her thick hair was pulled back and tied in a ponytail, which always made her feel younger. The calendar had just turned a page to March and it was cool in the mornings.

An assortment of ducks was making their way toward her across the water. They climbed on the bank and waddled in her direction. They then muttered and squawked a bit at her feet until they were convinced she had nothing to feed them at which time they headed back to the water and paddled toward another part of the small lake.

It looked to be a pleasant day; the sun was bright and there was a steady breeze out of the south coming toward her across the water. There were some white clouds on the eastern horizon that looked like they had been produced by some large explosion that had now turned into white flowering smoke. They looked to

Lauren like clouds did when they might turn dark and produce storms. But, at the moment anyway, they were white and shimmering in the morning sunlight.

Lauren smiled as she watched the small ripples on the lake as it was touched by the wind. Right at that moment, and despite the disastrous state of the world, she was not worrying about those things for which she knew she had no solution. She tried to pray for God's intervention, but she couldn't find any words that did not sound selfish and self-serving. Perhaps He would take that into account and listen.

In the past week, Lauren had listened to Charlotte as she revealed every concern, fear, hope, expectation, and wish of her short life. The two of them laughed, cried, worried, and fretted together as both the teenager and the mature woman shared their worlds and happily found there was a place for each in the other's. Lauren took great satisfaction in thinking of those things.

What of the world, though? she thought. *What if this all doesn't last? What then?*

There was no answer and she knew it. There never really was an answer even when the world was "normal," as if it ever really was.

Lauren gritted her teeth. She had done it. On this beautiful morning, she had given herself something else to worry about.

Par for the course, she thought.

Lauren smiled and began shaking her head. She slowly got up from the swing and started across the lawn to the house, breathing in the coolness of the morning. But after only a few steps, she felt a strange numbness in her legs as though they were no longer part of her body. They were still moving, but they felt like they were getting heavier with each step. Suddenly, her left leg gave way and she began to fall forward. She had that helpless feeling like she was a toppling tree as her body hurtled unhindered down to the ground. Despite her free fall, Lauren had managed to extend her hands in front of her which blunted the full force of her body's impact on the lawn. But she still hit face down with a jarring jolt. The aroma of the grass that had been recently mowed filled her nostrils as she lay still. Her first impulse was to draw her knees up so she could push herself up with her hands and regain her feet. There was one problem—she could not move her legs.

"Oh, no," she pleaded as she buried her face in the cool grass. "Not me, too. Not now."

* * *

Every day there were more changes. It was a matter of more and less, actually. There were more people in the hospitals and less on the streets and at the workplace. More people could not walk and less people could. More people were having trouble breathing and fewer people were breathing normally. More people were getting sick and fewer people were staying well. It was like a giant scale in which the abnormal was beginning to outweigh the normal.

It had become useless for Alex to go his office, as only a patient or maybe two could make it in on a given day. Besides, he was there by himself now as Emily had been taken down with the paralysis only the week before. She had fallen from her chair and could not get up from the waiting room floor until she had yelled loud enough for him to hear her. Alex then called her husband who came immediately to get her, and they were off to the hospital— even if there wasn't much that could be done there. Emily had even tried to make a joke as Alex helped her into her husband's car, but the fear in her eyes was evident enough.

If he had ever felt helpless as a doctor, he never felt it more acutely as he watched Emily and her husband drive away. It was true that Alex took Emily for granted almost every day of their association in the years they worked together. But he consoled himself with the thought that it was only because she was so much a part of him and his professional life. It sounded hollow now as he thought of it, but there was really no other way to think of her. She was part of him; he could not imagine his world without her. Alex now felt foolish that somehow he expected he could keep his own feelings out of their relationship. Somehow, his emotions always found him out.

With Emily gone and his office work almost nonexistent, Alex then had been going to the hospital to help in any way he could. This transition began to make him feel like a "real" doctor again, as he was taking histories and doing physical exams and screening patients for admission. There were still those patients who had other illnesses besides the paralysis that needed attention. The regular hospital staff doctors were inundated with work and were glad to see him there. He was given temporary admitting privileges by the hospital administration as well. Some of the other psychiatrists in the area had also begun showing up to help. Alex was glad to see that, as he knew that psychiatrists were sometimes viewed by the primary care physicians as second and third tier specialists that had little, if anything, of value to offer the practice of medicine.

Although he tried not to let this bother him, Alex also knew that some "real" doctors were defensive because they were afraid of psychiatry. They were also afraid of their own feelings, and like many whose personalities could be declared obsessive compulsive, were the world champions at ignoring them. Psychiatry was a constant reminder that people were not just flesh, bone, and physiological functions and could not be explained in only those terms. Good doctors knew those things if they knew anything about people at all.

Alex also knew that after the patient had been examined, probed, cut on, and sewed up, the "real" doctors were only too glad to hand them over to the psychiatrist for treatment if they didn't have anything else that could be repaired by the laying on of healing hands. Most of them wanted little to do with treating depression, anxiety, and any other emotional ills that could not be done away with a pill or a scalpel.

But despite their failings and foibles, doctors were human beings and most of them had a genuine desire to help their patients. The pay was usually good, but the hours were long and the responsibilities were staggering. They never seemed to stop grumbling about government meddling and tiresome interference from the insurance companies, but most of them kept on working although they labored in a country that was supposed to have a free enterprise economic system. However, now physicians often found themselves with their hands tied and reduced to the rank of indentured servitude. If the truth were to be told, there had been a crisis in the healthcare system in America long before the advent of this latest epidemic. But, right at the moment, no one was much concerned about the politics of the matter. Concerns of that nature had fallen by the wayside with the growing, unceasing tide of desperate, helpless people whose thoughts and emotions now turned to their own mortality.

* * *

Ballantines was located only a short walk from the Capitol and was frequented by a good many of the veteran politicos in Washington after hours. It was an elegant place—quiet, reserved, with dark wood-paneled walls and large, comfortable booths. The tables were generous in size with teakwood tops surrounded by chairs with curved arms and seats covered with rich, dark leather. It wasn't a private establishment, but it might as well have been as the Maître D was quite selective in who was seated. Even new members of Congress usually needed an introduction before they were granted entry. It was strictly off limits to members of the press. For that and other reasons, *Ballantines* became something of a haven for lawmakers in DC who didn't want to be bothered during a quiet dinner or drink. Hungry members of the press corps could sometimes be seen outside on the sidewalk hoping to catch someone coming out or going in and force him or her into an interview.

On any given evening, *Ballantines* was usually busy and filled near capacity. On this particular evening, however, fewer than half the tables and booths were occupied. It was quiet and the usual lively hum of conversation was muted. Even the waiters who were always attentive and moving with alacrity seemed to be in another, slower gear as they moved among the tables.

In one of the booths along a long wall of rich paneling two men sat with drinks on the table in front of them. Both men looked to be of a similar age; both dressed in suits; both looked serious and mirthless.

"Did you think we would've ended up here, Harold?" one asked. "In Washington?" as he drained his glass and motioned to a waiter. "Or maybe a better question would be, if we would end up like this, going out with a whimper instead of in a hail of bullets or the blast of an exploding mortar in Viet Nam?"

The waiter nodded and disappeared only to shortly reappear with another glass filled with ice floating in a golden colored liquid. He placed it on the table in front of the congressman.

"Thanks, Eddie," the congressman said.

The two men seated in the booth just continued to look at each other for a while with their hands encircling their drinks.

"Jesus, Sherman, you ask the damndest questions," the other man replied. "But I know what you're getting at. It has been a long road. We both could've had our asses shot off or blown to bits in 'Nam, but we didn't. Now we're here and it looks like we're going to lay down and die like lambs without firing a shot at the enemy." He looked down at his glass and then took a long drink from it. "Maybe if we knew who or what the enemy was, we could shoot at it."

Harold Janes then just shook his head.

"I guess that's what my English teacher would call irony—I don't think I ever quite understood the concept until now. Maybe that's the best way to describe my life—ironic." The politician sighed and started on his fresh scotch.

"When that lunatic pointed that automatic at me the other day and fired, I thought my ticket had been punched right there," Harold Janes said as he swirled what remained of the drink in his glass. "Two tours of duty in Viet Nam without as much as a cut finger, and then I get waxed by some nutcase of a doctor in the Capitol Building. Now, that's irony!"

"You feeling Ok, Harold?" the congressman asked.

"Just sore. I'm taking antibiotics and the doctors tell me I'm healing well."

"The security people still don't know how he got that gun past the detectors. They're thinking he may have had an accomplice, or accomplices."

"The enemy is getting harder to see, Sherman" Harold said as he drained his glass. "Evil never sleeps...I'm just glad the son of a bitch couldn't shoot worth a damn."

The congressman just looked back across the table.

"Indeed, Harold...indeed."

Another silence passed between the two as they both lost eye contact and fumbled with their drink glasses.

"You want to hear something else ironic?" Congressman Branch asked.

"You're the politician, Sherman, you make the speeches. I just listen."

The congressman's eyes narrowed as he looked at his lifelong friend.

"Three weeks ago, Harold, I was sitting in my study at home with my father's Luger in my hand listening to Beethoven on a Saturday afternoon. Marian was gone to Jennifer's and it was snowing outside. I had decided that it would be my last Saturday afternoon in this vale of tears." He paused and drank again from his glass. "I had never before thought of suicide, Harold. Those kinds of thoughts were for those who were cowardly and couldn't deal with life—losers. But, somehow things began to all make sense to me. Life had turned out to be a joke—I had turned into a joke—everything I stood for and tried to do was a joke. And then it seemed to follow that death was the ultimate joke. It was the only thing that made any sense to me."

Harold Janes just stared into his friend's eyes trying not to betray the surprise that jolted him.

"I couldn't lift that gun up to my head, Harold. I wanted to, but I couldn't. My hand wouldn't move. I know it sounds crazy. I was prepared to die. I was not afraid, but I couldn't make my hand and arm move."

The congressman looked past his friend as though his could see something in the blackness of the night outside the restaurant. He then emerged from his momentary absence of mind to face his friend.

"You know what I thought about, Harold?" He paused and looked into his friend's eyes. Not waiting for an answer, he continued. "I didn't think of Marian; I didn't think of Jennifer and the girls; I didn't think of my country and how it needed me still—all the things I love and have lived for and still do. But, I thought that if I raised that pistol to my head and fired it as I fully intended to do, I would never hear Beethoven again. I didn't know if I would go to heaven or hell, but I would never hear those beautiful strains of his glorious music again. That man who had composed the most haunting, exciting, exquisite music the world had ever heard despite being profoundly deaf. Now that is a happenstance thick with irony, Harold. The world's greatest composer who could not actually hear the music he had written. And if I could never hear it again, it would have been a needless, unnecessary, and unpardonable tragedy."

He lifted his glass and drank from it.

"Someday I will die, Harold. But it will not be by my own hand. I will let God decide when."

The two men studied each other without any more words passing between them—they were no longer looking away. There was no reason to.

A faint smile appeared on Harold Janes's face as he lifted his glass and the two friends drank together.

34

The changing face of the country was beginning to be apparent everywhere. There were vehicles abandoned on the streets, highways, and Interstates. Piles of uncollected bags of garbage cluttered the streets. The sanitary services were still operational, but at their own schedule which basically amounted to when there were personnel available to drive the trucks and make the runs. Those were the things that were always taken for granted and basically invisible during times when life was in its usual state of functional dysfunction and when the human race was not being threatened by extinction.

To say it was becoming unsafe to venture forth on the streets alone or even in groups was to beg the obvious. It was also true, however, that the paralysis was unblinking in selecting its victims, so the lawless and the law abiding were at equal risk. It appeared that the righteous and the unrighteous were affected without prejudice. The only emerging truth from this unwelcome metamorphosis was that the country was beginning to look like a frightful, desolate vision of a cataclysmic future in some horror movie. The only things missing were the zombies, werewolves, and vampires.

* * *

Alex wasn't sure what time it was. He had left his watch at home and there was no clock on the wall he could see. In fact, time had become something of a vague, meaningless notion for him. If not completely lost, at least unnoticed and/or unheeded for the most part. He stopped for a moment and looked out one of the windows of the emergency room area and was greeted by part of a blue sky and an oak tree with its budding leaves bathed in sunlight. At least he knew it was still daytime. His thoughts were drifting toward making the trip back to Washington for the committee meeting tomorrow. He got a queasy feeling in his gut when he thought of the wild eyed doctor standing just a few feet from him on the table the previous meeting. He now understood how those who survived violent episodes could have longstanding problems afterward. Going back to Washington would be a welcome break even if he took no real pleasure or joy in his attendance. The reluctant announcement by the people from Gardner last week was at the very least a narrow shaft of light in a current world of darkness.

For a moment, Alex didn't realize he was standing statue-like in the middle of the hall looking out the window. He didn't feel particularly tired, but he hadn't had any lunch and had been seeing patients without a break since he had arrived before eight. As he turned to look back down the hall, he noticed that the hallway was filling up from the other end with gurneys occupied by new patients. All the examining rooms were full and patients were now being seen wherever they were. There was no privacy to speak of and confidentiality was only some theoretical concept. Not that anyone was bringing a complaint. It would have served no purpose. There was crying and screaming to be sure, but the treating staff had no time to hear it.

As he walked down the hall and reached the point where the line of gurneys started, Alex was heading toward the triage desk to see where he might begin work. As he passed between the rows of patient carts, a hand reached out and touched his arm. He turned his head and was suddenly transfixed.

The hand that stopped him belonged to Lauren.

No words came out of him; no thoughts entered or left his mind; Alex simply stood and stared the stare of the disbelieving. Lauren tried to smile, but mostly failed. She did manage a self-conscious half grin as she tried to speak. No words would come from her either. Alex finally broke the bonds of his own momentary paralysis and grabbed her; holding her close to him, he then lifted her up from the gurney like a helpless doll. She wrapped her arms around him and the two were locked in a desperate, suffocating embrace. Time took no notice of their shared intimacy in the noisy hall. Neither one spoke; they just clung to each other as Lauren softly cried.

"What happened?" Alex asked.

"I fell in the yard and couldn't get up," Lauren replied. "I just laid there until your neighbor happened into his backyard and saw me. He called the ambulance."

The two were still clinging to one another as they spoke.

"I don't know how long I was there on the ground before he found me. I tried to crawl but I couldn't. Oh, Alex! I thought I was going to die right there on the grass! I was afraid no one would come." She burrowed her face into his chest and sobbed.

"Well, you're here now, baby. Can you move your legs?"

"No, they're like dead weights. I'm helpless and it's horrible, Alex! I'm scared!"

Lauren squeezed him tighter, and he could feel the rhythm of her shaking sobs on his chest. The clamor of suffering and alarm had all but disappeared in the crowded hallway for both of them. It felt like they were alone, but they were not lonely.

* * *

Flights into and out of DFW Airport were spotty and unpredictable at best now as Alex made his way through the terminal toward his gate. The crowds were smaller than usual, but people were rushing, hurried, and impatient as always. Security was lax now as well, which Alex considered a mixed blessing. He could only hope he would be able to get to Washington without incident. He was tired and not at all sure that his presence at the meeting would actually make any difference.

Lauren had been admitted to a ward in the hospital. It was makeshift and crowded, but they had made room for her. Alex had seen to that. Charlotte and John were both upset and wanted to see

Lauren right away. They came the afternoon she was admitted, and Charlotte didn't want to leave her. It was all Alex and John could do to get her to go home with them that evening. Grace had agreed to come and look after the teenagers after Alex left for Washington the next day. Alex didn't want to leave Lauren, either, but he was now more desperate than ever to see what Gardner had come up with that might be helpful or even curative. The stakes had grown astronomically high for him now. He had been a mere spectator before, but now he was a full participant in this unspeakable tragedy. His hands were now bloody.

* * *

Despite some problems getting a taxi out of the airport in Washington, Alex did make the meeting on time. He went directly to Harold Janes and after first inquiring about his health, told him about Lauren. Alex had heard of the "thousand yard stare" that combat veterans were subject to after extensive, unyielding experience on the battlefield, and there was no mistaking it in Harold's eyes when he talked of Lauren. She was under his command, and she had gone down on his watch. Harold didn't have to say it; Alex understood all too clearly. Even though Alex had no military experience or training, it was like the two men were now brothers in arms.

Congressman Branch filed in and commenced the meeting without fanfare. He looked directly at the two doctors from Gardner Pharmaceutical. There was no mistaking his agenda and everyone around the table knew it. Tension settled over the room like a morning frost and was just as chilling. There was no conversation around the table; it was quiet like death was quiet.

What was different at this meeting was there were security officers everywhere in the halls and several standing around the periphery of the conference room. Alex couldn't help but feel it was overkill and spooky.

"There's no reason to go into any detail about the events of last week," the congressman said. "The doctor was a misguided lunatic. Might as well call a spade a spade. We can only take some measure of comfort in the fact that Mr. Janes was not seriously injured and could be with us today."

Alex smiled to himself at the congressman's candor.

"We will now hear from Dr. Harris."

The doctor from Gardner did not stand, but suddenly began speaking as he looked into the unblinking eyes of Sherman Branch.

"We've only had a week, but here it is."

He cleared his throat, but spoke with confidence and clarity.

"We have isolated a compound that we think will arrest the paralytic symptoms we've been seeing and reverse them."

It was now like a sudden rumbling of a waterfall as the dozen or so people around the table awoke from their trances and began to gasp and mumble. Congressman Branch put up his hand and quiet returned.

"I can't speak with confidence. Much of what I'm saying is conjectural. If the circumstances were anything like normal, we would need to do extensive research and testing, but the circumstances are anything but normal." Dr. Harris paused. "Please don't ask me a lot of questions as I won't have the answers. The main issue we have is how to administer the compound. We can't give it by mouth since it's too dangerous and potentially lethal to go through the GI tract. We also have ruled out an intravenous route. It's also dangerous to administer it that way. Our best hope is to give it in an aerosol form similar to the way we distributed the Dynasane last year."

At that point, the murmuring and muttering started again and most everyone began to squirm in their chairs.

"You mean we're going to have to spray the whole country again?" one of the other doctors on the committee asked.

"If we're going to administer this compound to the nation, yes," Dr. Harris answered. "But it will need to be in a different way this time. This chemical compound is so unstable that it cannot be put in pressurized canisters like the Dynasane. It will need to be stored in a hard crystalline form and then exploded in the air sort of like fireworks over a wide area. It will then be dispersed by the air. It's the only way we have been able to determine that it can be distributed across the country and be effective. Trying to give it to each affected individual would be hopelessly expensive and impractical. And, ladies and gentlemen, we don't know if it will work or not. We think so, but there's no way we can be sure without time-consuming tests."

Dr. Harris held the questioner in a riveting stare as he spoke.

The murmuring stopped and there was silence again.

"What makes you think it will work, Dr. Harris?" Alex asked.

Without coughing, blinking, or hesitating, Dr. Harris continued.

"We've tried it on five volunteers in our research facility. Four of them recovered completely in two days' time and one died. The subject who died had other complications than the paralysis and likely died because of them. He had terminal cancer and pulmonary complications. He had volunteered as a last hope of survival and to participate in the trials. The man was one of our lead researchers and well aware of the risks. He insisted on being a volunteer."

The small complement of humanity sitting around the table suddenly became mute and still. Alex couldn't believe what he had just heard.

"The others are doing well?" Congressman Branch asked.

"Yes, sir. They all work for us and are back at their jobs," Dr. Harris answered with more than a bit of pride in his voice.

The congressman sat back in his chair and continued to look at Dr. Harris before he finally spoke.

"How soon to prepare this stuff for distribution?"

"If we begin right away, about ten days, sir."

"Dr. Harris, you had best get to it, sir," Branch added.

"There is one important caveat, sir," Dr. Harris replied.

The chairman just stared at him.

"There may be a number of people in the country who cannot metabolize the preparation due to their body's particular chemical makeup. Some may die. There's no way of telling how many might be affected. However, the potential for recovery in the vast majority of the affected population is great."

The two men continued to stare at each other without speaking.

"What are you calling this stuff?" Branch then asked.

"No name sir, just GRD 21. It was the twenty first preparation that we tried."

"Let's hope it's the one our nation needs," the congressman replied as he closed his briefcase.

* * *

There was a hard knot in Alex's stomach as he stared out the window of the jetliner with eyes that gathered light but a brain that had no abiding interest in what it was beholding. It appeared that the big jet was flying just above a floor made up of white clouds that looked like they might have been white cobblestones. He wondered what it would be like to be able to walk out across that vast expanse some thirty thousand feet above the earth. Just a few inches of plastic and metal separated him from seeing if he could. It was one of those miracles of aviation that Alex didn't completely comprehend—how a human being could be safely ensconced in a pressurized cocoon so far up in the sky that the air was too thin to breathe and live to tell about it afterwards. At least that was the hoped-for result. He knew it did not always end up that fortunately for some.

But the not always reassuring physical laws of nature and man's command of them were not the reason for the discomfort in Alex's gut. The constellation of emotions stirring in him now had been set in motion at the meeting. Could he dare believe that there might be a healing for this now worldwide scourge? It seemed that only a fool of the first rank would contemplate such an outcome; yet, that possibility is what had fallen on his ears just a few hours before. Could it be that the world would be able to dodge Armageddon for the second time in just a couple of years? Of course the first salvation had led to a worse damnation despite all the well-intended efforts that had been mustered against an unseen monster.

A wave of guilt began to wash over Alex as he thought of and Lauren and himself. They were just two people in the great sea of lives that had been upended by this cataclysm. Many had already died and had no chance of recovery even if that possibility should now exist for those who remained. Who was he to ask for some special dispensation for himself and those dear to him? Life and fate and happenstance and every other circumstance of what transpired on this fragile ball flying through space defied any explanation or meaning, or so it seemed to him now. How he wished he had more faith. But he was no different than anyone else. He wanted Lauren to live; he wanted Charlotte and John to live; he wanted to live.

There was no mystery to it.

* * *

When the meeting had broken up, Alex had hurried to bid farewell to Congressman Branch. He had made it a point to catch him before he got out the door of the meeting room. The congressman was gracious as always, but their eyes fixed on each other's and lingered a bit as they said goodbye. The finality of the moment was hanging heavily in the air. Neither could possibly know if and when they might meet again. The arrangements for the distribution of the GRD 21 would be left to Gardner and the military and carried out as soon as possible.

Harold Janes pressed Alex's hand more firmly than he usually did as they bid each other goodbye. His knitted brow and the narrowed look in his eyes were not lost on Alex. They walked different directions down the hallway as they parted.

There were no celebrations at the close of the meeting which everyone mostly assumed would be the last of the committee—as Congressman Branch had put it, "for an indeterminate time." The gathering just dissolved and those who had attended just dissipated with it.

* * *

The DFW Airport, which had always been alive with masses of people and busy with airline traffic, was beginning to take on the look of a once-thriving enterprise that had fallen on hard times. It was sort of like a shopping mall that had been vibrant with crowds and commerce but was becoming something like a ghost town where the people who used to frequent it had taken themselves and their dollars elsewhere. Many arrival and departure gates were closed and unused, and there were rows and rows of planes parked in neat order in certain areas of the airfield. Planes that were sitting there waiting to go somewhere, but with little likelihood of that happening. There were still places to go, but no passengers to take to them.

Alex was trying to think back a year or so to remember if things had seemed so bad during the previous crisis, and concluded that they hadn't. He had never seen anything like this. If Gardner could not get things ready for ten days, there might be no one left to save. It puzzled him how, if everyone in North America had been doused with the Dynasane at virtually the same time, why did they not come down with the paralysis at the same time? It was a queer thing, but he wrote it off to the differences in people and their physiology. Perhaps the researchers knew, but he doubted it. At best it was a moot point now. At any rate, he was just interested in getting to the hospital to see Lauren.

* * *

It was almost seven when Alex arrived. The emergency room was overrun with patients and running out of room to put them. He took little notice but immediately made his way up to Lauren's room—or at least the room that Lauren was sharing with about six other patients. It was a room designed for two patients. The beds were jammed inside the small space with just barely enough room for someone to get in between them. Makeshift curtains had been erected to create some semblance of privacy, but for all practical purposes, there was none. The stale air mingled with the usual medicinal aromas that hospital rooms always emanated, along with the distinctive stench of urine, feces, and other unmistakable essences produced by human beings—especially sick human beings.

Waves of repulsion, disgust, and unwelcome memories began to rise in Alex's chest. It put him in mind of his experiences working at the Tarrant County Jail. He had worked some shifts in the infirmary during his year of internship at St. Bartholomew's Hospital in Ft. Worth. Drunks, derelicts, hardened criminals, psychotics, and sociopaths who would kill their cell mates for a package of cigarettes were all in attendance at that county sponsored institution where many of them needed medical care from time to time. For the most part, this was the disenfranchised of humanity with little remnant of humanity left in them. They would urinate on each other in the holding cells, fight incessantly, and do whatever else they could to be transferred to the infirmary where they were isolated from the other inmates. Except for the occasional college kid who ended up there for getting drunk and disorderly, they were mostly those who had little contact with polite society except to rob, murder, and create whatever mayhem they could in the world. They were patients seldom seen by well-to-do physicians.

Had it not been for the fact that he and Maria were so broke when he was an intern, Alex would have just as soon skipped the experience altogether. But intern's pay in those days was at slave labor levels, and Maria was working as a teacher at a small independent school district outside of Ft. Worth, which did not pay much better. Most of the interns he knew worked outside jobs to make extra money. It was called "moonlighting" or "working on the farm." Most all his contemporaries interned either for the money or the clinical experience, or both. Somehow, though, Alex had never thought he would have occasion to think of it again. It was the kind of experience that was invaluable, but most doctors would just as soon have wanted to stay in the past.

Young physicians did that kind of duty because they knew that it would serve them well. There were others, though, who truly had altruistic goals for their careers. They wanted to help their fellow man and ease his suffering. They really wanted to find a cure for cancer. It wasn't that the rest didn't want to help others, but most realized that after their training, there were rewards waiting. Everybody knew that all doctors eventually got rich, didn't they? They just had to do a few years of indentured servitude and the rest would be streets paved with gold. Or, so the myth of medical practice in America had told them.

Alex never thought he would find a cure for cancer, but he did want to learn to help his patients. As he thought back on his career, he knew he had no reason to complain. There were some medical specialties that allowed their practitioners to earn millions. Psychiatry, however, was near the bottom of the pay scale. That had never bothered Alex. He made a good living. There were no streets of gold, but he could take good care of his family and have pretty much what he wanted in life. If he had one remaining conceited wish it was to be able to stroll into the local Lamborghini dealership, casually write out a check for several hundred thousand dollars, and drive the latest model home. Lamborghini— that Italian Marque whose cars, even though thirty or more years old, still looked sleek and modern. But Alex knew he would need to win the lottery to make that fantasy come true.

Maybe someday.

"Oh, hello, Dr. Madison," one of the nurses said to Alex as she appeared suddenly from behind one of the curtains at the far end of the room. "I guess you're here to see Ms. Marsh?"

Alex was rudely shaken from his unpleasant memories and more pleasant wishful fantasizing.

"Yes...yes, that's right. How is she? Any change?" Alex asked as he tried to remember the nurse's name. He had worked with her in the emergency room on several occasions. The nursing staff was now filling in wherever they were needed most around the hospital.

"She had a seizure last night. Dr. Thompson said it might

have been from some of the meds she was given. Does she have a history of seizure disorder, Dr. Madison?"

Alex stood like a mannequin before he finally said anything.

"Uh... I don't know. We had never talked about it. She had never mentioned it to me, ah..."

"Ellen, sir. Ellen Bradly."

"Yes, of course, Ellen. I'm sorry. To answer your question, I'm afraid I don't know."

Alex was blushing and doing his best to look professional but failing miserably, as he realized.

"I didn't know things had gotten this bad on the wards, Ellen. It must be terrible for the staff as well. This is pathetic. I don't know if I can leave her here, but I'm not sure I can take care of her at home, either."

Alex was standing at the foot of Lauren's bed as he spoke with the nurse. Lauren looked to be asleep. Her eyes were closed and her breathing displayed that steady cadence of slumber. She was dressed in a hospital gown and her long chestnut hair was thick and matted on her pillow. Her face was pale and sallow. Waves of unsettling emotion kept rising and falling in Alex's chest as he stared at the sleeping woman on the bed. She seemed like a stranger. There was a sense of relief in him that he did not have to speak to her. He wasn't sure what he would say. Alex knew he loved her, but although he was a physician, he was not prepared for what he was seeing now.

"Her respirations have been erratic, sir, but she has not yet needed any breathing assistance. We've been watching her carefully."

"Thank you, Ellen. I do appreciate it. I know you and the others do good work even under these conditions," Alex replied and managed a wan smile.

Now the nurse was blushing and trying to hide her embarrassment. She looked down at the floor.

"It's been terrible, sir. We can't keep up. We don't have a chance. We can't begin to help these people, but they just keep on coming."

She looked into Alex's eyes for the briefest moment and looked away again.

"I know, Ellen. But there may be some help on the way." Alex wasn't sure what he should or shouldn't say. There was no secret service issue now; it was day to day life and the very real likelihood it would end soon for many if not most of the people here in this very room.

"There's a new drug being developed right now and it should be available in a few days. I can't say anything more, yet, but I promise I will tell you about it when I know something more."

He looked at her and again tried to smile.

"Please keep that to yourself for now, Ellen. I know that's a tall order, but it will be better that way. I'll let you know."

Alex took one last look at Lauren then turned and left. As he got into his car to head for home, he wondered if he had done more harm than good by saying what he did.

We'll find out soon enough, he thought.

35

Military transport trucks began to make their appearance on the streets of Dallas, Ft. Worth, and the Midcities—the several smaller communities located between the two large metropolitan centers. This also held true in every other city of any size in the United States. The various branches of the military had been hit hard by the paralysis, but the president had decreed that a military presence in the larger population areas might quell some of the lawlessness that was worsening in the country. It was more or less a bluff of sorts as the numbers of uniformed personnel were dwindling, but those who were able bodied carried weapons that marauding gangs might respect. The president was also hopeful that the military presence might stave off the impending anarchy that everyone was now expecting along with the total disintegration of civil order. Everyone who had eyes to see and ears to hear knew it would not be long in coming. The apocalypse that every naysayer and would-be soothsayer had been trumpeting was imminent.

* * *

"She's worse, daddy," Charlotte said as Alex walked into the room Lauren was now occupying at the hospital.

She had been moved after she could no longer breathe on her own and now the rhythm of the breathing machine that was keeping her alive was cycling through its unsettling wheezes, hisses, and clacks. Lauren's chest rose and fell with each inspiration and expiration brought about by the noisy apparatus connected to the plastic tube that was in turn connected to a tube in the tracheostomy in the front of her neck. There were two other patients in the room also being sustained by mechanical respirators.

Charlotte turned away from her father and looked back at Lauren whose eyes were closed. Alex put his hand on his daughter's shoulder and squeezed as he looked on. He sighed almost imperceptibly, but the expression on his face did not change.

"I know, baby, but the machine will keep breathing for her. It won't let her die," he said as he put his arm around Charlotte's shoulder and pulled her to him.

"Oh, daddy, she can't die, she just can't." Charlotte began to sob as she buried her face into her father's chest. "Don't let her die, daddy."

Alex had no ready words for his only daughter. He had witnessed and welcomed the attachment that had grown between the two—one on the cusp of womanhood and the other whose womanhood looked like it might have already been spent.

John was standing on the other side of the bed. He had looked up when his dad arrived, but then turned his gaze back down to Lauren as he stood mute. His hands were in front of him clutching the bed rails. His knuckles were white.

"Dad?" John looked toward Alex. He did not need to say anything else.

"I don't know, son. We'll just have to wait. I haven't heard anything from Washington yet about when the drug will be ready for the planes to distribute it. It should be soon."

"Can she live much longer this way, dad?" John asked.

"As long as there are no other complicating factors, son. Like if she developed pneumonia or another kind of infection or something like that, it could be more serious. But, she's strong and healthy. If she can make it until the medication is distributed, I think she will be Ok."

John stared at his father for another moment and turned his face back to Lauren. The machine continued its irritating but life sustaining cycles as the three of them stood and looked at the dark haired woman lying quietly on the bed.

* * *

The schools were all closing now and most services and many businesses could no longer stay operational. Looting was escalating and there was gunfire and fighting in the streets. The military presence had been little, if any, deterrent to the mayhem that was becoming more deadly and commonplace. Those in uniform had little option in most cases but to return the fire of people who had armed themselves and taken to the streets individually and in gangs to steal, murder, and destroy what little was left of the domestic tranquility. National and local authorities made appeals for peace and restraint, but by that time, the beast had been loosed on the streets of America.

There was no restraint; there was no reason; there was no peace or apparent desire for it; there was only escalating violence and chaos. Burning buildings were everywhere now and bodies were piling up in the streets. The nation was lapsing into a scattering of what were now little more than armed camps. People looked to what military presence was left for protection. Most now knew that venturing outside their homes was suicidal. Food, water, and other necessities were becoming scarce and a compelling reason to fight with or kill one's neighbor. The meek were not going to inherit the earth unless God interceded, and there was no evidence of that so far in America.

The nation was shocked and disbelieving. Perhaps only those unfortunate few who had experienced the devastation in Europe in the years before and during World War II could have any notion of what was going on and what might lie ahead. It was unlikely any of them wanted to see it again.

* * *

The activity at the emergency room had slowed considerably, but Alex had concluded that this was because people were either

276

reluctant to come in or could not get in due to the rapidly worsening clamor and danger in the streets. Ambulances could not effectively run any longer and people who could not walk or move their legs could not drive themselves. The military brought in some people who were now the only new patients that were being seen. Despite this, Alex continued to work in the EOR and do whatever he could to help the other staff. Supplies were growing short and it looked like the availability of food and water in the hospital was going to become a serious matter shortly. He had brought John and Charlotte to be with him at the hospital as he felt they would be far safer there than at home. There had been violent incidents in the neighborhood; people were arming themselves and treating their neighbors like enemies.

Charlotte spent most of her time on the ward where Lauren was now located and helped the nursing staff there. She was scared and anxious, but soon discovered that throwing herself into the work helped and kept her mind off the new, devastating realities of her world.

Ginger was dead. Her father's wealth could not buy off the respiratory arrest she had suffered along with the paralysis. And Charlotte did not know what had happened to Trudy and the others. She often thought of Amy, but had not been able to contact her. She tried, but cell phone service had become spotty at best or nonexistent. Even if she could have gotten through, she was not sure Amy would have responded. Charlotte knew it was hopeless, but her feelings for Amy would not go away. They were friends forever despite Amy's rejections. That notion left an unsettling, nauseous feeling in her stomach.

Proper credentials for the ancillary staff in the hospital was now not even a consideration. Anyone who could do anything to help did so. John stayed in the EOR and helped Alex and the other doctors, doing whatever they asked him to do. It was early spring and his thoughts were on baseball. He wondered if he would ever play again.

Alex was thinking he had never before spent so much time with both of his children than in the last few days. He thought of Maria and wondered how she would feel if she could see them all now. Just two years ago, none of them could have envisioned the scenes that were now startling realities in their lives. Maria was gone; John and Charlotte's lives were to be forever branded by the disintegration of their world; and the woman Alex now loved looked to be soon gone as well. Who, indeed, could count that kind of cost? Alex knew better than to think about what was fair—he knew there was no fairness in the world that anyone could count on. The world was what it was; life was what it was; there was no fair and unfair. There was just life as it had been for thousands upon thousands of years. Just ask anyone who had survived Dachau, or the assault on Omaha Beach, or lived with and survived a malignant cancer, or the death of a beloved spouse. No one gets a free pass. Loss comes to everybody sooner or later.

These days, loss would be coming to everyone and all too soon if nothing changed. Alex could only feel a stabbing pain in his gut. He felt it whenever he thought of John and Charlotte. They would be the real victims. They still had dreams and desires and had not been battered about by the maelstrom of life until now. But what they didn't know about, they could not miss. Or so Alex consoled himself by thinking.

There was a buzzing sensation in Alex's coat pocket that startled him a moment until he realized it was just his cell phone. He was surprised as he had very few calls in recent days. He wondered if there was any service at all anymore. The guitar riffs from *Born to be Wild* continued to get louder until he swiped his thumb over the "Answer" icon on the little screen and put it up to his ear as he said, "Hello."

"Alex? Harold Janes here. Hope I didn't get you at a bad time, but I guess that's actually an oxymoron. There aren't any good times these days, I'm afraid."

"Well, Harold, it's good to hear from you. I'm glad you called," Alex replied.

"I just wanted to let you know. I just heard from Sherman Branch that the planes are flying in two days...on Thursday at first light." He paused a moment and Alex thought he detected a sigh from him as well. "I thought you'd want to know."

"Oh, yes, Harold. I'm glad to hear it. I'm happiest for Lauren, though. She's not been doing well. She's on a ventilator now."

"Oh, I see. I'm distressed to hear that, Alex. Is she holding her own? Is she going to make it?"

There was a pause—a pause that was unsettling for Alex.

"She's stable, Harold. There have been no further complications so far, but that could change anytime," Alex replied. "How are things with you and your family?"

Another long pause ensued.

"My oldest son was stricken last week. His mother and I are worried, of course."

"I'm sorry, Harold. If I could be of any help, I hope you know I would."

"I know, Alex. I hope this stuff from Gardner can do something. My wife and I have moved into my office at the FPA Building. We have some security forces here and it gives us some measure of safety, but it's not very comfortable as I'm sure you could imagine."

"Well, your and your family's safety comes first, Harold. I hope your son will improve. I'll tell Lauren you called the next time I can talk to her. She's been unconscious for several days now."

"I'll be thinking about her, Alex, and saying some prayers, too."

There was still another pause on the line. Alex cleared his throat.

"I hope we'll be talking again soon, Harold, and the news will be better."

Alex bumped his thumb against the "End Call" icon on his phone and slowly put it back in his pocket.

36

That suspended moment between sleep and consciousness defies clear or easy description. When sleep bathes a person in quiet repose, his or her mind is not unconscious at all. There may be all sorts of brain activity with complimentary images assaulting his or her senses. Getting from that state of mind to wakefulness, however, can be disorienting and distressing.

First, there was a shadowy rectangular shape that Alex could barely make out and a soft but eerie glow that seemed to be coming from someplace else. Neither one of those phenomena would hold still. They were in slow but constant motion as though they were revolving in his head like the projections of a reflective ball in a dancehall.

Suddenly, Alex's head jerked forward and the disorientation he was experiencing disappeared. The rectangular object was a window casing and the glow was a night light in Lauren's room at the hospital. He had lapsed into slumber in a chair by Lauren's bed. The respirators were still on their relentless march sustaining the existence of the three patients in the room. Lauren's chest was still rising and falling to the dictates of the machine attached to her. There had been no change in her status since he had come in to see her and fallen asleep by her bed around midnight.

Alex looked on the other side of her bed and saw the two forms of John and Charlotte in their sleeping bags lying on the floor. Their rhythmical breathing told him they were asleep. They were all ensconced at the hospital now, trying to make things as comfortable as possible. John and Charlotte had not disappointed him. He wondered if their youth helped them to accept the horrors they now had to endure. They had not seen much of life and did not have the baggage of jaded adulthood to hinder them. Whatever the reason, he loved them even more now. A smile warmed him inside as his mind turned to the fact it was now Thursday and the planes would be starting their runs soon.

Alex looked at his watch. It was nearing five.

He stood up and stretched and breathed deeply. He was dressed in jeans and a rugby shirt along with his running shoes. Dress code had been largely abandoned for the sake of comfort by most of the staff. Some of the doctors still wore suits and ties, but they were the same ones that would wear suits and ties to sit around the swimming pool. It would take more than a worldwide crisis threatening the destruction of mankind for some people to change anything about their daily habits.

It didn't matter now, Alex thought.

What did matter was what happened in the next few hours and, indeed, the next few days. It had become that primal—certain extinction of the species or perhaps a chance for life to continue. As Alex thought about it, it seemed dramatically Shakespearean, but he couldn't think of a different or better way to put it. When those words from Hamlet, "...perchance to dream..." rolled off his lips some several hundred years ago, it spoke the often unspoken question living in every human being who had ever taken a breath and dared to think about tomorrow.

Alex took a lingering look at Lauren before he turned and walked out the door and down the hall. He then pushed open the door that led to the stairs. He walked up the two short flights of steps that ended at another door. Once there, he pushed the bar forward, opened the door, and walked out onto the roof of the hospital.

The March air was cool. There was a breeze coming out of the south that brushed at Alex's face. He closed his eyes and breathed it in. The hospital was only five stories high, but from that height, Alex could see a good distance. He walked to the edge of roof that was guarded by a short wall that reached up to his waist. It was dark and still except for the lazy breeze that rose up and then lingered. There was almost no traffic on the streets. He saw a police cruiser slowly moving north on Cooper Street. The abandoned cars and trucks that dotted the street had been pushed aside to allow traffic to pass. Some of the street lights were still functioning—the ones that had not burned out or escaped being shot out by random gunfire.

There were also some fires burning across the landscape he could see. Alex couldn't tell if they were burned-out stores, businesses, homes, or perhaps campfires for those with no other place to go. Despite the nature of current events, though, it was unusually quiet. A siren sounded in the distance, but faded as quickly as it came. Alex thought it must have been an emergency vehicle on Interstate 30. Despite this apparent death knell for the country, there were still signs of life.

Alex was thinking about what the word "surreal" meant. It kept coming into his mind. That term had been used to describe movies he had seen like those by Fellini and Bergman. The characters in those films walked, talked, and acted as if they were alive, but somehow the things they did and said seemed out of place and unreal—like in a dream. Perhaps that was what "surreal" was supposed to mean. He was thinking that the situation he found himself in now should be a perfect example of it, but it did not feel that way to him. It felt normal in that the days and nights came and went; there were still people doing what they always had done; people still put on clothes and talked to one another; they still laughed, smiled, frowned, got angry, complained, and loved and hated each other. It didn't feel surreal or like a dream to him. He kept thinking he should be feeling something more—something befitting the occasion of the world coming to an inglorious end. All that was left was the yearning that arose inside him for Lauren—the one thing that still made this moment real to him; and the cruel, unspeakable fate that awaited John and Charlotte. Alex only wished he could take up arms and fight for them.

But, there was no great battle; there was no final confrontation with hoards of warriors rushing toward each other with weapons drawn, ready to strike.

There was only quiet as if time was waiting for beleaguered mankind to simply disappear. The earth was billions of years old and those beings who could be called human had been inhabiting it the better part of only a million or so of them. The way geologists reckoned time, it was almost like they had never been here at all.

The planes will be here soon, Alex thought as he walked back toward the stairs.

Right then, all he could think about was being with Charlotte, John and Lauren.

* * *

There had never been a time in her career that she did not love to fly. Sometimes she wondered what it was that had attracted her so strongly to such a thing, but she never stopped feeling the rush and excitement of it. She had always presumed that it was the time her uncle had taken her up in a Piper Cub when she was fifteen, but she wasn't sure about that. More likely, she thought, was that brief moment of weightlessness as the plane left the runway and was free of the earth as the thrust from the engines pushed her back into her seat. There was just no other of life's experiences that was quite like it. There were some things that rivaled it, like the first time she and her husband Ray had made love on the carpet of her living room floor, but none that surpassed flying through the air at incredible speeds in a machine that was under her control alone.

Colonel Edwina Marie Fox was tough. She had always had to be. Her chosen profession was dominated by men some of whom had no qualms about trying to make her life as a pilot an endless misery.

Winnie, as she came to be called since her high school days, had barely made the height requirement for future pilots when she entered the Air Force Academy in Colorado Springs. She was petite, blond, pretty, and smart. She was also friendly and likeable, but those who took those traits for weakness soon learned otherwise. People often told her she might be more at home in Hollywood than in the cockpit of a jet fighter. Everyone could see she was pretty, but not everyone could see her strength and determination. In her training, she learned to deflect or ignore the good natured jokes, the crude, derisive comments about her sex, and the constant questioning of her abilities. But she never traded her femininity to prove she was "one of the boys."

As a student and fledgling flyer, she struggled with self-doubts about her abilities, but she left those somewhere aloft as she streaked through the heavens at dizzying speeds in a jet plane. Winnie was a United States Air Force Officer as well as an outstanding pilot who just happened to be a woman. It was also sweet retribution to have some of those arrogant jerks who had caused her unyielding tribulation during her training now having to salute her.

Winnie knew today's mission was as critical as missions could get. She, her husband, and two sons had moved to the base when it became too dangerous to stay at home. She had flown with the armada last June in the "exercise" that had been shrouded in secrecy. On that occasion, she and her co-pilot Major Andrew Harvey had led her command on the mission over the north Texas area.

On this day, she was in the cockpit of her aircraft along with Major Harvey to lead the group again. She and her co-pilot were taxiing to the head of the runway with dozens of planes behind them. The big aircraft arrived at the head of the runway as Winnie maneuvered it around to face southward and stopped to await takeoff instructions. She turned and looked at her co-pilot for a long moment. Their eyes met in a ritual that had begun some years before when they began flying together.

She batted her eyes and winked at him and he nodded in return.

Only they knew the true significance of the exchange, but when they had first met, it had not been auspicious. He had given her all kinds of grief, mostly because she was a woman in a man's domain, and women in Major Harvey's estimation belonged at home attending to the needs of their husbands. Despite that beginning, however, he and Winnie had become friends and she knew that when and if the shit hit the fan, she could count on Andy. When she was promoted to Colonel, he was the first to congratulate her.

There was none of the overblown secrecy over the mission this time. Everyone knew what was at stake, and everyone involved knew everything that anyone knew about what was to take place. There had been news announcements about when the flights would take place and where. It was recommended that people open the windows of their homes and buildings for maximum penetration of the GRD 21. The effects of the compound would only last for about six hours or so. If it was effective as expected, relief would come in two to three days. If it was not effective, it was recommended that people continue to pray for God's intervention and guidance.

"Do you know how this stuff is supposed to work, Winnie?" Andy asked.

"You've got to be kidding! Biology and biochemistry were my worst subjects, Andy. I don't have a clue," Winnie answered as she looked sheepishly at him. "All I know is that if it doesn't work, we're pretty well cooked."

The two pilots sat in silence for a long minute or so.

"I also heard that there's no guarantee this stuff won't kill people, too," she added.

"Well, I guess that's the icing on the cake. If it doesn't cure you, it'll kill you. One way or the other, it will fix the country's ills." He smiled. "Maybe we should just keep on flying today and head for a tropical island somewhere. What do you say, Colonel? I think you'd look good in a grass skirt."

"At last my hopes and dreams have come true! I knew all along that you really loved me, Andy. I'm going to put it in my diary."

"And put it under your pillow, too? What if Ray finds it?"

"Who cares? He's such a drag. Seventeen years of marriage and two kids later, I think I need someone new and exciting—someone to bring out the real me."

Andy just stared at her pokerfaced.

"Winnie, you're so full of shit," he said with a drawl.

"Why, Andrew, whatever do you mean? Ray tells me the exact same thing! You men are all alike! You're all impossible!"

Andy was busy shaking his head and smirking when the radio suddenly came to life.

"Armada One, Armada One...this is the tower...all is a go... repeat, all is a go...you are cleared for takeoff..."

"Roger, tower...this is Armada One Leader ready for departure," Winnie answered.

Winnie looked at Andy. Their eyes lingered on one another a bit before she turned to look down the runway. For a moment, her thoughts went flying back home. She could still feel Ray's rough, unshaven face on her cheek as he held her with his big, bearish arms before she left.

"Love you, little fly girl," he had said.

"Love you, too, my man," she replied and kissed him softly.

"Bring that big bird home and come back to me, now."

Their eyes met as he brushed his finger lightly against her nose.

Her two teenaged boys were asleep when she looked in their rooms. She did not awaken them. Now, she wished she had.

Winnie sat motionless and stared down the long runway as the big jet's engines whined. The seconds ticked by and she still did not move.

"You got it, Winnie?" Andy asked as he looked at her. "You want me to take it?"

She said nothing, but only continued to stare at the empty runway. A heavy, uncomfortable knot that felt like a bowling ball suddenly settled in her gut and a half breath caught in her throat. She tried to swallow, but could not. She hadn't felt any sensations like that in an airplane since flight school.

Winnie finally took in a deep breath and slowly pushed forward on the thrusters with her right hand. The huge plane shuddered as it began to inch along the empty runway. The whine of the gigantic turbines turned to deafening thunder as the aircraft began to roll faster. It looked like a big, black ungainly bird as it gathered speed in preparation for its escape into the dark blue of the morning air.

Winnie looked over to her left and saw just the emerging rim of the orange, viscous ball as it was breaking the surface of the horizon. It almost seemed like the first light of day was racing her across the landscape as the plane's wheels left the ground. Winnie continued to push the thrusters forward until the big plane was at last free of the earth and bound for the waiting sky.

It looked to be a glorious day.

BLACK ROSE writing™

CPSIA information can be obtained
at www.ICGtesting.com
Printed in the USA
FFOW03n1459030714
6180FF